LOFTING

LOFTING

ALMA MARCEAU

STUDIO LOPLOP
LOS ANGELES

Studio Loplop
Los Angeles, California

Manufactured in the United States of America
First Edition

ISBN 0-9677459-0-X
CIP 99-69887

Portions of this book appeared in slightly different form under the
title "Tout à Fait Une Femme," in Volume 21, Number 2 (1997) of
The Annals of Cloistered Fornication (Paris & Dublin). To the editors
of that unjustly obscure journal I extend my sincere gratitude for
having given these pages their first glimpse of daylight.

The quotation appearing on page eighty is from William Strunk Jr. &
E. B. White, *The Elements of Style*, 4th edition. Copyright © 2000
by Allyn & Bacon. Reprinted by permission.

I

PATROQUEEET: Harlot!

PARAPRAXISTA: Andres! Amigo mío! Good to see you. Be kind. I'm drunk. What's doing?

PATROQUEEET: Not much, querida. Just sitting here, foundered in the blackest depths of morbid depression.

PARAPRAXISTA: Oh *no*! Why?

PATROQUEEET: Well, you weren't around all evening, so naturally I assumed you'd been stricken by tragedy or romance—tragedy either way for me, of course.

PARAPRAXISTA: Silly gander! No tragedy here. No romance either, unfortunately. Took my dinner solo, in fact.

PATROQUEEET: Chophouse counter?

PARAPRAXISTA: No. Local sushi emporium.

PATROQUEEET: Mirugai on 34th Street? I love that place—it's a classic. You got schnockered? Why?

PARAPRAXISTA: Oh . . . I dunno. Compensation for a cruddy day, maybe? A patient—you'll remember him: Rafinesque-Schmalz . . .

PATROQUEEET: The neurosurgeon with OCD?

PARAPRAXISTA: Yes, that one. Anyway, the malcriado finished his session by dumping on me, and I lost control and lashed back—then spent all afternoon punishing myself for it. But all is well: I've stewed my regrets into insignificance.

PATROQUEEET: Did you dine at table, or consume your parasitic worms at bar?

PARAPRAXISTA: Haha! At bar, of course. You know I'm hideous and introverted: sitting at the sushi bar makes it seem like I have friends. But I thought the parasite problem had been taken care of— isn't there some treatment now they do to the fish?

PATROQUEEET: Incorrect, and no. That's a Sushi Bar Protection League canard, disinformation meant to allay the fears of the yuppisan—justified fears, in this case. Cause there's no such thing as risk-free sashimi: you bites your fishy, you takes your chances. "All is fugu," as the sages saith. But listen, this warm Mountain Dew runs right through a fellow. I must perform the ancient Okinawan rite of "urinato." I shall return.

PARAPRAXISTA: Andres, yer a total loon tonight! The latest batch of crank must be purer than usual.

PATROQUEEET: Stove-top meth; ready in five minutes.

PARAPRAXISTA: Go pee, already.

PATROQUEEET: <——back, and relieved . . . and quite jolly. Wasn't it Proust who remarked on the olfactory pleasure of asparagus piss? Not, mind you, that I've actually read Proust: just a bit of trivia I picked up in the trenches at Dien Bien Phu. I never read books over 150 pp. in length, for religious reasons.

PARAPRAXISTA: For religious reasons? I suppose you're a Zoroastrian.

PATROQUEEET: Not at all. I'm one of the tribe. Fallen, of course—but no less proud of our heritage of Abraham, Moses, Marx, Einstein, Freud, and Jackie Mason.

PARAPRAXISTA: *Jackie Mason?* I *hate* Jackie Mason!

PATROQUEEET: I hate Jackie Mason, too—but he's a lot harder for the gentiles to appropriate than the others. They always fuck it up. But with Mason, the worst possible consequence is still only bad schtick. Not so with the rest. Look what happens, for example, when a goy like Mao gets hold of Marx: the Great Leap Forward and the Cultural Revolution. Need I ask which is worse: a boring night of alter kocker comedy in a run-down hotel in the Catskills, or a terrible hecatomb: millions of Chinese sacrificed to an insane ideology? I think you see my point.

PARAPRAXISTA: I see your point. But what about this supposed religious prohibition against long books?

PATROQUEEET: Oh, that. It's stated clearly in Leviticus, right between the admonition to avoid tattooing because ("think, think for once") you are going to be somebody's grandmother one day, and the proscription against blasphemy because God jealously protects his damnation franchise. Read your Bible, girl—but do it on your own time. This is costing me by the minute.

PARAPRAXISTA: You shit! I'm the best damned thing that ever happened to your minutes.

PATROQUEEET: Well, you're right, of course. You know, it occurred to me today that if I could write, I might make a decent poet.

PARAPRAXISTA: Haha! This was big news for you?

PATROQUEEET: No, you don't understand. I have great titles for poems—dozens of them. I can't stop myself; they accumulate like delivery pizza discount coupons on my mantel. I'm not inclined to do anything with them—I don't eat pizza—but I can't throw them away. It's like a wartime mentality.

PARAPRAXISTA: You were in the military?

PATROQUEEET: No, I never served: flat feet. Flat and wide. E-flat feet. Of course, I've been known to tell youths in taverns that I saw heavy action in the Montagnard brothels up on the Laotian border at U Thant. I'm the right age and I say "frag" and "Special Forces" and shake my head a lot, but that's a tall tale. My closest experience to actual combat was the time I shouted "Incoming!" while standing in line at the post office. But I didn't mean I had a soldier's mentality. It's home-front deprivation that haunts me. I have unexplainable urges to horde cooking oil, for instance.

PARAPRAXISTA: Maybe you should contact poets who have great poems but no titles?

PATROQUEEET: Sure, I'll run an ad. But aren't you going to ask me for an example? They're funny. Though I warn you, I'm no Hoffenstein.

PARAPRAXISTA: That's okay, I'm no Bunny Wilson. And, sure, I'll take an example.

PATROQUEEET: Such fucking enthusiasm. Remind me to dedicate my first volume to you: "For Claire: who saw what others missed."

PARAPRAXISTA: Titles, please.

PATROQUEEET: Okay . . . here's one: "The Distrait Sullenness of an Iranian Pistachio Merchant at the DMV." What do you think?

PARAPRAXISTA: I'd prefer to reserve judgment until I've seen the entire oeuvre. Give me another.

PATROQUEEET: "Xebecs, Muscle Cars, and the Interpenetrability of Teenage Girls."

PARAPRAXISTA: That one has promise. Too bad you aren't big in the content department. I'll take a third, if you're up to it. And I have a suggestion: maybe haiku would be a way to start.

PATROQUEEET: Bashō must go on.

PARAPRAXISTA: Christ, that was terrible. But quit stalling. Give me a title.

PATROQUEEET: Okay, this one survives from some experiments with automatic writing: "Goa Mutton Curry Nothing to Reproach Her for But the Equable Temperament of a Ugandan Marxist; this Ebon Flow, this Turning Hegel on his Head to Catch the Inevitable Plummet of Change from the Pockets of Synthetic Trousers Bound for Exile."

PARAPRAXISTA: Look, Andres . . . about your not being as funny as Hoffenstein: you shouldn't put yourself down. It leaves me less to do.

PATROQUEEET: Haha! God, yer cute when yer being cute. Wanna cyber?

I paused. We'd been typing back and forth in a fury, and I was having so much fun my neighbors were probably getting very concerned for the mental health of the woman next door, laughing and snorting to herself in the dead of night. I knew Andres was kidding about cyber, but I'd secretly been dying to know what it was all about. I had refrained from asking him only for fear that he might have misinterpreted a query as a request—not a wild surmise, if he was the aficionado that some of the roomies claimed. His introduction of the topic, however, seemed like the chance I'd been hoping for to talk about cybering without implying anything more. Still, just in case he actually meant his joke to be expeditionary, I decided to offer a preemptive opener.

PARAPRAXISTA: Sorry, Andres, I don't cyber. I thought I told you that we were strictly forbidden to touch ourselves here at the convent. But—if you don't mind my asking—what gives with you and this cyber thing? According to Mayan Ingenue et al., you have quite a reputation.

PATROQUEEET: Interesting. Does she claim to know from personal experience, or has she seen a scholarly paper on the subject? And who the hell is Al?

PARAPRAXISTA: Aww . . . c'mon, Andres. You know Maya—she doesn't lie, at least not so as anyone can prove. And she *specifically* said she didn't cyber, herself. (I had to put that comma in, or you would have jumped on the double entendre, bastard that you are.) She was matter-of-fact about it. You're saying it's not true?

PATROQUEEET: No, it's true. I won't deny it. Not to you, Claire. It's not something I'm proud of, mind you. I'd have to describe my feelings more as, well . . . arrogance.

PARAPRAXISTA: You are a bad man!

PATROQUEEET: Yes, I am. But just *how* bad, my little liebfraumilch, you will never know. <efg>

PARAPRAXISTA: "<efg>"?

PATROQUEEET: "Evil fucking grin."

PARAPRAXISTA: Oh! Haha!! I learn something new every other day. Will you tell me about this?

PATROQUEEET: Sure. I won't tell you about *me*, but we can talk about anything else.

PARAPRAXISTA: Okay. I'm interested in what's going on in the room—in the loft. Tell me about that.

PATROQUEEET: Oh, well, that. Nothing but ephemera: transient couplings that leave no memory of themselves. Negligible distortions in the space-time continuum of love, baby. Cupid as mayfly. Passion grown squishy, wan, and feckless. Shall I go on?

PARAPRAXISTA: No. And while fairly funny, not good enough. I want to hear your expert interpretation of the phenomenon. (Take note: that was a stroke.) And I promise I won't read you "the wrong way." And—it should go without saying— I won't repeat a word to anyone.

PATROQUEEET: Oh, well, in that case: what are you wearing?

PARAPRAXISTA: Haha! Control-top pantyhose and a homburg. What are *you* wearing?

PATROQUEEET: A gingham jumper and a titanium cock-ring—as you might have predicted. Hang on a minute.

PARAPRAXISTA: Hanging, patiently. :-)

A longish pause followed, and I was sure Andres was puzzling over my sudden interest in cyber. It was a full minute before he typed again.

PATROQUEEET: Okay, Claire. Back. Sorry, I had to get a Cactus Cooler out of the fridge. I'm parched. Now I'll answer anything you want to know. But first you have to take my word for one thing: there's a world of difference between "cybering" and "cybering." Does that make any sense?

PARAPRAXISTA: I'm not sure. Is it the quality that's different?

PATROQUEEET: Yes, that—but there's more to it as well. Like anything else, you can talk about two things being the "same" because they have a formalistic resemblance. So, Leroy Neiman and Willem de Kooning are both painters, in the sense that they apply pigment to rectangular, stretched canvas. But their art springs from two entirely incommensurable wells of sensibility and intent. You can easily see this by comparing their work: despite years of strenuous effort, self-discipline, and passionate desire, de Kooning never succeeded in capturing the essence of the jump shot. That's what I'm getting at.

PARAPRAXISTA: Haha! Okay, I think that makes it clearer. But, still, what is it exactly that you do? I mean, the idea of two people sitting in front of their computers, masturbating, seems so silly. And, for the life of me, I can't see how one does it and types at the same time.

PATROQUEEET: Yeah, it's silly.

There was another long pause, though this time I was certain Andres hadn't gone for another soda. Somehow I'd said the wrong thing.

PARAPRAXISTA: Andres, please . . . You know I didn't mean that *you* were silly; I just don't understand the mechanics of it. It's the technical part that seems so unreal to me. I've talked it over with Maya, and she said the same thing. Please explain this to me . . . I'm truly in the dark.

PATROQUEEET: Look, Claire, I like you a lot, and you have a very perceptive and analytical mind, but . . .

PARAPRAXISTA: But *what*??

PATROQUEEET: But, you will never comprehend this through abstract reasoning. I hate to say this, because I can't prevent it from sounding like a come-on (which is the *last* thing I want it to sound like)—but if you wanna know what hot is, you gotta knuckle down and suck the jalapeño yourself. Description is no substitute for sensual experience. *National Geographic* doesn't really bring you face to face with the majestic crab-eating macaque of tropical Borneo. That's an illusion created by TV. The medium is not the message. A stitch in time . . .

PARAPRAXISTA: Okay, okay! Enough. I get the point. I'm slow—not dead. You watch way too much public television.

PATROQUEEET: Sorry, I get carried away. And, yes, I'm addicted to de rerun natura. But look . . . if you really want to understand, you'll have to find someone to play with. Just make sure it's someone who knows what he's doing. Then cyber will make sense to you, and you'll see why your questions about the technical stuff are misdirected. This isn't about technology, Claire. It's not about computers, or modems, or jokes about getting jizz on your monitor. The hipsters writing about the "Net" for pop-culture rags and the TV-newsmagazine helmet-coifed fuckwits who chuckle each time they say "cybersex" know nothing. They are sans clue, sans clue very much. Christ, they couldn't recognize clue on a bet. Allowing them to truck with the subject of cyber is like having Dan Quayle moderate a Samuel Beckett symposium. Every time I see it, I feel like I'm going to rupture a major vein. Anyway, Claire, I hate to cut you off, but I have to get up early for a meeting, and I'm only going to get 3½ as it is. I have to say tah. Be good and we'll talk soon. (Be bad, and we'll talk sooner— yuk, yuk.) Kisses***

I typed a hasty goodnight, but Andres had signed off before receiving my message.

For a long while I lay in bed, unable to sleep. The conversation with Andres had gone poorly. Not only had I failed to get my questions answered, it appeared I'd alienated him in the bargain. And now, as I thought about it, I realized that our talk had stirred up conflicting emotions, and with them, the beginnings of self-doubt. Could I have mistakenly pre-judged cybersex? Did common wisdom have any better claim to oracular accuracy regarding the erotic than it did regarding anything else? Was cyber, as Mayan Ingenue and others had claimed, really so laughable a notion? I'd wanted it defined, but Andres' reaction indicated that the very request implied a misunderstanding.

Despite all this turmoil, when I awoke the next morning, I suddenly knew that I wanted Andres, or at least —since he was married and I wasn't yet ready to suggest he come out to New York for an adulterous weekend—that I wanted him to type me off.

We'd "met" half a year before in a chatroom. I liked him right away—his limber mind, his convoluted sense of humor, and the frank way he took on disputants: with a javelin forthrightness that made him cold and cruel and generally horrid to those who worshipped at the shrine of circumlocution—and irresistible to me. The attraction, however, seemed strictly one-sided: for the longest time he paid me so little attention that I began to doubt my opacity. Then one night, out of the clearest blue, months after I'd begun frequenting the room, he'd suddenly IMed me:

> PATROQUEEET: Heyas. Just wanted to tell you I thought that was right funny.

> PARAPRAXISTA: Heyas, yourself. That you thought what was right funny?

PATROQUEEET: Your joke from a few minutes back: "If Anne Rice married Edith Piaf . . ." I couldn't laugh at the time because the ATF was at the front door of the compound and I had to help our leader with the reloading. I'd hate to think you thought I didn't appreciate you.

I thanked him for the compliment and for appreciating me, and then we chatted for a while. The next morning, I had e-mail from him:

Dear Parapraxista,

Happy day! Just wanted to tell you how much I enjoyed our little indaba last night. I will forever regret having taken so long to make your acquaintance. From what I could gather in three sentences, you seem bright, funny, and incredibly gullible. That's a winning combination in my book. Let's talk again soon.

Andres, dba Patroqueeet

I laughed, and then ran to look up "indaba."

Short greetings and how-do's soon lengthened into hour-long conversations. I learned that Andres was fifty and "a Pegasus with Andromeda rising." He had been married for twenty-five years, though beyond that he refused to discuss his personal circumstances. He worked in the Denver offices of a large brokerage firm where, using computer-modeled econometric analysis and "a sort of gut-level hunch, a feeling like a pocket of methane in the descending colon," he evaluated the ripeness of securities for sale or purchase.

We'd exchanged photos. He was tall and lanky, as advertised, though a little stooped at the neck, as if he were anticipating passage through a short doorway. He appeared in dark, soberly styled suits in most of these shots, from which I formed a visual impression ("conservative; traditionalist; safe") that seemed rather at odds with his eccentric on-screen persona. Not, however, that I found the contradiction difficult to live with. My father was an animal physiologist who'd dedicated his life to teasing out the mysteries of thermal regulation in some Alpine salamander. He epitomized the unkempt scientist, the schlumpy egghead, and because he had abandoned my mother and me when I was four, that look epitomized in my eyes male irresponsibility. As a result, no doubt, of a reaction to this, the trim, comfortably fastidious businessman was definitely one of my types.

Now, however, I had a problem. Although I'd acknowledged my hankerings for cyber, I could be certain that their fulfillment, the traverse from point A to point B, wasn't going to be that simple. For although I'd seen Andres act downright obscene in room chat, whenever our conversations had taken even the slightest sexual turn, he'd invariably developed acute discretionary avunculitis. It was therefore unlikely that he would respond to the sort of indirect suggestions I might find sufficient courage to make, and so I knew that I was going to have to beg him for sex—a job for which I had neither aptitude nor appetite.

For the next few evenings I resisted the urge to sign online. I was feeling a little discomposed; not unhinged, but wobbly enough that the casement could stand to have its edges tamped in and its screws tightened a turn. I'd need some time to collect myself before taking any further steps. I told Andres by e-mail that I was busy with work, but that I looked forward to seeing him when things settled down. Then, on an impulse, I took off for a long weekend.

I drove to Connecticut and checked myself into the King Arthur's Court, a cozy lodge of the variety that maintains a rustic facade but sits over updated plumbing. (I've learned to avoid any inn calling itself a "Bed and Breakfast"—mostly a charming euphemism for a room without a toilet. I don't want to meet my neighbor or his smells when I wake before dawn to pee.)

I hiked through miles of woods, all in bare winter aspect, save where a few straggling patches of late autumn foliage clung to the trees. As I clambered over boulders and rock-hopped across streams, working out the kinks in muscles atrophied by urban disuse, I took stock of my life. My work was still good: a source of satisfaction and challenge, a refuge from excessive introspection. And things on the personal front were improving. The depression that followed my breakup with Glenn was nearly gone; I could claim a steady remission, if not yet full recovery. I saw it as a healthy sign that my longing for a lover had grown into a persistent ache—and that my erotic imagination was undergoing a sort of renaissance after a long dormancy.

I returned to the city physically relaxed, mentally refreshed, and determined to bring Andres around. Desire was going to have her way with me, and treading water was no longer an option. For better or worse, I'd come to see him as the supreme representative of virtual sex, and—if his reputation were any indication—my best choice for a guide. After unpacking I signed on. Andres was there—though, from his delayed responses, apparently occupied. But I was nervous as a cat on stilts, and foresaw no relief until I had a chance to speak my mind. I asked him for his ear; he asked for five minutes to wrap up his other IMs; and then we started.

PATROQUEEET: What up, Claire? You absconded to CT? How was it?

PARAPRAXISTA: Yes, to Litchfield. It was beautiful, and nice to get away from the three A.M. trash pick-up.

PATROQUEEET: I bet. Though all that rural silence can be pretty scary, too. The nastiest things come unannounced, you know, skulking across meadows under cover of pastoral gloom: sylphish stoats creeping on silent ferret feet.

PARAPRAXISTA: I should have been scared?

PATROQUEEET: No, it's best to live in ignorance. Although, come to think of it, just last week, probably not more than an angstrom or two from where you were, a mink stole up on a blue-hair in the night, mistakenly drawn by the similar shade of her pelage.

PARAPRAXISTA: Her *pelage?*

PATROQUEEET: Yes. But certainly faux ermine on *that* dowitcher: poor old bird hadn't a cent. Quite a stir when the maid stumbled upon her the next forenoon: jocular vein and lateral caryatids bit clear through by canines and paired, pointed adjutants.

PARAPRAXISTA: Sacré cur! You've been reading too much Stephen King.

PATROQUEEET: Who?

PARAPRAXISTA: Haha! I love it when you feign ignorance of the popular culture. But it's pseudo-snobbery. Everyone knows you know everything.

PATROQUEEET: I'm a psnob's psnob. But, verily, I know nothing. Certainly not like that Armenian girl—the one who got all the "A's" in school. What was her name? Something "Valedictorian?"— I forget. But what was this thing you wanted to discuss?

PARAPRAXISTA: Not really a "thing." Just some thoughts I wanted to run by you.

PATROQUEEET: You have thoughts?

PARAPRAXISTA: Shush! I'm serious now!

PATROQUEEET: Okay . . . sorry. All ears . . . I mean eyes.

PARAPRAXISTA: Look . . . this is hard for me—so be patient and sweet, promise?

PATROQUEEET: Sure.

PARAPRAXISTA: I've been thinking about what you said—everything you said—and I've come to the conclusion I was stupid, or at least that I was judging something I know nothing about, which is the same thing. Also, you probably think I'm some sort of prude, and I wanted to set the record straight: I'm not. So there. The truth is I'm fascinated by the cyber thing. And I've decided I want to try it . . . to see for myself.

PATROQUEEET: What made you change your mind?

PARAPRAXISTA: Well, I don't know that I've really changed my mind so much as started to heed my heart. Well, actually . . . lower down than that. Anyways, I was afraid before—that cyber would be ridiculous or embarrassing, or, even worse, not much fun. I trust your judgment, Andres. And your good taste. I figure if cyber is something you're into, then it must be something good. Or, really more to the point, if cyber is something that other women are doing with you, then *you* must be good. <g>

PATROQUEEET: Your intuition tells you I'm like a Chinese restaurant?

PARAPRAXISTA: *What?*

PATROQUEEET: You know: the way you pick a Chinese restaurant when you find yourself in an unfamiliar part of town. Go for the one that's packed. If you can, go for the one that's packed with Chinese. The logic is flawed, of course, resting as it does on the reverse racist assumption that "those other people" are universally gifted with refined palates. I bet you didn't know that the Chinese employ the identical strategy when they visit the States: the best McDonald's is the one with the most white devils.

PARAPRAXISTA: Christ, you're making this difficult.

PATROQUEEET: I only do that to reassure you I'm not an impostor. But go on, you were saying . . .

PARAPRAXISTA: Okay. Here goes: I wanted to ask if you'd "take me by the hand," so to speak. If you'd show me.

There, I've done it, I thought. Ten agonizingly long alligators later Andres responded.

PATROQUEEET: Claire . . . Oh, dear Claire. Look—first of all and foremost—I am very flattered by your request. And tempted. Very

tempted. (Did I mention that I was tempted?)
But I have to say no. You'll have to find someone
else. I like you very much—and that's the crux of
the matter. I have real doubts that our friendship
would survive something like this. And our
friendship is something I don't want to risk.

PARAPRAXISTA: I figured you'd say that, but I like
you a lot, and I've come to the conclusion that,
contrary to what four out of five doctors and
Redbook would tell you, this won't "tear us
asunder." I really want to do this: with *you*.
Please don't make me beg.

PATROQUEEET: You mean you'd beg sponta-
neously?

PARAPRAXISTA: Haha.

PATROQUEEET: Look, Claire . . . let me think
about this for a day or two. I'll need to crunch
some data, consult some consultants, maybe
sacrifice a ewe or two—you know, read some
entrails, that sort of action. One thing, though:
if I say yes, you have to agree to a couple of
conditions.

PARAPRAXISTA: Sure. Which couple?

PATROQUEEET: Okay, #1: Total discretion: I don't
kiss and tell, and I expect the same from my part-
ners. I hate all the gossipy shit online. I mean, I
love it—I just don't want to be its subject.

PARAPRAXISTA: Mais of course, Andres. That's not my style.

PATROQUEEET: I know it isn't. But OSHA requires me to ask.

PARAPRAXISTA: So what's #2?

PATROQUEEET: #2 is easy: you promise to answer all my questions with absolute honesty, and you agree to do anything I say. That's my deal: you want to go on this trip, grasshopper, you make me journey master. You may be unsure along the way (I hope so); you may get into crocogator-infested waters (if all goes well); and you'll certainly have to fight your natural resistance (I have ringside seats for the main event). I'll be there to answer your questions, but I'm warning you: I will tolerate neither excessive willfulness nor any sort of power play. If you want to be "equal" in this game, then beg off now—no hard feelings. Okay?

PARAPRAXISTA: That's a bit ominous.

PATROQUEEET: You agree to the terms?

PARAPRAXISTA: Yes.

PATROQUEEET: Good. I'll send you e-mail by tomorrow evening with my decision. Goodnight for now, Claire. I'm glad we had this little talk. Sleep well.

Throughout the next day I vacillated between fretful desire (I was worried Andres would say "no," and I'd be left out in the cold) and nervous anticipation (I was now just as worried about the consequences if his answer were "yes," for he'd shown a very stern side of himself when presenting his conditions, like a sexually charged version of the severity he brought to bear on snerts in the room).

That evening, after an attempt at dinner that left the food on my plate rearranged but undiminished, I logged on to check e-mail. I clicked open Andres' expected message.

Dear Claire,

I've decided to accept your proposal, subject to the conditions I stipulated last night. As you read this, my double-billing, pseudo-intellectual property attorneys are having a paralegal draft our contract, while they drive to a deposition for another case. Meet me at midnight, Greenwich Village Mean Time. Send e-mail if that's inconvenient.

Yours in Christ,
Andres

2

I VOWED TO KEEP AWAY FROM THE COMPUTER until the hour of our assignation. Instead, I sat on the sofa in front of the TV, sipping sherry and flipping channels, finally settling on Porcel and his overstuffed sirens, in the hope that buffoonery might calm my nerves. But at eleven-thirty, weary of the predictable order in which the Spanish-language commercials for stomach-control foundational garments followed those for flamboyant Dominican astrologers, I gave up and signed on.

This was no improvement. I couldn't seem to lose myself in chatroom antics, nor achieve that state of absorbed attention which made time fly online. I found myself once again regretting my failure to honor any of my past resolutions to master Vipassana meditation. How splendid it would have been to sit in stillness, watching my thoughts, noting their arrival and passing with perfect equanimity, my consciousness unshackled by ignorant desire. Instead, I picked compulsively at my cuticles and wished I had a cigarette, and could barely manage to sit at all. So deeply and disgustedly preoccupied was I with my own undisciplined mind, that, when the IM bell finally sounded, I'd nearly for-

gotten the subject of my wait. The chime pulled me out of
myself and back to the screen fluorescing before me. It was
Andres.

PATROQUEEET: Claire! How are you?

PARAPRAXISTA: Oh, there you are! I'm fine,
Andres. Actually . . . I've been a little distracted
today. How are *you?*

PATROQUEEET: Why distracted?

PARAPRAXISTA: I was anticipating your answer.
To tell you the truth, I couldn't concentrate on
anything else.

PATROQUEEET: Oh, good! I like that.

PARAPRAXISTA: Bastard! <g> You were screwing
with my head, weren't you?

PATROQUEEET: Oh, no—not at all. When we
talked last night I honestly wasn't sure what I
would do. Still, I'm glad the delay wound you up:
I like my women high-strung. They're more
pluckable that way.

PARAPRAXISTA: Ha. But I'm not a lute, I'm just
nervous.

PATROQUEEET: Don't be. This is supposed to be
recreation, after all—not surgery. Look, if it
helps, I'll make you a promise: all scars will be
discreetly hidden under the armpits.

PARAPRAXISTA: That's very reassuring. So what do we do now?

PATROQUEEET: Draw the curtains. I'll be over there in a minute to sever your phone lines. (I'm kidding, really.) Let's start with some questions. Take your time, but answer me truthfully. Neither hem nor haw, okay?

PARAPRAXISTA: Okay.

PATROQUEEET: Do you have some wine?

PARAPRAXISTA: Yes—but over by the couch.

PATROQUEEET: Red or white?

PARAPRAXISTA: Red.

PATROQUEEET: Fine: go over and get it—I'll wait. If you spill, remember two words: "baking soda."

PARAPRAXISTA: Okay.

PATROQUEEET: Back?

PARAPRAXISTA: Yes, back. Sipping comfortably.

PATROQUEEET: Okay, good. I want you to start by describing your breasts to me. You don't have to take off your blouse, unless you find it easier that way.

PARAPRAXISTA: I wouldn't know how to do that— how to describe my breasts.

PATROQUEEET: Yes, you would. You write well, and you're a careful observer. Just start. Plain description. First, tell me about the size and shape.

PARAPRAXISTA: Okay. Well, my breasts are smallish, but not tiny.

PATROQUEEET: Shape?

PARAPRAXISTA: Rounded; a little low-slung. But firm—not saggy. They've always been that way, ever since . . . well, ever since—

PATROQUEEET: Ever since they sprouted?

PARAPRAXISTA: Yes.

PATROQUEEET: Do the nipples point downward?

PARAPRAXISTA: No. Upward. My breasts aren't pendulous or pear-shaped; they're just not the high-on-the-chest, Nubian maiden type. From the very beginning. I mean, since the sprouting. It's not a gravitational thing. Actually, they're quite dense and firm; I look good décolleté.

PATROQUEEET: What color are your nipples?

I hesitated. Not from embarrassment but uncertainty: I've never been all that good at defining color. For example, I could never quite fix a distinct image of "ecru" in my mind's color wheel. My answer was a guess.

PARAPRAXISTA: Kind of a chocolaty-pink, I'd say. They're medium sized, and nicely shaped—if that isn't an outrageously immodest claim to make. The aureole is proportional—bigger would have been unaesthetic on my breasts. The nipples are always hard, even when I'm not excited. I'm very happy with them, come to think of it. They protrude quite a bit, and make points in my blouses; I like the way that feels, and the way it looks. I only wear bras in winter.

Andres was right: once I'd gotten started, I'd had no difficulty at all describing my breasts. It even struck me as odd that I'd never done so before. I liked telling him about them. Not that there was anything erotic to what I'd typed. I'd deliberately avoided pornographic expressions, adopting instead what seemed to me a comfortably neutral approach: the reportorial style of the Sunday science supplement. I might have been describing a new species of sea life, or perhaps relaying geographical details from the surface of a strange planet. In any case I was enjoying the leisurely-paced challenge of whatever it was we were doing.

PATROQUEEET: Claire, that's lovely. And you're performing beyond all expectation. In fact . . . Yes! There it is! We've just received confirmation: the East German judge has awarded you a 9.8 for the artistic portion.

PARAPRAXISTA: Haha! I miss the East German judge.

PATROQUEEET: We all do. A divided Germany was a safer Germany.

PARAPRAXISTA: Haha! Yes—the downside to the New World Order. One thing, though . . . I thought we were supposed to be having sex?

PATROQUEEET: Sex? With me? Now who's kidding? You've been misinformed—probably Maya again. She's a veritable *Pravda* of falsehood and half-truth. But let's carry on. Are your nipples sensitive?

PARAPRAXISTA: Sometimes.

PATROQUEEET: Good. Please go to the icebox right now and fill a big bowl with some ice. Put it next to you.

PARAPRAXISTA: What?

PATROQUEEET: Do it, Claire.

PARAPRAXISTA: Okay.

I ran to the refrigerator. Although I had some idea what the ice was for—at least I knew that we weren't going to be mixing highballs—this request struck me as more playful than anything else. I can't say that anything we'd done so far had been much of a turn-on, but neither did I feel ridiculous, even as I filled a glass salad bowl with ice cubes.

PATROQUEEET: You back?

PARAPRAXISTA: Yes, *Sir!*

PATROQUEEET: None of that shit, please. No "Sirs" with me—okay?

PARAPRAXISTA: Geesh. Okay, okay.

PATROQUEEET: Is it cold in your apartment?

PARAPRAXISTA: Yes, a little.

PATROQUEEET: Okay, grab a blanket. Let me know when you're back.

PARAPRAXISTA: Back. With the blanket.

PATROQUEEET: Are you wearing a skirt, Claire?

PARAPRAXISTA: Yes.

PATROQUEEET: I want you to pull it up over your hips, now. Tell me when you've finished.

PARAPRAXISTA: Skirt now gathered over my hips. Sitting back down.

PATROQUEEET: Bare legs or hose?

PARAPRAXISTA: Bare legs.

PATROQUEEET: Part your thighs now—just a little—then lay your right hand on the inside of your right knee, palm down. Let it rest there for a moment.

PARAPRAXISTA: Okay.

PATROQUEEET: How do you feel?

PARAPRAXISTA: All right, Andres. A little odd, frankly.

PATROQUEEET: Well, you are odd. That's why I like you.

PARAPRAXISTA: Yes.

PATROQUEEET: Don't worry. You are making excellent progress. Now, please bring your hand up along the inside of your thigh . . . slowly—then let your fingers caress the flesh of your thigh as you move upward—moderate pressure. Make sure you don't go too lightly, Holly: you should feel the resistance of your muscles under your fingertips. I want an impression of the curve of your leg and the texture of your skin as you touch yourself.

Andres paused then, presumably so that I might have a chance to carry out his instructions. Stroking my leg, sitting with my thighs parted, exposing myself to this "voice" on the monitor in front of me, I suddenly felt quite lewd—titillated, I decided, by the exhibitionistic quality of it all: a reasonable conclusion until I remembered that I was alone in my room. *Exhibitionism?* Nonsense! I'd only been exposing myself to myself. At most I was having a playdate with an imaginary friend.

PATROQUEEET: Claire, when you masturbate, do you use your fingers or a vibrator?

PARAPRAXISTA: My fingers. Sometimes a vibrator.

PATROQUEEET: Do you put your fingers inside yourself, or only on your clitoris?

Before I could answer, Andres' IM chimed again. With a shock I looked up at the message on my screen:

PATROQUEEET: Take your hand away! I did not tell you to touch yourself. Remove it—*Now*!

Surveying my lap, I discovered that I'd unintentionally lifted my hand from where it lay at the top of my thighs and brought it to rest on the fabric of my underwear. I saw, too, that I must have pressed down, because the white cotton was furrowed where it had been forced between my labia. Suddenly, a chill infused my neck and shoulders: impossibly, yet undeniably, Andres had known I was touching myself. There *were* two people in my room!— and one was watching everything I did. For several fearful moments I scrambled after a rational explanation, reminding myself that my lifelong disbelief in the paranormal rested on a solid scientific foundation, and that coincidence and plain old materialistic psychology could easily account for what had just happened. Andres was highly intuitive, and very lucky. That was all. There was no need to go off the deep-end with supernatural speculations. I managed thus to calm myself, but when we continued I still hadn't entirely shaken off the eerie sensation that I was being observed by an immediately present yet invisible entity.

PATROQUEEET: You still there?

PARAPRAXISTA: Oh, yes. I'm sorry, Andres. I

didn't know I wasn't supposed to do that . . . to touch myself.

PATROQUEEET: That's all right, Claire. But please promise me you won't exercise any more initiative for the time being. Just follow now, okay?

PARAPRAXISTA: All right.

PATROQUEEET: Answer the question: do you put your fingers inside yourself when you masturbate, or do you only manipulate your clit?

PARAPRAXISTA: Both. It depends, I guess. Sometimes both—sometimes just my finger on my clit.

PATROQUEEET: Do you use lube, or do you get wet enough on your own?

PARAPRAXISTA: I get pretty wet; sometimes I put my fingers in my mouth first. Are you going to be taking a smear for the lab?

PATROQUEEET: We can play sports trivia if this is boring you.

PARAPRAXISTA: No. Sorry. Carry on.

PATROQUEEET: Buy some lube this week. If we go further with this, I'll need you to be very, very slick.

PARAPRAXISTA: Yes. Okay. Updating my grocery list. Should I buy in bulk?

PATROQUEEET: Claire, please unbutton your blouse now. And, without removing your bra, reach inside and pull your breasts out, so that they rest on the collapsed cup with the nipples exposed.

PARAPRAXISTA: Okay. Wait a second.

I lifted my breasts out of my brassiere and arranged them as instructed. Like a still life, it seemed to me: tangelos balanced on the rim of a platter. Truthfully, the feeling wasn't bad. I imagined I looked very tart-like in my deshabille: a "C" girl pinup from one of the second-tier men's magazines of the late '50s, a few clicks below Betty Page. Then all of a sudden there was a rush of blood to my nipples, followed by a dull but unmistakable spasm in my groin—just one pulse, as if my heart were compensating for a skipped beat. A soft, humid heat now began to radiate outward from my center.

PATROQUEEET: Tell me how you feel.

PARAPRAXISTA: With my hands, Andres. How do you feel?

PATROQUEEET: You *really* want to know? I feel like you'd rather give me shit than have sex— which is stupid, because in fact you're horny. But I have to tell you: I'm growing tired of the fleering edge you can't seem to keep tucked inside your attitude. Perhaps you'd like to take over?

PARAPRAXISTA: No . . . okay . . . Christ. I'm sorry— again.

PATROQUEEET: Jesus, Claire. Just put yourself on hold for a few minutes—it won't kill you. I promise. Talk to me about your feelings. Tell me your thoughts—whatever they are, positive or negative. Describe your mental conversation. But please stop trying to hide. Cool is bullshit. I would have thought you were old enough and wise enough to know that. Or... maybe you'd rather we stopped? I can find other things to do...

There was, I knew, something fundamentally wrong with my approach. Why couldn't I let go? I suddenly realized that I'd been trying to perform an impossible wire-walk between a posture of world-weary cockiness—eyes jaded by a phony been-there, done-that arrogance, lips sneering round a rouge-stained Gitanes—and what I really wanted: unconditional surrender to my body's demands for sexual gratification. The first, the ironic stance, was uncompromisingly defensive; it would permit no bargaining with the second: hence my snotty rejoinders to Andres' questions. But my sarcasm was about to make him renege on his decision. I knew I had to stop the wisegirl act at once, or face the likelihood of getting cut off.

PARAPRAXISTA: Look, Andres, please continue. I promise to cease and desist. And I'm sorry about before: I was being a snit. I wasn't sure about all this at first; it's all very different. The honest truth is that I *want* different. I really do. But at the same time I'm scared of it. Does that makes any sense?

PATROQUEEET: Yes. Perfect sense. And apologies accepted, of course—but irrelevant. It's up to you, Claire: do you think you can do this without the mocking 'tude?

PARAPRAXISTA: Yes ... oh, yes. I promise. I'm very excited right now—for the first time in a long time. Thank you for that. There is one thing, though ...

PATROQUEEET: Yes?

PARAPRAXISTA: It's about the way I'm sitting here ... all alone ... almost nude. Please tell me that I'm not ridiculous.

PATROQUEEET: Oh, no, Claire ... darling, no—absolutely not. Don't you ever think that. Quite the opposite: what you're doing is very hot. And you're certainly *not* all alone. I know this is difficult, and the newness is strange, but please don't worry about looking ridiculous: you could never be ridiculous in my eyes. Especially when you're naked. Trust me on this: men never laugh at naked women. I'll explain later. Just know that your responses to my words are making me very hard.

PARAPRAXISTA: Really?

PATROQUEEET: Yes, really.

PARAPRAXISTA: Thank you, Andres. What should I do now?

PATROQUEEET: Now *that* was a good question. Bring the hand that's lying on your thigh to your throat—just under your chin.

PARAPRAXISTA: Okay.

PATROQUEEET: Now extend your index finger so that you're pointing at yourself—as if to say "look, no dewlap yet."

PARAPRAXISTA: Ha!

PATROQUEEET: Make contact with your skin, and, as you do, rotate your finger so that you can feel your nail.

PARAPRAXISTA: Okay.

PATROQUEEET: Very slowly now, run the edge of your nail down the middle of your throat, stopping when you reach the soft cup between your collar bones. You may take your hand away to type, but directly afterwards I want you to replace it exactly where it was.

PARAPRAXISTA: I'm there. Entre clavicules.

PATROQUEEET: Good. Continue downward, taking your time—but with increasing pressure. When you get to just above where your cleavage becomes visible, where the swell of your breasts begins, come to a halt.

PARAPRAXISTA: Halted.

PATROQUEEET: Fine work, soldier. At ease.
I want you now to concentrate with me. I'm
watching closely—so closely I can smell the
perfume rising from your breasts on the little
updraft your chest makes when you inhale.
A falcon could souse on that sublime thermal;
I can't, but I do have eagle eyes. So do exactly
what I say. Get it?

PARAPRAXISTA: Got it.

PATROQUEEET: Good. Let's resume. Slowly, and
with care. Look down at your breasts; remember,
I am using your eyes. Press the point of your
finger until your breastbone resists, and your
juices run clear. Done?

PARAPRAXISTA: Done. Oh! "Done"—haha.

PATROQUEEET: Move with me now: my hand on
yours along the top of your left breast, tracing the
crest of the dune with your fingernail, slowly and
smoothly: fluid motion. Make the center of your
nipple our end point, our bearing mark. And
mind yourself Claire: you mustn't pause as you
approach the nipple—mustn't hesitate across the
border where the color goes deeper. Are you still
with me?

PARAPRAXISTA: Jesus. Yes, Andres . . .

PATROQUEEET: Good. Gradually increase the
pressure through small increments, bringing

more force to bear as you get accustomed to each
level of intensity.

PARAPRAXISTA: OK.

PATROQUEEET: Now push hard!—all the way to
the tip. Be brave for me, Claire: let me see the
sharp red mark . . . let me feel the burn and the
cut . . .

PARAPRAXISTA: Y!

PATROQUEEET: *Ice*, Claire! Grab a handful and
press it hard to your skin. Freeze the pain. Hold
the ice to your nipple until it goes numb and you
feel nothing except the heat between your legs . . .

I'd done exactly what Andres had asked: pressing my nail
into my breast, I'd raised a welt like a scarlet wake across the
delicate pale flesh. But so mesmerized was I by the process,
so astonished at my own recklessness, that I registered discomfort with only the lesser part of a divided mind. Then,
just as Andres had anticipated, I'd suddenly demurred at the
border of my nipple, fearful that visiting the lacerating pressure of my nail upon the extreme sensitivity of my aureole
would bring more agony than I could bear. But when my finger at last made land on the nipple's darker, more densely in-
nervated skin, pain unexpectedly gave way to a strange, aus-
tere delight, a feeling that seemed to crystallize and expand
upon contact with the ice. And then the epicenter of sensation quickly surged from my nipple to my genitals: I felt first
a nagging ache, a subsonic thrumming like the purring of a

cat in my lap, and then a warm gush. I looked down to see that the crotch of my underwear had been soaked to translucency.

> PATROQUEEET: Claire? Are you okay?

> PARAPRAXISTA: Yes, oh. I'm sorry Andres. I must have spaced out for a minute. More like blissed out, actually. I'm fine, though.

> PATROQUEEET: You blissed for two minutes, Ms. Potatohead. Bulova watch time. I think you liked that, Claire: I could feel your pussy melt.

> PARAPRAXISTA: Christ, Andres! How the hell did you know that?

> PATROQUEEET: My sources are confidential. Are your nipples numb?

> PARAPRAXISTA: Yes. Very.

> PATROQUEEET: And your pussy, comment va-t-elle?

> PARAPRAXISTA: Wet; very :-)

> PATROQUEEET: Take off your underwear, Claire.

At this point I would have liked an intermission, a moment to figure out what had just happened to me, to try to reconcile exorbitant and contradictory emotions—frustration and pleasure, shame and lubricity. Andres clearly had other ideas.

PATROQUEEET: Earth to Planet Claire: do you copy?—Over.

PARAPRAXISTA: Yes. What?

PATROQUEEET: Um, about that underwear?

PARAPRAXISTA: Yes, okay. Sorry. She is off.

PATROQUEEET: Thank you. Excellent technique, by the way: one leg at a time. Nothing fancy, but *very* reliable. Listen, though: from now on I don't want you to type unless I ask you a question. Just do what I say. Cross the i's and dot the t's. All right?

PARAPRAXISTA: Yes; I promise.

PATROQUEEET: Move your right hand to your pussy. Put the tip of your index finger into your vagina: mull it around until it becomes slick. Once you've done that, type "y."

PARAPRAXISTA: y

PATROQUEEET: Push a little further, Claire: go in past the first joint.

PARAPRAXISTA: y

PATROQUEEET: Now hold still. I'm making your finger my finger . . . thicker, longer than yours: a man's finger. I'm in you, but not moving in you: hard as bone, daubed with your nectar and your scent, poised for the plunge. I like having my finger in your cunt, Claire. But tell me: does it feel good? Or shall I remove it?

PARAPRAXISTA: No!

What Andres was doing felt exquisite: my vagina was swollen and liquid; my clitoris hard and so sensitive it throbbed at the slightest vibration. Badly in need of relief, I couldn't bear a premature ending, particularly since taking my finger into my own hands was no longer a desirable option: Andres plainly had a destination in mind, and I had committed myself to holding out for that orgasmic ne plus ultra which, I reasoned, had to exist to justify all this tribulation.

A sudden internal enlargement, a forcing open of my vagina ended my reverie.

PATROQUEEET: Two fingers, Claire. Sliding two fingers into your pussy—deep.

PARAPRAXISTA: y

PATROQUEEET: My two fingers...hold them in you, hold them tight in your pussy. Still your hand, Claire—no motion yet. Can you hold still?

PARAPRAXISTA: y

PATROQUEEET: This is difficult for you, isn't it, Claire? Fingers so quiet in you, and you needing so badly to fuck.

PARAPRAXISTA: y!

PATROQUEEET: I want to move in you, Claire— but gradually, slowly—just enough so that your muscles crimp against my fingers, the reflex before you open to me. I'm afraid, though. Afraid that if I gave it to you—a little motion, a gentle rocking—you might disobey me, you might rush things. Can I trust you to listen to me? You *do* want me to fuck you, don't you?

PARAPRAXISTA: y

In fact my body had already begun to rebel against Andres' commands: my hips were turning spiral volutions, and with each orbit my vagina would engulf my fingers a little more. And Andres' last question—that arrogant, blunt challenge— served only to further inflame my body's revolt. Like modern women everywhere, I'd always thought of myself as incorrigibly clitoral; for me, unsupplemented intercourse was strictly an open-ended pleasure. But perhaps because of this unusual clustering of circumstances—my psychological surrender to Andres, my unsettled state of mind, the indefinitely extended prologue—I felt my usual need for some auxiliary application of finger or toy evanesce. Suddenly, satisfaction meant penetration, tout court. I wanted Andres to slam his fingers into me, to truly fuck me, with all the power and fury implied by the hard-clatter ending of the word.

PARAPRAXISTA: Please, Andres ...

PATROQUEEET: Please what?

PARAPRAXISTA: Please fuck me, Andres.

PATROQUEEET: Put three fingers in your pussy.

PARAPRAXISTA: 3?

PATROQUEEET: Yes. Three. Now. Bury them deep—as far as they'll go. But hold them there. No rocking, no squirming. No more cheating.

PARAPRAXISTA: Oh, God, okay. 3. Fuck.3

PATROQUEEET: Listen to me now, Claire: no typing—just "y." I know you want me to fuck you hard—and I will. But only if you listen to me, only on condition that you do exactly what I tell you.

PARAPRAXISTA: y

PATROQUEEET: Place the tip of the index finger of your free hand on your clit.

PARAPRAXISTA: y

PATROQUEEET: Pull the skin back enough to retract the hood slightly. Now let the hood slide forward. Now pull it back again. Do it slowly. Take a few moments, establish a tempo. Is your clit swollen for me?

PARAPRAXISTA: y

PATROQUEEET: Slip it between two finger tips and rub: I want to feel it under my fingers.

PARAPRAXISTA: y

PATROQUEEET: You're perfect, Claire. And now I want to see everything. Spread yourself wide for me . . . show me your pussy. Don't hide from me: let me linger over you—your thighs and belly, the soft curl of hair on your mound, fingers buried in the wet groove of your cunt. Are you spread for me, Claire?

PARAPRAXISTA: y

PATROQUEEET: Pulling my fingers out of you slowly—follow me now—twisting my hand, corkscrew turnings: feeling you tighten against my fingers, muscles clutching, clinging . . . Too bad for darling Claire. She'd rather I kept my fingers in her cunt, wouldn't she?

PARAPRAXISTA: y!

Penetration had brought extreme pleasure: the female gratification of enclosure, of ingesting and hosting the living other—an intensity of feeling that only increased as the hand inside me began to execute its assigned instructions: retracting its fingers millimeters at a time, twisting them until the rolling wedge of knuckle produced a rippling friction against my vaginal walls . . . incomparably delightful movement that was, alas, about to end—and far too soon. Suddenly, however, Andres changed his mind.

PATROQUEEET: Stop now, Claire. Reverse direction. You've been obedient, so I'm going to give you a little more. Slide your fingers back into

your pussy—three fingers—all the way. Hold still
now. Remove your other hand from your clit.
Hold still, and swear to me you aren't moving.

PARAPRAXISTA: y

PATROQUEEET: I know you can't stand very
much more of this. But we have to talk about
something before I allow you to continue. I want
you to know how I see you: naked and panting;
belly and breasts shining with sweat; thighs
spread apart; my fingers buried in your pussy.
Look at your cunt: the flesh so swollen, your hole
so dripping wet the seat below you is soaked. An
accurate picture?

PARAPRAXISTA: y

PATROQUEEET: Look at yourself, Claire: you're a
whore. My whore. More egregious yet: you're not
even being paid. And that feeling between your
legs, Claire—my fingers in you? Your cunt is
mine. I own it now. We both know why you're
here, how you got to this place. You're a whore
because I made you one—and that's exactly what
you wanted, isn't it, Claire? Now, don't even
think of objecting! Before you start to protest, or
to rationalize with some clever lie, do one small
thing: taste the words on your lips. Do you recognize them? We both know the truth. You've been
praying that I'll fuck you, Claire. You can't deny

the name in your mouth. You're my whore and you like it.

I hated those words and I hated Andres for saying them. But most of all, I hated that he was right: for here I sat, exactly as he described me: pregnable, wanton, depraved. And neither could I gainsay his proprietary claim: his hand was in my pussy, and for as long as it remained there, he would control me sexually. He would, as he put it, own my cunt. Only acutely urgent self-interest prevented me from punting myself free of our conversation with a keystroke.

PATROQUEEET: Tell me what you want, Claire.

PARAPRAXISTA: For God's sake, Andres! You know I want you to fuck me . . . Please fuck me!

I couldn't believe what I'd typed! Responding without deliberation, I'd intended to blast Andres for his selfishness and cruelty, to damn him for abusing his power over me. But, to my surprise and consternation, I saw that I had instead accomplished the exact opposite. "Please fuck me!"— no words could have better affirmed my subordination, my total capitulation to his will.

PATROQUEEET: Put your hand back on your clit, Claire. You can diddle there, but remember: a good slut keeps her thighs spread. You've let your knees come together again. I'll have no more of that. I want to see everything when you fuck yourself. Do you understand?

PARAPRAXISTA: y

PATROQUEEET: Good. Begin by sliding my fingers out of your pussy, twisting as before. Slide them all the way out . . . then into my mouth. I want to lick them, to eat what you've made for me. I want to taste your cunt from your fingers, Claire. Spread your pussy for me. I'm going to spit into your hole, then push my fingers back inside you—to the depths of your cunt. Sliding out again, then back in—hard now. You want hard fucking, don't you?

PARAPRAXISTA: y

PATROQUEEET: They say never kiss a whore, but I want your tongue to suck. Now grip my fingers with your cunt while you fuck yourself. Fight it, Claire: long, fast strokes against the tight trammeling pink. Fight it—hold my fingers fast—don't let me go—slam my fingers into your sweet tight cunt. Come for me now! Show me how a whore comes! Come hard for me, Claire . . .

But by the time Andres typed those final exhortations, I was already in the staggering throes of a violent orgasm—my hips lurching and snapping like a pinball flipper as my vagina clamped down with reflexive desperation upon the three fingers that jerked and twisted within her like invading spirits. With the outrush of tension, my body convulsed and my limbs contorted so grotesquely I must have looked as though I were in danger of losing my life. A low moan ended in an incoherent, guttural cry; then the cry was repeated, and at last I recognized the voice and the plea as my own: "Fuck me, Andres, fuck me"—a prayer of entreaty becoming one of benediction as crisis faded into satiate calm . . .

I sat stunned and silent for a few minutes. As though taking care not to disturb the bubble of tranquillity in which I floated, Andres said nothing aside from a simple iconic kiss, "*." After I'd recovered sufficiently to type, I thanked him. He asked me if I felt all right; if I was out of breath; if I would like an analysis of my cardiovascular capacity and output—all part of what he called the "post-game review." Sensing that I was having trouble keeping awake, he suggested I get some sleep. He called me "a groovy chick," thanked me, and bade me goodnight. Then he was gone, signed off into space.

I crawled into bed, shivering with delight as my body, still warm and damp from sex, slid against the cool crispness of newly laundered sheets. Then I began to laugh. A man I'd never met had just fucked me to a magnificent orgasm, in whose afterglow I now basked, feeling neither strange nor regretful. If I had any other thought at all, it was an excited hope that what had just taken place portended greater pleasures still, and perhaps, ultimately, even contentment itself. I fell asleep with my mind cradling this tantalizing yet unexpectedly calming thought.

As I slowly awakened to the reveille of my morning shower, the feelings of the night before remained with me, unadulterated by remorse and undiminished by the light of day. I dressed for work, but found it difficult to transition into my customary contemplative preview of the day's cases. Sitting down with my first appointment, I became aware of a mellow voluptuousness between my legs, although I was uncertain whether it represented the lingering physical memory of recent activity or the onset of new stirrings. In either case, I'm afraid that the incongruously happy smile with which I met my first patient almost certainly confused her.

When my eleven o'clock had gone, I sat alone for a while on the little verandah of my flat, soaking up a welcomed dose of late winter sun and mentally reliving *My Cyber with Andres*, as I'd christened the event. Memory served, if anything, all too well, for all of a sudden my pussy began to throb with nagging persistence. I glanced around to verify that I was unobserved before unbuttoning my blouse to bare my breasts to the sun's rays. I licked a finger, used it to coat my nipples with saliva, then watched as the moisture evaporated from the edges to the center, cooling the flesh into hard buds as it was drawn up into the warming air. Impatient with desire, I pulled up my skirt, drew my underwear to one side, and put a finger on my already swollen clitoris. Then, forgoing all preliminary soundings, I penetrated my vagina with two extended fingers of my other hand. There was no difficulty: I was almost excessively lubricated, as if my body had anticipated its own need. I masturbated with rapid, reciprocating strokes, though I didn't neglect the twists Andres had made me impose on myself. Now vividly liberated from their text, Andres' encouraging words ("Come for me, Claire!") echoed in my ears as I reached climax. I cried my response in a needful, rasping whisper ("Yes, Andres . . . yes . . .")—but then, in

the very midst of orgasm, I suddenly recognized my unintended paraphrase of Molly Bloom and burst into uncontrollable laughter.

By the time I signed on that evening, I was anxious
and excited to see Andres, though what I wanted most immediately from him wasn't a replay of the night before, but
rather a chance to talk about it. For hours I'd been generat-
ing theories—psychological, sociological, and aesthetic hypotheses about virtual sex—and I was dying to compare
notes. Perhaps, too, I was concerned that I might have been
a victim of self-delusion (or worse, a victim of a self-delusion
that couldn't be repeated!), and I was hoping for some reassurance.

PARAPRAXISTA: Hola, Andres!

PATROQUEEET: ¡Hola, chica!

PARAPRAXISTA: Hey!—how the hell did you do
that upside-down exclamation point??

PATROQUEEET: Sorry, kumquat, that's a closely
guarded professional secret.

PARAPRAXISTA: Fuckknuckle.

PATROQUEEET: Fuckknuckle? But dearest, from
where does this appellation spring? On second
thought, don't answer. The only thing that
matters is that I'm *your* fuckknuckle.

PARAPRAXISTA: Si, querido. You got a minute?

PATROQUEEET: For you, baby, I got two minutes.

PARAPRAXISTA: I'm honored, I'm sure. Listen, I wanted to thank you for last night. Morning is long gone, and I don't really care if you respect me, but I did have a few questions.

PATROQUEEET: And I have a few answers. And of course I respect you, Claire. I respect all the sluts I cyber (insert "kidding" emoticon here). And don't worry about herpes—mine's in remission.

PARAPRAXISTA: Yuk, yuk :-) Okay. Seriously, what happened last night—I liked it a lot. I'm not quite sure how to say this so that it doesn't sound ridiculous or too fawning . . .

PATROQUEEET: Don't worry, I loved *Bambi*. And the sequel: *Anal Bambi does the Stags of Europe*. Not much of a rack on that doe, though.

PARAPRAXISTA: Shut up, Andres.

PATROQUEEET: Sorry. Please go on.

PARAPRAXISTA: Mostly I've got good feelings about all this. But I'm bothered by the thought they could be completely self-generated. What happened last night was very satisfying in a way I didn't expect. I *want* to believe it was "real"—that we communicated—that I didn't simply invest your words with emotional content that wasn't there. I wanted—

PATROQUEEET: Claire, you pretty little fool, shut up.

PARAPRAXISTA: What?

PATROQUEEET: Just slow down for a second, would you? Let's take this a step at a time. You've put a lot on the table already, and I'd like to comment a bit before you go on and I lose the spoor of your gist. I'm not as spry as I once was, lassie.

PARAPRAXISTA: Sure, Gramps.

PATROQUEEET: Thanks. First off, let me just say that your concerns aren't paranoid. *You* might be, but that's a different topic. This stuff can be misleading. That little box on the screen can operate like a kind of virtual confessional. IM encourages people to unburden themselves, and we tend to idealize those we entrust with our darkest secrets. So, self-delusion is possible— though I don't think it applies to you, at least not last night. You didn't make that up. Of course, you're the doktari, so I won't presume to lecture you on the dynamics of interpersonal communication...

PARAPRAXISTA: Lecture away, but know that I'm not going to sleep with you for a better grade.

PATROQUEEET: That's fine: a simple blowjob in the parking lot at the Christmas faculty/student mixer will suffice. Now, my theory (which is mine) is this: the danger of the idealization I mentioned is greatest for those who come to this medium fundamentally unhappy or disturbed. Needy, fucked-up folk get frisky with each other. Ten minutes later they're talking "soul-mate." A month later, one of 'em is abandoning job, spouse, and kids to move to Comedo, Oklahoma, where love and bliss reside, sight unseen. Nutso facto. Frankly, you don't strike me as the sort.

PARAPRAXISTA: You know of actual cases?

PATROQUEEET: Absolutely.

PARAPRAXISTA: Incredible. Oh, by the way, I'm arriving on United Flight 334 at noon: Gate 6B. Can you pick me up, or shall I arrange for a cab? All the furniture is going by rail.

PATROQUEEET: Very funny, Claire. Come if you want: I'm typing from a prison cell. But to return to my rant, this can be a lot of fun, as long as you go into it attentively.

PARAPRAXISTA: Which means?

PATROQUEEET: Well, okay, for example, it's possible I'm not really as tall and debonair as I've described myself to you: deception is the amaranthine handmaiden of virtual romance. (Please don't ask me what that means.) Physically, I might be Balzac[3]: "Can I offer you another eight dozen oysters, monsieur?"—A rational person knows that, accepts it as a real, if relatively negligible, risk, ignores it for pragmatic purposes, but ignores it consciously. Likewise, no matter how good I make you come, you are not (I hope) going to attribute princely qualities to me—beyond my due, of course. You shouldn't imagine that I never snap at my wife, that I never get depressed, that I never cheat on my taxes, or that my flatus smells of gardenias after the dinner buffet at a Burmese bar mitzvah.

PARAPRAXISTA: Myanmar.

PATROQUEEET: What?

PARAPRAXISTA: Myanmar. Burma is now Myanmar. Thought you might like to know.

PATROQUEEET: Yes, of course. Can I finish?

PARAPRAXISTA: Sure.

PATROQUEEET: Thanks. Okay, I know this answer is already epic in length, but I want to say one more thing about what happened. It was real. I'm a real person—probably not too unlike the person you've imagined, except for the lacy underthings I wear when I talk to you. You are sufficiently sound of mind that you wouldn't idealize an online lover. I mean, at least not any more than you would a real lover. Of course we're all selectively blind to the faults of our romantic objects: his eyes fail to linger on your weak chin; you choose to ignore a fat-to-muscle ratio that has more status value on the Indian subcontinent than Stateside; he takes no notice of your pigheaded refusal to signal left turns; you smile sweetly through his displays of wine snobbery. Nevertheless, I meant my words to you, and you responded to them. You responded to me. Look at it this way: your orgasm is your receipt for experience experienced.

PARAPRAXISTA: Can I write it off?

PATROQUEEET: Yes. "T & E."

PARAPRAXISTA: You don't think I was just masturbating?

PATROQUEEET: No. I'm not saying that this is identical to body-to-body sex, but it certainly isn't the same as wanking solo. You didn't just make up what happened—at least not any more than you make up the other bits of experience that constitute your world. And, excuse me, solipsism is a dead end. If you and I share a brisket sandwich and then talk about how it tasted, we have no problem understanding one other. We can talk about the crispness of the bun, the tenderness of the meat, the callipygian wonder that is the waitress who served it—and we make sense to each other because we shared the same experience; we didn't just create the fucking sandwiches in our heads, nor did we simply imagine Dolores' magnificent glutes.

PARAPRAXISTA: What we talk about when we talk about brisket?

PATROQUEEET. Yes. Very clever. Now, please be quiet, please? Seriously, Claire: all that French Lit department epistemological crap is baloney. We're not absolutely free to imagine reality. We discover it and talk to it, and it talks to us—but it constrains us, too. You can't drive a brisket sandwich to work, no matter how many times you deconstruct it.

PARAPRAXISTA: The brisket sandwich?

PATROQUEEET: The brisket sandwich; yes. I deconstructed one once: got gravy all over a nice white dress shirt, and right before I had to give an important presentation. It's fucked, but that's the way life is.

With a sudden pitter-pat of joy, I realized that Andres and I shared the same obscure bugbear: postmodernist relativism. The subject could get me worked up the way football franchise deals or sit-com cancellations put others in a stew. Whenever I heard someone reducing something to "text," I wanted to bitch-slap the malefactor, subject her to the Ludovico cure, force her to read Adorno in German—make her suffer until she knew in the kishkes that you couldn't just explain away pain and injustice through reinterpretation, not even the slyboots sort with the long pages of endnotes.

PARAPRAXISTA: Andres, I'm so excited!

PATROQUEEET: You are? Did they find Alan Greenspan and Jeanne Kirkpatrick murdered in coito?

PARAPRAXISTA: No, no—nothing *that* good.

PATROQUEEET: Then what?

PARAPRAXISTA: Okay. But I have to ask you a question first.

PATROQUEEET: Shoot.

PARAPRAXISTA: What do you really think of postmodernism?

PATROQUEEET: Oh, that's easy. There's no such thing.

PARAPRAXISTA: No?

PATROQUEEET: Well, okay—that's a little too categorical. It exists as an architectural movement. But outside the definable style that has brightened the malls and corporate façades of our fair land with gumball-hued columns and gables, there is no pomo.

PARAPRAXISTA: That's pretty extreme. I mean,

I agree. But I'd like to know what you mean, Zachary.

PATROQUEEET: Sure. Here's the *Reader's Digest* condensed version: everything postmodernism claims for itself—the way it differentiates itself from modernism—is already manifest in Duchamp's ready-mades and, in particular, his urinal. So, if Duchamp is the archetypal modernist—which is not an assertion that takes one very far out on a limb—then postmodernism is nothing but modernism with a superfluous prefix.

PARAPRAXISTA: Thank you. I love you.

PATROQUEEET: Wow. That was easy. If I say "Derrida," do I get head?

PARAPRAXISTA: You get head anyway. If you say "Derrida," you get good head.

PATROQUEEET: There's bad head?

PARAPRAXISTA: Trust me. I've been with men who thought the clitoris was up past the gall bladder.

PATROQUEEET: Heather Gray's anatomy.

PARAPRAXISTA: Who?

PATROQUEEET: Porn starlet. Ring-spun blond,

great tates. Short, brilliant career during "The Golden Age"—circa 1977. Listen, Claire, light of my day, I must run off. RL rears its hideous hydra head. See you tomorrow?

PARAPRAXISTA: I hope so. Marvelous talking to you.

PATROQUEEET: Same here. And remember what Albert Camus said: "Don't be a stranger."

When I'd broken up with Glenn six months earlier, I'd resolved to hunker down and heal before exploring the possibilities of my new single life. Not only did I have serious doubts about finding true love with Cousin Irene's gynecologist's brother, Schmuel, the actuary, but I'd had enough vicarious experience of the pitfalls of the rebound relationship to understand that women in my situation were tragedy magnets. They attracted losers, borderline personalities, and manipulators as reliably as lame hares drew ravens in a Russian winter.

Yet pleasure could be a dogged and powerful advocate for its own aggrandizement, and it wasn't too long before I found that I'd grown practically dependent on Andres for my sexual satisfaction. This I knew was a dangerous situation: to safeguard my own fragile happiness I would have to stave off any hope of an expanded relationship—of a life together, in other words. To fail to do so would be to risk heartbreak and disappointment, and perhaps even that worst nightmare of the single women of late spring: an alcoholic, trailer-park spinsterhood—pickled old meat, waiting for a married lover's eternally forthcoming divorce . . .

Nourished by regular stimulation, my libido bloomed rampant. Beside the usual exorbitance of my erotic dreams, frequent waking fantasies began to affect me: bondage, bisexuality, various combinatory permutations, troilist picaresques in town and country—pretty much anything, in fact, short of bestiality and the coprological. These fantasies would come on without warning and were no respecters of situation—as, for example, the time I was having lunch in a small cafe near my apartment and found myself unexpectedly transported into a pornographic daydream. I'd been sitting quietly alone at my table, when my eyes suddenly began projecting images of obscene exertion; soon the white tablecloth before me was obscured under a living congeries, an aggregation of flesh-moving-against-flesh, rendered in the blithe, hyper-saturated hues of early color stock. This dream was more elaborate and finely textured than any I could recall. Most strange was the way it seemed to occupy its own timeline, to have an existence concurrent and partially corresponding with mine, yet independent of my foreknowledge. It was as if I had been thrust into a stream of events that told a story in which I'd been assigned a significant part, a story which reflected my obsessional universe, but one whose authorship I could not claim.

I recognized my own body: figures stood or sat around me, indicating me as the hub of interest. I was on a bed, naked and damp with my own sweat, wreathed by bunched and tangled sheets. My pussy was sore, as though I'd been recently penetrated. Someone I'd never seen before (yet whom I recognized somehow as my lover) was easing me down onto all fours. He crouched before me, stroking my brow and gently brushing his fingers across my eyelids, admonishing me to be "a good girl," while another man, behind me and out of sight, slid his cock down the crack of my ass until it was positioned at the opening of my vagina. I made noises of protest, but my lover reminded me firmly that I had agreed to submit to his wishes. He made it clear he would brook no attempts to renegotiate: I was to obey and remain silent. Defiant, I began to argue, but he pushed his hand, the pad of muscle and flesh at the base of his thumb, hard into my mouth. Then I heard him say he loved me, and a moment later the man at my back was forcing himself deep within me. Immediately upon reaching the limit of penetration, he pulled back with a violent tug, as if he'd been stung or burned, wrenching his cock almost clear of me before again plunging to my depths. This time the action was like the jab of a truncheon wielded in anger, an intention my assailant confirmed when, thrusting full bore, he began to curse me, spitting his revilements into my ear ("bitch," "cunt," "whore") with the septicity of a rapist. On the third stroke of his cock, I could feel the entire organ swell, and—to my utter horror—I began to climax as his semen flooded me.

He was still extracting his penis—he seemed to have lengthened as he detumesced, so that I felt as if a yard of garden hose were snaking through me—when I heard a door open and footsteps approaching, again from behind. The newcomer, too, was beyond my angle of vision. I saw my lover look up, his face expressionless. He uttered no word of greeting. Instead, with the tone a brutish employer might use with a menial, he spoke a single command: "Clean her up." Nimble fingers touched my sex, and then into the breach a tongue softly extended, lapping and waggling as it siphoned away the semen that clung within.

My lover smiled and said, "Thank you, Eva. You can finish her off now,"—and with a pang of excited surprise I realized for the first time that a woman had been performing these ablutions. Eva began again to lave my genitals with her mouth, and if she was still under orders, there was assuredly nothing at all impartial or janitorial in the slow, adoring strokes with which the spongy flat of her tongue burnished my clitoris. Spurred by her obvious passion, I came again— and with that crisis the dreamscape abruptly dissolved.

I got up from my untouched salad and walked in a daze to the ladies' room, where I entered a stall, lowered the lid of the toilet, sat down, and began to shake, and then to laugh. I stayed holed-up for several minutes, waiting for my pulse to normalize and for the trembling in my limbs to abate. Unsure how closely identified I was with my daydream alter ego, I was afraid I'd made a spectacle of myself in the dining room. For all I knew, the rapture of two orgasms had played over my face in full view of the waiters and customers, who, ready with smirks and ridicule, now awaited my reappearance. Praying for unobstructed passage and the diversion of a busboy breaking a plate, I conceived a plan to quietly drop the money for my check onto my table while slinking undetected through the restaurant and out the door. But as I smoothed my skirt and fortified myself for my exit, I again succumbed in laughter to the ridiculousness of my situation: sitting on the can in the ladies' room of a Greek restaurant, a hostage to the machinations of my rampaging libido. I made myself go back into the cafe and pay the check at the register. When I left, no one so much as bothered to lift an eye from his dolmas to pay me notice.

3

ANDRES AT LAST SUGGESTED A PHONE CONVER-
SATION, and I jumped at the chance: I'd been longing to hear
his voice, and I looked forward to exempting myself from the
laborious and distracting replications of verbal emphasis and
vocal gesture required for successful dirty typing.

I was pleased to find that his actual voice closely matched
the voice I'd synthesized from his writing. Even his conversational style was the same, except for an irksome tendency
he had to finish my sentences whenever I paused to deliberate longer than a beat—particularly annoying because most
of the time he finished them correctly.

We hadn't been talking long when he seemed to trail off
into silent reflection. After a while he said, "Claire, I love
talking to you—but you didn't just want to chat, did you?"

"Umm—no," I laughed, a little nervous even though I'd
expected this detour would come sooner or later.

"Go get your vibrator, I want you to come for me."

"I don't have to 'go get' anything, Andres. I have it right
here."

"Haha! What a girlscout. But for this badge you're going
to have to fuck yourself for me."

"Yes," I laughed.

"What's so funny?"

"My best friend is always asking me to go fuck myself?"

"Haha! True. Count your blessings. Sure you still want it?"

"God, yes, Andres. You know I do . . ."

"Then follow my directions."

I followed his directions: first spreading my legs for him and then alternately penetrating my vagina with the vibrator's tip and applying its buzzing head to my clitoris. I didn't have to ask if he was stroking his cock: his exertions were audible, their fluctuations of pace and forcefulness tracking the changing tempo of his phrases. The longer he spoke, the more intensely the passion in his voice burned, until it began to spark with a crude excess that his written prose had, I now understood, only imperfectly conveyed. I was powerfully affected by the barbarous element in Andres' lust; its marbling of egotism and mongrel voracity soon had me sticking to my seat. A paradox of sexual arousal, I thought: the hotter the fire, the more one drips.

"Bury the vibrator slowly in your pussy, Claire. I want to hear your voice as you fill your cunt . . ."

Impelling the tool from behind with my hand, I nearly lost my fingerhold on the fluted sides of its base. It seemed rather more to have been pulled than to have slipped into me, as if my vagina, scoffing at the meagerness of daintily served tidbits, had swallowed the white plastic cylinder whole. In any case, I had no difficulty interpreting the dildo as flesh—as Andres' flesh—for the column gave up its al-abaster chill the moment it was lodged in me, and its inanimate rigidity was supplanted in the same instant by a kind of living hardness, as of an antler in velvet.

"...here's my cock for you now, Claire. Take it in your hand...spit on it...rub the head against you...work the slobber into your clit. I want you to show me what a desperate begging little cunt you are..."

I pulled the dildo from my vagina and pressed it against my clitoris until its vibrations shook my entire body like a palsy: even the bones of my inner ear seemed to rattle with the tremor. Meanwhile, Andres' obscene fusillade continued unchecked, his voice wrung into a snarl, his epithets—aggressive, defamatory—bristling with the rapaciousness of animal ego.

"Spread wide for me, little bitch...push my fingers into your wet cunt...hard slick ring of muscle around my knuckles...squeezing two fingers into you, scraping past my cock...fingers and cock in you...spreading you...filling your cunt...oh fuck...sweet fuck...my Claire likes me in her rank little fuckhole, doesn't she? You'll beg for it, Claire, like you always do—you'll beg me to fuck you. Skank whores beg...you'll beg for my cock..."

Suddenly I recognized (for I had already long "understood") just how much I loved being Andres' object; just how much I loved being put to lewd uses. Then all at once I found myself at the orgasmic threshold.

"Andres...oh dear God, fuck...I'm going to come..."

"Not yet, Claire. Pull your fingers out of your pussy—and toss the dildo aside."

"What?"

"Stop, Claire. Now."

"Christ."

This was a wrenching about-face; I was shaking, a moment away from climax. But I complied.

"Okay, Andres, I stopped. Shit. You almost killed me."

"Shut up, Claire. You'll do what I tell you. Or maybe you'd prefer to be excused?"

"Fuck, Andres, yes . . . I mean no. I don't want to be excused. And, yes: I'll do whatever you want—you know that . . ."

"Good, Claire. You're going to take my cock in your mouth—but not right away. First I want you to imagine in detail how you're going to please me. For a little while you're going to stop being so selfish."

Hitherto I'd always been sexually passive with Andres: he assigned me roles; I played them according to his wishes. And while I certainly took pleasure in submission, much of my tractability had been about the practice of the possible, since I'd known no other way to satisfy him than through eager but relatively silent deference to his will. But it seemed to me now that Andres had cracked a window of opportunity: I saw an invitation to exercise power, to invert the relations of seduction. Tentatively at first, I began to turn the tables on him.

"Andres, I *have* been thinking about how to please you. I've been thinking about how to suck your cock. Seriously— that's what you said. Seriously—the way a whore sucks."

"Claire—yes—just like that . . ."

"I remember, Andres. Don't be nice, you said; don't be the girl next door. Fuck the girl next door, you said: she's pretty but sexless . . . she gives lousy head . . . she hates the taste of a cock ... she hates the taste of come. I remember what you told me: cocksucking isn't supposed to be nice; you didn't ever want me to be nice. You said you'd teach me to be your whore. I like that you teach me."

I paused to listen for a moment: Andres' breathing was growing deeper, his exhalations more labored. I loved my new role as coquette: teasing was getting me everywhere. I resumed my soliloquy, now with greater confidence:

"Do it like a whore, you said: stroke with one hand ... suck the head ... then down the throat to your balls—all the way—throat tightening around your cock. I promise, Andres, I'm going to suck your cock like that. Hard, like you told me, like a whore: licking and sucking for a quick finish, sucking hard because time is money ..."

"That's it, Claire ... fuck ... you're a good little slut ..." But his guard was down, his voice, straining with feral hunger, stripped of its usual authority.

"Andres ... my pussy aches from before—it hurts. I can't stand it. I need to touch myself. May I please touch myself?"

"Yes. Fingers on your clit."

"May I take your cock in my mouth?"

"Look up at me, Claire: I want to see your eyes while you suck me. Stroke your pussy, and look up so I can see your face, your mouth around my cock."

I'd taken Andres' call at my desk, and there I'd continued to sit. Now I slid to the carpet and cowered down onto my calves, balancing slightly forward on my toes. I wanted to feel as indecent as I sounded, and the idea of masturbating in a squat suddenly appealed. And, indeed, within seconds it seemed to me that I turned incredibly, wantonly vulgar—like some biker chick whose boyfriend was making her expose herself to his ex-cellmate. (How little I'd had to deviate from my regular behavioral commute to feel a world apart!)

I crooked the phone into my neck to free my hands, then proceeded to describe for Andres what I'd done and what I was doing: the luscious shiver I felt as the damp cleft of my pussy, parted between thighs spread in a low crouch, suddenly took the air's chill; how I'd shoved two angled fingers into my vagina, and then drove each stroke down to the web of my hand; how my cunt bucked forward to meet these thrusts, its muscles clutching at my fingers like a bog sucking a wader's boot; how I could smell myself, the scent of sex—musky, fungal, lacustrine—rising from between my legs; how delicious I tasted when I touched my fingers to my tongue, and how delicious I would taste on his.

I'd reached a frenzy of self-induced excitement, and now, as I imagined myself sucking Andres' cock, sucking it as though I were dying and his semen were my antidote, a charge of the lewdest exhortations tore from my mouth. I was shocked at my own salaciousness: exceeding what until this very moment I'd believed were insuperable bounds—of modesty, of decency, of my notions of good taste and narrative restraint—I begged Andres to fuck my face, to stop my glottis with his glowering prick, to scald my throat with the milty plasma that seethed and gurged like boiling oil in the hot cauldron of his testicles. (And if in this heedless rush to produce a grand effect I had perhaps trod past the obscene into the ridiculous, my barrage of words elicited no such complaint from Andres, who in fact had ceased talking altogether, ceased even the dutiful, repetitive "yes" with which he had been responding to my every suggestion, so that only moans and sighs signaled his imminent crisis.)

At the end, Andres exploded with a magnificent taurine bellow, while I flailed around on the floor, my body racked by climax, my legs battering the furniture like those of a strangulation victim in her final struggles. I was certain I could feel his cock dislodge from my throat, pulsing and twitching as it pulled away, and then endless jets of come, their spray coalescing into an unctuous, liquidy sheet, flowing across my tongue and lips, my belly, and the furrow of my cunt.

The illusion was as perfect as what it depicted was false: Andres and I were together, and he had been fucking me, in my pussy and in my mouth, and I could taste his come mingled with my perspiration and the saline drip of exertion that ran from my nostrils to my upper lip. The intensity of the climax had stunned my mind to a blank quiescency. I fell asleep, then awoke a moment later to Andres' voice.

"Claire, that was wonderful. Thank you."

"Mmm . . . Andres . . . what? Thank me?" I was giggly and less than coherent.

"Yes, thank you—for the chocolates and the flowers. Hey, are you okay? How many fingers am I holding up?"

"Oh, of course!" I answered. "Perfect—sorry. Two fingers and a thumb"—but like a simpleton who had just discovered her navel, I couldn't stop my demented giggling.

"What's so funny?" he asked, a little defensive.

"Oh, nothing, nothing, Andres. Don't worry—you were fine."

"I wasn't worried that I wasn't 'fine' Claire. I was just wondering what was so fucking funny."

"Oh, well, Andres dearest . . . maybe it's just this vision I have of myself: sprawled on the floor, naked and wet, recovering from the most intense and—I'm ashamed to say—most satisfying orgasm of my career as a sexual being. And I was on the phone the whole time. I'm laughing because I'm an absurd fucking sight."

"Who's looking at you?" interrupted Andres, his tone suddenly reproachful.

"What do you mean?"

"I mean, who's looking at you? You say you had a vision of yourself—but what you described seems more like someone else's vision. Someone very, very uptight."

Andres was right, of course. Again I'd made the mistake of judging myself from a perspective that regarded "going all the way" and "foreplay" as real entities in nature, rather than artificial (and arbitrary) demarcations.

"I know what you're saying, Andres. It's just that I'm of several minds on this—each with a different take, and all the takes mutually exclusive."

"Let's keep this Sybil, shall we?"

"What? Oh . . . haha."

"Go on, Claire. Please. I've always loved you for your minds as well as your bodies."

"After I come with you, Andres, for a few beautiful minutes I know that what I have with you is real . . . is good. But then, later, part of me sneaks up from behind and chides the rest of me for being idiotic and delusional."

"Aww, honeybunch—that's just your ANA talking."

"What?"

"Your ANA—your "Adolescent Nemesis Archetype"—one of the great universal, transcultural, meta-temporal images that Jung missed. (Another reason I hate Jung. Except neo-Jung... and nothing after *Harvest*.)"

"Yeah, Andres. You, me, Ma Barker, and the colored balloons. Anyway, I can tell you're dying to explain. Knock yourself out."

"How you indulge me! What I mean is that no matter how realized you are as an individual, no matter how completely free you think you've scoured yourself of the despotic and hypocritical mores of the dominant culture, there still lingers this persecutorial incubus somewhere inside who won't stop calling you 'weird.' I have a pet theory (unkind people have called it 'unsubstantiated conjecture' and 'a crackpot idea') that Freud was only half-right when he attributed the formation of the superego to early childhood. The nastier, more atavistic bits actually originate in junior high school. They're teen contumely internalized."

"Have you ever noticed that you talk in parentheses?"

"You kiddin'? Alla da time, people stoppin' me onna da street to tella me dat. And it's true. I even see the little opening and closing lunules as the words come out of my mouth. You have some sort of problem with a parenthetical style?"

"Not really."

"Good answer—haha!"

"Would you mind terribly, though, if we finished with this particular aside? I want to get back to the main lecture."

"You're asking me to put aside my aside?"

"Exactly."

"Okay. In conclusion, Ladies and Gentlemen: the super-ego is constructed partly from our parents' normative beliefs (and their parents' beliefs—ad regressum, ad infinitum, ad reinhardt), all inculcated before we're fledged. The rest we get from our adolescent peers, who—just in case you've forgotten—were evil, cretinous fucks who spent their waking hours scanning us for the least sign of nonconformist behavior. It is their mocking expressions and bigotry that form our internalized standard of the acceptable. A chilling fucking thought, ain't it? I tell you, Claire, I feel for gay kids: it's got to be a living hell. And gay kids with recalcitrant nodular acne? Where is their savior? Who is their Kevorkian? It behooves us to remember: the sleep of reason breeds tiny monsters when the first animal is jettisoned."

Usually I loved Andres' flights, the way he cobbled together whimsy, serious ideas, and disparate cultural fragmenta into something that resonated like the best surrealist poetry—even as I was aware that this was also his method for effecting graceful transitions from "fucking" into conversation. But somehow this particular segue had been too facile. A feeling of emptiness blossomed in the pit of my stomach, a feeling that something important had been neglected.

"Andres, I was wondering: did you like what we just did? You never said anything, and here I am glowing, dying to tell you how great I feel, ready to embarrass myself . . ."

"Claire, querida—please. I *loved* what we did. Loved it. And I came good. It was positively marvelous. It's just that after the conjugal fact I get strong and silent—old, overripe

Camembert that I am. If you'd prefer, however, I could hand you a line . . ."

"Yes, Andres."

"Haha! You're serious! Christ! You chicks are all the same: you want shmooze—even if it's insincere."

"That's true. We want shmooze. Honesty and originality are nice but less important. It's a girl thing. I don't expect you to understand. Just say it."

"Okay, Claire. How's this: the quality of our virtual sex-life couldn't be better."

"You romantic fool. Is that really the best you can do? You're pitiful." I laughed, but somewhere within me a seed of disappointment split its husk and extended a rootlet to my heart.

"All right. How's this, instead: Claire, I want you to know how much I care for you, and how much I love what we do together. I love the sex, and I love talking to you and having you as a friend. I know what we have isn't completely 'full' or 'normal'—but that doesn't mean that this relationship is hollow or false. As you know from your experience with Glenn, there are plenty of 'real life' relationships that are less substantial than ours—"

I hung up the phone. It was a stupid reflex, a childish impulse, but I was insulted and hurt. I hadn't expected a declaration of love from Andres, merely some emotion, a word or two that reflected the intensity of our sexual moments. Instead, I'd gotten objective analysis and impartial assessment. Fuck him, I thought, as I slammed down the receiver. Fuck him.

I burst into tears. Then a moment later I was consumed with regret for what I'd done. Suddenly I was afraid that, having given Andres a glimpse of a madwoman, I might have lost him.

I now needed desperately to talk to him, to explain myself, and I felt a tightening in my chest when I remembered that I'd never gotten his phone number. I signed online and searched his name for hours, but in vain. By the time I fell asleep, as depleted as my well of tears, a sad yellow morning was already beginning to sift through my bedroom shutters.

When I awoke, I wrote Andres a letter. I wrote bluntly and without preamble, assuming that my best chance to mend things lay in concise explanation and honest apology, and in avoiding the sort of beating around the bush that might be interpreted as psychotic calculation.

Dear Andres,

I'm sorry. I was unfair and rude, and you deserved neither. This is the reason for my behavior: I want more. It's normal, and I can't help it, and I get pissy because I don't know what to do about it. This isn't about you. I know that, and it is very important to me that you know that I know that. My disappointments aren't your fault, and my happiness isn't your responsibility. And what we have brings me great joy. So please don't take my occasional outbursts as accusations. They aren't. I hope very much that I can still be your friend, and, in particular, your "virtual hottie." I can't deny the depth of affection I have for you. Please don't let that be a threat. It should be a reason for continuing what we have—whatever it is that we have—and not a reason to change it or end it.

Love,
Claire

Andres called the next day, his voice calm and cheerful. I was relieved to hear it and grateful that he'd spared me the agony of a long wait.

"Oh, Andres, I'm so sorry. I didn't want you to think that—"

"Hush, Claire. I read your letter. You don't have to say another word. I understand. I mean it. Wanting more is normal: you're a smart, wonderful, incredibly sensual woman with broad hips perfect for childbearing, calves like pillars, and the constitution of a dray horse: you should be conquering the wilderness and founding a dynasty. What we have is great, but it isn't everything."

"You aren't mad?"

"Mad? No effing way. Annoyed? Yes. Irritated beyond belief? Quite. But mad—never! You keep forgetting I'm a guy: I'll put up with a lot to get laid."

Andres seemed totally unperturbed by my tantrum of the night before, and with the tiniest bit of horror I realized that part of me was disappointed we weren't going to have a row. I shook my head, unsure if this perversion came from a compulsion to repeat, or a morbid need for the diversion of dramatic conflict.

"You know, Claire: what you said in your letter didn't come as a total surprise to me. I've been thinking about these things a lot recently—though I'm not really too worried."

"Worried I might go nuts on you?"

"No. Haha! Worried that what we're doing might be keeping you from meeting someone in real life. Fact being that I think you're going to meet someone very soon."

This prediction struck me as risible, as silly as a palm reader's boilerplate prophecy. It was also very unlike Andres to dabble in prophecy: his skepticism of psychic phenomena, I knew, was as absolute as my own. I challenged him on the spot.

"I'm going to meet someone soon, eh? How the hell do *you* know? Has Madam Zoltar been talking in her sleep again?"

"Oh, no. Zoltar's a silent REM type: those all-seeing Romanian lips never part until the cock crows. But that's strictly academic now: Zoltar has passed from our dimension. I am the new Bombastus. I have efficacious modalities. I am qualified and certified. I hold a degree from the University of Illinois at Paranormal. I possess that knowledge which can only be gained through repeated near-life experiences. And do you know what I see when I gaze into the ether?"

"I wouldn't even dare to venture a guess."

"A wise call. Best to leave these things to professionals. What I see, in any event, is a sophisticated Manhattan crypto-proto-sybarite, recently become aware of the warped sexual self at her disposal. Namely her own. She asks me for advice. I tell her what I would tell an ugly sister: "Carpe lingam." Wisely, she heeds me: she finds a man; she seizes him; they live happily ever after. In fact, Claire, my loon, you are ready to meet someone—someone right. And you will.

You mentioned that people have been remarking on a change in you. The change is bound to be remarked on by some highly eligible bachelor or adulterer. It's in the stars: you will soon leave me. My destiny is to be replaced and left heartbroken."

"Nobody's going to replace you!" I laughed, cheered by Andres' banter. "Not even a real-life nobody. And if I do meet someone—and Japan will run a trade deficit with America before *that* happens—I'll just cheat on him with you."

"Whoa! Wait one damned second, Claire! Whom met who first, eh? You'll be cheating on *me* with him. I insist."

"You insist what?"

"I insist both ways. That you cheat on me, and that it is me who gets cheated on. You got a problem with that?"

"Not at all. In fact, I'm hugely enjoying this scenario of a love triangle with me as the hypotenuse."

"Querida, that's 'hypoten*euse*'—pronounced like 'chanteuse,' not like 'mongoose.' If you're going to manage a ménage, you gotta get the jargon right."

"I'll work on that. By the way, don't you hate it when folk pepper their conversation with foreign phrases in order to show off?"

"Absolutely. It's not only pretentious, it's discourteous. Only a poor memory prevents me from quoting Messrs. Twain, Orwell, Strunk *and* White in support of exactly that opinion—"

"Hold your horses," I interrupted, probably nipping something epic in the bud. "I've got one more question: isn't it *just* as annoying when people try to show off by dropping the names of literary figures?"

"Of course. That's even worse. Indubitable evidence of an unoriginal mind, quite. Was Strunk a literary figure?"

"Quien sabe? You mention him in every conversation. He must be acquiring literary-figure status from sheer frequency of use."

"I venerate *The Elephants of Style*."

"Oh, God! That's a *terrible* pun, Andres. It's not even remotely funny."

"Perhaps, but it's insidious. Never again will you find it possible to glimpse the slender spine of that smugly synoptic volume, its title so regally teal, so aristocratically avec serif, without immediately thinking to yourself: 'Ah, *The Elephants of Style*'—and then collapsing in paroxysms of uncontrollable laughter, overcome by a vision of Babar in Armani on a catwalk. For you see, querida, in this world there are inexorable antiphonies—breakfast antiphonies if you happen to wake hungry for gospel—associations that come to mind as predictably as the response of a church choir to Mahalia Jackson's call. If I leave you with nothing else of value, I leave you the eternal mnemonic treasure of *The Elephants of Style*. Never forget, Claire: 'rather, very, little, pretty—these are the leeches that infest the pond of prose, sucking the blood of words.'"

"Haha! That is all rather fascinating, Andres. Some might even find it funny. But let's get back to me as the pretty little love object of two very devoted, handsome, and sexually evolved men. Frankly, I love the idea. Alas, it will never happen."

"No, Claire, it will happen—if you really want it to. But the subject doesn't wow me. I'd rather name-drop, something closer to my heart. I believe in it. I practice it at every opportunity. I'm willing to defend it with energy, tenacity, and a battery of quotations from the greats of antiquity, mediocrity, and modernity."

There was nothing to do but let Andres talk. Once he'd gotten his teeth into a subject that interested him, attempts at re-direction were useless. I would have to content myself with strictly private thoughts on the question of threesomes and Pythagoras . . .

4

As if the Fates had conspired to prove Andres right, or merely as a result of one of those lucky coincidences whereby life lends credence to the plot conventions of made-for-cable movies, I soon met someone.

Nick came to my office complaining of anxiety attacks. He'd been referred by his former therapist, retired since they'd last seen each other. On the basis of this initial consultation, I concluded that his problem was physiological, and so referred him in turn to a psychiatrist who could prescribe medication for him. I didn't think talk therapy was likely to cure him, and I never take a patient unless I believe I've got better-than-even odds of doing him some good.

Nick thanked me, but seemed hesitant to end the interview. He asked some questions about my work and the kinds of patients I treated, and as I answered, I felt the concentration of his gaze sweep slowly over my face, and then take what looked to be an impertinent turn downward toward my breasts. But before his stare went below my neckline, it reversed direction. Suddenly his eyes were locked with mine and he was giving me a wicked, satisfied smile, as if he were pleased with himself for having elicited—then promptly disappointed—my accusation of leering machismo.

"Look," he said, rising from his chair, "I know you must get a lot of guys who become infatuated with their therapists. That's transference, right? But since you're not going to be my therapist, and I'm not infatuated with you—I mean, not yet, though I think you're beautiful and you've got a great voice, and I'd like to find out about the rest—if you'd consider it, I'd love to take you to dinner sometime." With a flourish he pulled a business card from his wallet and placed it on the edge of my desk, opposite to where I was sitting, flustered now, coloring with embarrassment. "This is my work number," he continued. "Please call. I swear I'm not a creep. If you don't believe me, you can check with my mother. Let me know."

Nick smiled, warmly now, still without a trace of self-consciousness, then turned on his heels and was out the door before I could think of something appropriate to say.

Who the hell was that? I thought, lifting his card from my desktop. "Nicholas Pericolo: Artist," I read—and laughed: to promote yourself that way you had to be either very good or very foolish. I tried to recall his face: a pleasant enough gestalt; hazel eyes behind long, dark lashes; swarthy complexion; day-old scrub of beard. His hair was thick: swept up and over in front, the sideburns left longish. In fact, his whole look—the white, open-collared dress shirt, the black leather car coat, the black Levi's and black cowboy boots— seemed like a consequence of that glossy black pompadour. The effect was rockabilly and somewhat theatrical, though fortunately more Dave Alvin than Elvis impersonator.

I made Nick to be in his late thirties, smack dab in the middle of my preferred age range. But he was too cocky for my taste, and I had an impulse to snap his card into the wastebasket. Two considerations checked the urge. First, it had been a very long time since I'd been asked out; and secondly, although Nick had dumped a big pile of flattery on my office carpet, he'd been polite enough not to trample in it by asking for my home number or forcing me to turn him down on the spot. I've always appreciated a man who packages a graceful way out into his propositions.

Nick's card stood propped against my desk calendar for a week, and after looking at it and fingering it and intermittently toying with the idea of a date, I decided to call him. I had no other plans, and I figured there were worse ways to spend a Saturday night than dinner with someone who was likely to make a big effort to impress me. As I was about to dial his number, my phone rang.

"Dr. Lerner? This is Nick."

"I'm sorry—Nick who?" Like someone running around the house looking for the pair of scissors she held in her hand, I'd been so preoccupied with what I was preparing to do that I'd momentarily failed to connect Nick whose number was staring at me from my bureau, with Nick whose voice now faltered on the other end of the phone.

"Umm . . . you know, 'Nick the Schmuck.' The guy who was calling to ask you out, but has decided instead to open a vein in his wrist . . ."

Explaining my confusion as best I could, I apologized, and then offered to take him to dinner to make amends. After some polite protest, he accepted. We discovered we were both free that evening, and decided there was no sense in postponing our date until the weekend.

Nick picked me up in a newish Mercedes sedan. I was

surprised: based on the haircut, I'd figured him for an old Mustang, maybe a Mini Cooper. Our dinner reservations weren't for another hour, so we decided to have cocktails first. Nick suggested a place he knew, a supper club that featured what he called "bad Caucasian funk." But the music didn't start before ten, he said, and until then the bar was quiet, dark, and cozy.

I liked it right away, and I liked the bartender and the patrons, who all seemed to know Nick. They bantered freely and razzed each other like old friends. Everyone was extremely nice to me, and a collective effort was made to include me in the conversation. I soon gathered from certain comments that I was hardly the first woman Nick had brought here. I decided it was time to gauge the mettle of the man, and have a little fun in the bargain. With a smile I turned to him and asked (sweetly, but loudly enough for the others to hear): "Nick, are you a dog?"

Like the cast of a sitcom pausing in unison to clear airspace for a punchline, everyone in the bar suddenly fell silent. Nick met my assessing gaze with an unembarrassed smile: "Yes, Claire," he replied, "—as a matter of fact, I *am* a dog. That's not a problem for you, is it?"

It was a decent return, but I was ready with another volley.

"That depends. Are you a *good* dog?"

"That question could mean a lot of things," he laughed. "Do you mind if I call you Dr. Lerner?"

"Yes, Nick, as a matter of fact, I do."

He was charming, and much more subdued than I'd expected after his cheekiness at our first meeting. Unusual for me in a non-professional setting, I ended up asking most of the questions. He wasn't at all secretive about his personal life, but my inquiries into his work at first elicited only the vague datum that he was "an illustrator." After I insisted on detail, he launched into an exhaustive description of wood engraving, an archaic method of printmaking for which he claimed a natural talent. His was nearly a lost art, he explained, very much in demand by his advertiser clients, a technique yet to be replicated by a computer program. "I'm indispensable," he laughed. "I've got at least six months before they replace me with graphics software."

We left the bar and decided to walk the few blocks to the Indonesian restaurant where I'd made reservations, a kosher rijsttafel buffet called "Bali Chai." Nick was good company; he had an offbeat sense of humor, and I liked looking at his face, which, I decided, was more than easy on the eyes. He was also appealingly self-assured, much less swaggering than he'd seemed at first impression.

After dinner, Nick suggested we go to his place. "I mean, if you want. It's still early, and I'd love to show you my studio and some of my work. The pieces are all block prints, by the way. I don't do etchings, so you're totally safe. And I never tie women up on the first date."

As I agreed to the plan, I knew I was taking another step toward the fulfillment of Andres' prophecy.

Nick's studio was a combined living and work space in Tribeca, unlike anything I'd ever seen or imagined. The lofts of the most frenetic of the original action painters were less disorderly, or at least their chaos somehow congealed, like the splatters and drips of their canvases, into a recognizable whole. Nick's chaos, on the other hand, was the fragmented miscellany of the garage sale or junkyard. Gray metal partitions divided one large room into ceilingless cubicles—three for living, three for work—each lit by a bare bulb hanging from the rafters at the end of a long black cord. The furniture was hideous: shelves and file cabinets that looked as though they'd been gleaned from an S & L bankruptcy sale; high-backed office recliners in dark maple, circa 1974; battered cutting tables that were already antiques when the ILGWU began its unionizing drives in the sweatshops.

This was much more furniture than one person could use, although that one person would have been hard pressed to find a single square inch of bare space upon which to work, for every horizontal surface was cluttered with stuff: computers (in and out of boxes), piles of speakers, CD players and power tools, and everywhere wood blocks and wood shavings, chisels and gouges, paper and ink. All of the merchandise looked as though it had just been off-loaded from somewhere, and none of the art seemed completed. Everything appeared to have been frozen in the midst of activity, like a workshop at Herculaneum suspended in time by a torrent of lava.

Nick excused himself to attend to a messenger who had buzzed from below, so for a few minutes I pursued my explorations unaccompanied. The visual mayhem, I saw, extended into another plane, for all the studio's vertical surfaces—including the concrete columns that mushroomed from the floor at regular intervals to support the roof—were densely postered with memorabilia and art. I poked around in search of groupings and patterns, interested to discover if this wall-to-wall "gallery," apparently the result of haphazard accumulation, might betray some hidden organizing principle. To be honest, I was pulling for randomness: it would confirm my intuition that Nick was the anti-Glenn, at least aesthetically. (Glenn's tastes were certainly refined enough, but he was unbearably prissy about his habitat; to make the least alteration or addition to home decor could cost him hours, sometimes even days, of agonized indecision.)

I picked out a square meter of wall at random, and reviewed its contents. The transect contained, in part: two unmounted contact photographs in the style of the Rayograph; a faded and fly-specked miniature reproduction of the *Mona Lisa* set in a passe partout whose edge bore a sticker that read "Sullivan Art Store, Topeka, Kansas"; a recipe for "3-Alarm Tex-Mex Chili," torn from a magazine and stuck to the wall with a steel pushpin; four Belle Époque erotic postcards depicting plump tribades cavorting on a divan in front of a painted backdrop of trees and suburbicarian ruins; one of Nick's own signed pieces: a small, densely intricate landscape built up from dots and fine lines that looked like a study of one of the Dutch masters, maybe van Ruisdael; two ancient Hasselblad brochures showing cameras specially designed for the lunar landings; a menu from the Musso & Frank Grill in Hollywood, California, with prices ($1.75 for a sirloin steak) that momentarily transported me to a time before the last generation screwed things up so badly for us, the next generation. Then my eye fell disbelievingly on a treasure: flanked by a two-year-old receipt for an Ohaus electronic laboratory scale (metric calibration) and a postcard of a "Jackalope" was a small gouache painting in an antique gilt frame. The style wasn't one I was likely to misattribute, and the signature confirmed my hunch: the work was by Klee. When Nick returned, I asked him about it. He promptly wormed out of a discussion of its provenance, but was very happy that I recognized the artist and liked the piece.

It had grown late; Nick helped me into my coat, promising that "on our next date" he would not only complete the tour of the loft, but give me a full demonstration of his woodcutting prowess. Although we hardly said a word to one another as he drove me home, I felt at ease in the silence, contented by Nick's smile and the press of his hand on mine.

Nick walked me to the front of my building, and for a moment we simply stood there facing each other. Then he drew me to him and kissed me on the mouth, and I kissed him back, and we lingered like that for a minute or two in view of the street. I felt like a lover in a Robert Doisneau photograph. This was new for me; all my previous sexual dealings with men—including Glenn—had had what I called a "dormlike" inception: you were hanging out with friends, usually in a dorm room, then you were alone together, then you started making out, then you went to bed. Now, leaning into Nick's arms, I lifted one foot off the ground with a bend of the knee to see if that cliché of cinema romance carried a feeling. (It didn't, but I was forced to flex my toes in order to arrest the slide of my pump, which completed the big screen effect.) Nick broke our kiss at last, though his hands kept a gentle hold on my forearms as he slowly pulled away.

"I had a wonderful time, Claire; I want to do it again. Very soon. I mean—if you do."

"Yes," I laughed, and then he hugged me again, and I had the distinct sensation of an appliquéed felt letter pressing against my breast.

Nick walked back to his car, but as I slipped my key into the lock of my front door, I heard him shout: "Goodnight Dr. Lerner!"

"Stop that!" I called out, turning back toward him. But he had already driven away, and my words dispersed, unheard, out across the empty street.

That night I made up my mind I would sleep with Nick the next time we saw each other. He was obviously something of a player, and his unapologetic answer to my "dog" accusation meant he wasn't likely to be shamed out of it any time soon. But suddenly I didn't care—a non-feeling I interpreted as a healthy relaxation of my predilection for prerequisites. I realized with pleasure that I had no interest in reforming him: I wanted to make him my lover, impure and simple.

Just now, however, I was faced with the decision of what—once Andres had made his inevitable demand for a report on our date—I ought to divulge to him about my feelings for Nick.

PATROQUEEET: Hey Claire! There you are! Did you fuck him?

PARAPRAXISTA: Jesus Christ, Andres! I can't believe you asked that.

PATROQUEEET: Sure you can. I'm clearly a
Federation-class yenta. Alors?

PARAPRAXISTA: Alors, what?

PATROQUEEET: Alors, did you fuck him?

PARAPRAXISTA: Damn you, Andres—I did not.
And if I had, I wouldn't tell you. Did you take
special classes to learn this kind of interrogation?

PATROQUEEET: Yes, a correspondence course
from Pinochet's CIA handlers. Anyways, I was
just being direct. You hate the oblique,
remember? And besides, you *have* to tell me.
It's part of our bargain.

PARAPRAXISTA: What bargain was that?

PATROQUEEET: The bargain where you agreed,
in return for my devoted services as your long-
distance-cyber-virtual-phone-incorporeal-lover
thang, to recount for me the intimate details of
your erotic life. If you perform over time, you also
get a new automobile: a Faustian compact car.

PARAPRAXISTA: Boo. Hiss. That was truly abom-
inable. And you're more yeti than yenta, if you
ask me. And I entered into no such bargain.

PATROQUEEET: Yes, you did. I have the docu-
ments, signed in blood. I bribed your phle-
botomist, in a land called "Honah-Lee." Look,
you know the nature of my thing: I live vicari-

ously through other people as a redundant substitute for personal experience. So you are under obligation as my dearest friend to provide fodder for the grist of my imaginary mill, if you'll excuse my fucking up a couple of old tropes.

PARAPRAXISTA: You know something, Andres? Your wife is a saint.

Flouting current courtship convention, Nick called me the day after our date. I had to temper my giddy elation, for fear of sounding vapid or too needy.

"So, you're good?"

"Yes, Nick. I'm good."

"Good-good. I want to see you again, Claire—like tonight, or tomorrow night, if you're available. I'm sick of playing boy-girl games, so here goes: I like you a bushel and a peck. Last night was great. Let's make babies."

"Sorry, Nick, no breeding. I'm committed to a life without sippy-cups. My germ plasm dies with me."

"Okay, bear with me, I'm writing this down . . . no babies. Can we still date?"

"No."

"No? Are you serious? No?"

"I'm serious. No."

"Wow. Okay, I *guess*. Got a sister?"

"Oh, I think you misunderstand me, Nick. It's not that I don't want to *see* you, I just don't want to *date* you. Capisce? Listen, I'll make dinner for us. How about tomorrow night, at my apartment?"

"What about your sister?"

"No go. She only likes smart and handsome men."

"È vietato entrare."

I rescheduled some appointments to free up the next afternoon. I loved to cook for others, but it had been a long time since I'd had the opportunity, and now I wanted to putter enjoyably through the preparations without regard for the clock. I went shopping: fresh flowers and vegetables from the street market; spirits and sweets from Zabar's; focaccia from the Italian sandwich shop next door. To obviate last-minute scrambling, I chose a menu that could be completed in advance and reheated. Then, carried away by the pleasures of the kitchen, I went glass for glass with the coq au vin until a bottle of wine, a Beaujolais in the very prime of youth, lay void and dispirited atop the recycle bin, exhausted from the unequal contest. By the time I began to dress, I was glowing as warmly as if I'd just had a jacuzzi and a rubdown. Ten minutes before Nick's expected arrival, I made the vinaigrette, popped the bread into a warm oven, and lit some candles. When I stepped out onto my balcony to wait, the sky was just giving up its last salmony residue of daylight.

Nick arrived at the appointed hour. He thanked me expansively for inviting him, then ran smiling around the kitchen, lifting lids off pots, sniffing at them with approving anticipatory sighs, and complimenting my culinary skills. We had a glass of the champagne he'd brought, and began to talk while I served up the meal.

Not five minutes later, and despite my self-avowed indifference toward the subject, I was already asking him about his womanizing.

"You know, Nick—you never really answered my question the other night in the bar."

"What question?"

"I asked you if you were a good dog, don't you remember?"

"Geez, Claire—it's a little rough around here on the newcomers, don't you think?"

"Maybe a little. More hearts of palm?"

"Look, I'd be happy to complete your survey. I'm not out to make any false impressions. And besides, I've been reformed. I'm still a hound, but now at least I'm honest about it." As he handed me his plate he smiled, and with relief I saw that he was more amused than rankled by my line of questioning.

"This isn't a survey, Nick. I just wanted to know a little about your life. I'm interested, and I won't judge."

Nick cocked an eyebrow at me, then snorted with exaggerated mirth.

"What's so funny?" I demanded.

"You are, Claire. Funny, and full of shit."

"I was being sincere."

"I believe you. You're *sincerely* full of shit. And of course you're going to judge. The fact is, how I answer your question is going to determine whether you have anything more to do with me after tonight. If that's not judging, I don't know what is."

I was ashamed. Nick was absolutely right. And although I'd never been a stickler for etiquette, I certainly knew it was impolite to administer exams to dinner guests. I must have stopped eating and blanched, for suddenly Nick was hovering over me with a look of concern.

"You okay? Are you sick?"

"I'm okay, Nick—thank you. I'm not sick. I just feel very bad about giving you the third degree. I was out of line. I don't know what to say. I'm sorry. It was a shitty thing to do."

"Oh, that's okay, Claire—really. I can take it. I'm a manly man." Then, after a thoughtful pause, he added, "You *were* rude, of course. But straight. I like that. I'm on a sincerity kick. I'll tell you anything you want to know."

"Really?"

"Really."

"Good. Start at the beginning. I want to know everything."

According to Occam's Razor—a rule of thumb in both science and perjury that posits that, all other things being equal, one should choose the explanation that most simply accounts for the facts at hand—lies and bad hypotheses are thought to betray themselves through excessive complexity. But in my experience all other things have never been equal: the most intricate and convoluted stories are as likely to be true as any other, and perfect cogency as often as not turns out to be the hallmark of autobiographical dishonesty. And so it seemed to me that the story Nick now related, full of explanations that looped and backtracked and second-guessed themselves, was closer to the bald truth than most.

Nick, I learned, was the third son of thrifty, hard-working, and perennially unlucky Bolivian immigrants, a couple whose dedication to the American dream carried them time and again to the threshold of success, but never across it.

After a series of small business failures (a corner market, a carpet cleaning service, and the last, a restaurant called "Chez Guevara" that featured "platos tipicos de La Paz") had wiped out the Familia Pericolo's moderate store of hard-won capital, Nick was sent off to live with cousins. He earned his high school diploma and entered a trade college to study graphic arts, but left before graduating because he could no longer afford the tuition. He worked for years as a bike messenger, then as a taxi driver, and then as a real estate agent before finally realizing his dream of becoming an artist. In the meantime, he explained, he'd made some shrewd investments in commerical property, and when he reached his late twenties, these began to pay off—better than he'd ever dared hope.

"I like to think that it was money that turned me into an asshole. Then again—Who knows?—maybe I was always an asshole. With bucks, though, I finally had a chance to prove it. Anyways, I followed the dick-with-dinero plan to the letter. I bought a ton of crap I didn't need. I did a lot of drugs. In one year I spent more than my parents had earned their whole lives. And when it came to sex, I had absolutely no conscience. I treated cars better than women."

"You never waxed your women?"

"Haha! No—I lied to them. I never lied to my cars."

"Why did you have to lie?"

"I lied to get laid—told them what they wanted to hear. Then I lied when I wanted to dump them, and if that didn't work, I treated them like shit until they packed up. The way I thought about it was this: it was straight business—they were with me for the dinners and the clothes and the trips; I was just a ticket to a better grade of fun. In return, I got sex and an armturner on my head. It never occurred to me I could hurt someone. I thought it was a game—like negotiating a contract. But some of these girls really thought I loved them. They thought I'd promised them a future, or at least a shot at a future. I was a complete schmuck, and there were a lot of girls."

"Then what happened?"

"Haha! Did I say something happened? Still the same old same old . . ."

I laughed too, but I studied Nick's expression all the same, just to be certain his kidding was in earnest. I ran to the kitchen for the dessert tray, and then he continued.

"Well, I suppose this should be the usual morality play where the guy loses everything up his nose, then repents and dedicates the rest of his life to Jesus or Krishna or Bill-fucking-W. But the truth is I never went out of control: business stayed good, and I didn't go into hock on the credit cards or anything that stupid. I didn't change because I had to. I changed because I thought I'd found what I really wanted. The second that happened, I stopped being a player. Cold turkey. No looking back. Gave up the screwing around . . . gave up all the phony friends who were just along for the lush ride. *Then* I got fucked over. Haha!"

"Who was she?" I asked, impatient to learn what sort of woman had been able to stall out Nick's hedonic flight, and then lay him low.

"You're going to think I'm nuts.

"I doubt it, Nick. I know what nuts is. Who was she?"

"I met her online."

I nearly choked on my coffee.

"What is it, Claire? What's wrong? Oh, haha! You must be online."

"Umm, yes. A little." I dabbed my chin with a napkin and tried to appear unruffled.

"Liar," Nick laughed, shooting me a look that said, "I'm on to you."

"Please continue," I said, feigning confused innocence.

Nick stared at me for a moment, then doubled over laughing—so hard his eyes went wet with tears.

"What's so damned funny this time?" I asked.

"Oh, a lot! You keep cracking me up. I just hope you let me hang around long enough to find out about all the stuff you keep hidden."

"Hidden? I'm transparent."

"Yeah, sure. Clear—like mud."

"Please, Nick," I begged, "Can we just get back to the story?"

"Para servirle. But I'm not letting you off the hook. Mark your calendar: we're coming back here sometime soon. Entiendes?"

"Sí."

"Good. Anyways, I met this woman—Anna-Cecilia—in a chatroom. We didn't hit it off right away. I thought she was obnoxious, and I gave her shit for a long time, and she gave me shit back. But after a while we called a truce, and then we became friends. She was funny and outgoing, but not completely 'of the sun'—if that makes sense. Not evil-dark—there was just something about her: a depth . . . a feel for the serious shit in life. And she was beautiful, at least in her photographs. We started doing cybersex, and then phone-sex. You know what phone-sex is, right?"

"Yes," I said, resisting the temptation to elaborate.

"Good," he smiled. "I didn't want to have to explain." Eyes sparkling with mischief, Nick leaned back and ran a hand several times through his hair: sensuously, contemplatively, like someone stroking a favorite cat. Then he winked at me and said, "Would you mind if we get into the rest later? I'm dying for a cigarette."

We bundled up, and I led him out onto the balcony. He lit a cigarette, and we stood together in silence, watching the smoke roll out like cotton batting under the eaves.

After a while Nick's hand found its way to the depression between my shoulder blades. It rested there for a moment, then rose up my spine in a gentle glide to the nape of my neck. Using his fingers as a comb, Nick drew my hair upward, then let it to pour down between his outstretched fingers. He repeated the gesture, and I inclined my head into his palm, becoming the cat now, greeting the stroke.

I wanted him, and wine had already diluted the dregs of my inhibitions. Yet I was unsure how to put the question, how to ask him to stay. It occurred to me that I would have had no difficulty initiating sex online—with typed words— whereas now, in real life, the appropriate phrases eluded me. In the end, I trusted an instinct that he wouldn't refuse a direct appeal, and a sudden insight that the most direct appeal wasn't verbal at all.

Nick was standing with his back propped against the balcony post, one leg bent so that the knee jutted out. Facing him, I grasped his elbows for support, then planted my feet on either side of the projecting limb, straddling it like a hobbyhorse. Then, looking him directly in the eyes, I lifted my dress and pushed my crotch down onto his thigh, sliding backward until my pubic bone contacted his kneecap through my underwear.

He showed absolutely no surprise at my brazenness, maintaining his nonchalance even when I began to hump his leg. Eventually, however, I saw that this indifference was a sham: for though he remained expressionless, his eyes were paying meticulous attention to my face, searching it for the effects of my impromptu frottage. Driven by vanity and also perhaps a certain competitive spirit, I rubbed myself against him with greater and greater insistence, hoping thereby to provoke a reaction. At last I felt his leg rising to meet my undulations, and I responded by angling my hips so that I could direct the pressure onto my clitoris. My breath came faster, but just as my movements were galvanized into a kind of half-controlled gyratory posting, as of a novice rider on a capering pony, Nick stopped pumping his leg, seized me by the shoulders, and forced me to sit still on his knee.

"Wait a second, Claire. I want to tell you something."

"What?" I was as bewildered by this solemn declaration as I was by Nick's abrupt cancellation of my efforts.

"It's just that, well, until now I would never have guessed you were just another slut."

I waited, but his face refused to soften into a smile—the smile that would have transformed his statement into the verbal equivalent of a friendly poke in the ribs. Finally, I realized that his impudence was intentional, the charge meant as a challenge and a question. *How would I take it?* Nick was asking—*as a criticism or an invitation?*

Put to me a year earlier, the question would have enraged me. Certainly, I'd have instantly branded as a misogynistic yahoo any man who so much as implied I was a slut. But Andres had changed me. Under his tutelage I'd come to see how critically important context and intent were to the hermeneutics of vilespeak. And Andres' intentions had always been clear: he thrilled to my orgasms, he was committed to their multiplication and eternal recurrence.

The question pressing upon me most immediately, however, concerned not him, but Nick. Specifically, whether *his* animus, like Andres', was sex, rather than control or cruelty. My instincts favored a charitable interpretation: that although Nick and Andres were far too different to be called brothers in the spirit, they nevertheless shared the same genius loci in one locus at least. If cocks had daemons, my intuition suggested, these two boys were identically possessed.

It was in accordance with this benign version of Nick—perhaps rashly adopted at the time (though in the end to prove accurate)—that I chose to accept his proposition. The decision made, however, I found myself stymied in its expression—muted by timidity and every explicit and rumored convention of what it meant to be a "good girl" that had ever introjected itself into my unconscious.

Having lost my nerve and my voice, I reverted once again to purely physical expression. I threw my head back like a conductor preparing to bow to applause, then ground my sex down on Nick's knee—with such momentum that the angle of thigh and calf supporting me collapsed. I went into free-fall, coming to rest, head level with his waist, arms and legs wrapped willy-nilly around his body, a baby lemur clinging to her mother after a hard-landed leap through the trees. Nick stared down at me, then gave a raucous laugh before helping me to my feet.

"Get a hold of yourself, would you, Claire? I'm going to finish my drink out here, and have another cigarette. Please go inside and sit in the living room where I can see you. When you're settled, spread your legs and play with yourself. I want to watch while I smoke. I'll be in in a while."

As if carbureted by Nick's request, the warmth between my legs flared and intensified. Pulling my dress high up on my thighs, I dropped into the green leather chair that faced the verandah and hooked the backs of my knees over the arm rests. I could see the double flame of Nick's lighter, once through the glass door and ghosted again beside it as a reflection on the pane; I could feel him staring at me from the darkness as he smoked.

To my surprise, my concerns took a thespian turn: carefully considering my movements, I tried to visualize how each might contribute to the realization of the scene I had, as I saw it, been asked to improvise. I brought my hands to my breasts, cupping them through the silk of my dress so that the draping defined their curves. Under the fabric, my nipples felt flat, like covered buttons, but I quickly roused them with a few hard flicks of my thumbs. Then I arranged my underwear—black and minimalist—so that the actual theater of operations would be screened from view, and my observer forced to deduce the nature of my hands' actions from the rise and fall of muscle and tendon across their backs.

Thus prepared, I began lightly to stroke my vulva, the glide of moisture wicking between fingers that I carried dripping to my lips, then sucked and licked with exaggerated gestures, then replaced between wet nymphae.

Startled by the sound of the glass door truckling on its rail, I looked up to find Nick watching me from just within the doorway, hanging back as though reined in by a respectful unwillingness to intrude upon my mis en scène.

It was time to heighten the drama. First, I rotated myself in the chair so that I faced Nick squarely, allowing him his first full glimpse of what Andres, in a moment of supreme silliness, had once called my "dainties." Then, forming my left hand into an inverted "v," I spread the lips of my pussy from above, while with my other hand, which I had in the meantime squeezed forward along the guiding bezel made by the crack of my ass, I prepared to make entry from below. I deliberately prolonged the first penetrative motions, but my excitement was so great that as soon as my first finger had been fully inserted, I followed it with another, and then a third, and their combined churning soon spackled my thighs and pubis with flecks of billowy emulsion. At last a poignant pleasure burst within me, and above the gurgles and squelches of fingers sliding against smooth wet membranes my cries rang out, then faded to a soft echo as I slipped, insensate, oblivious to my voyeur's hungry stare, fast into the netherworld between sleep and consciousness.

I was —teen, Sharon a year my senior, both of us "Equestrian Counselors" at a sleep-away camp in the Adirondacks, hired on for the season—trading three months of strenuous, stall-mucking labor for a token salary and the privilege of riding in our spare time. I was tall and timid, with olive complexion and a sun-streaked auburn mane; Sharon small and confident, her face all Irish contrasts, flawless skin creating a pleasing pale distinction to a frame of black hair. Though probably plain to an unbiased eye, to me she was beautiful—everything about her, but especially her shoulders: broadly set for a girl, the angles tanned and rounded like brown eggs, they beckoned to my fingers; never before had I known such a desire to caress.

Deferring to Sharon's superior knowledge, I followed her lead as we worked in the paddock and barn and took campers on the trail. She seemed happy for my company and assistance, and clearly enjoyed as much as I did the opportunity to discuss bits and saddles, to argue schools of equitation, or simply to exchange horse platitudes about Hanoverians and Thoroughbreds, Arabians and Swedish Warmbloods. I was surprised and gladdened when, little by little, as if she were testing a decision to befriend me, she began to share with me more personal thoughts. Before very long, she confided to me a sad story of alcoholic parents and a childhood of neglect and emotional abuse.

I was deeply gratified that Sharon had made me her confidante, a role which was new in my experience. I was sensible of a need to reciprocate, and perhaps because I had no story to offer that was comparable to hers in pathetic depth (and perhaps, too, because I had an unconscious need to unburden myself), I began to detail every experience or thought that had ever caused me emotional pain or mental turmoil. With almost saintly patience, Sharon listened while I described my insecurities, fretted over my chronic asociability, agonized over my appearance. Through it all she remained tranquil, sympathetic, uncritical—until I mentioned my obsessive escape to self-pleasuring, whereupon she suddenly raised a quizzical eyebrow.

I was mortified. Had I made an awful mistake? Had zealousness clouded my judgment, leading me to attribute a liberality to my confessor she didn't possess? I felt cold perspiration beading on my forehead as waves of humiliation and dread washed over me. My face must have gone ashen, for Sharon noticed my discomfort and asked if I was feeling sick. I hesitated, unsure if I should explain the true cause of my sudden distress. Something benevolent in Sharon's expression—the genuine concern I saw reflected in her gaze, or a sympathetic inclination I read in the curve of her neck—decided my answer, and in that instant it seemed to me that I was making a great wager, risking a friendship that, although only days old and more incipient than fulfilled, had already become profoundly important to me.

I blurted out the truth: that I feared my admission of excessive masturbation had repulsed her—then awaited her reaction with a nearly unbearable sense of impending loss. Her answer was to gather my head to her breast and start giggling. *What was this?* I asked myself. Was she making fun of me? But if so, why the tenderness?

Still smiling, Sharon explained that it wasn't my masturbatory habits that had given her pause, only my description of them as "obsessive." Sexual release, she said—whether by self-stimulation or otherwise—had always been as natural to her as breathing. And no one, she added, would call themselves air-obsessed.

"Oxygen, Claire. You look like the type who needs it all the time. I'm going to tell your friends!"

I laughed and hugged her to me, holding back tears of relief as the tension broke.

The next few days at camp would have been perfect but for the rapidity with which perfectly enjoyable days pass. I spent as much time as I could with Sharon: we rode and talked, raked out stalls, fed and watered the horses—the dirtier the job, the more fun we had.

I was aware that my attraction to her was more than platonic. My pulse quickened in her presence; her looks and touches made me wet between the legs, and I understood exactly what that meant. Yet at the same time I had no idea what to do with these feelings, nor was I sure whether they were at all mutual. I certainly had neither the skill nor the confidence to initiate any sort of investigative foray.

On the day before camp was to end, Sharon and I were alone in the barn, working—tidying up for the last time, making an inventory of lost and damaged tack. Outside there poured a steady thin rain, and it seemed as though the day's drear were reflecting the unspoken sadness we felt at our impending separation. Sharon lived far from the city and, somehow, despite our mutual promises to visit and write, there was a tacit understanding between us—a stoical acceptance of probabilities—that we were at the beginning of journeys that would soon take us in very different directions. We knew, in a way that usually only adults know but rarely acknowledge, that our good-byes the next morning would likely be final ones.

Our chores finished, we stood side-by-side, reclining in the manner of horsewomen, with our backs and the flats of one boot against the exposed studs of the barn wall. Sharon lit a cigarette, cadged from one of the maintenance crew, which we silently passed between us until it burned down to the filter. Then, as though punctuating a decision, she crushed out the fag-end with the twist of a heel and turned to face me.

"I love you, Claire," she said suddenly, and held my eyes with her own as she draped the back of her hand on my bare shoulder.

Surprised and overwhelmed by this sudden fulfillment of a secret wish, I began to tremble with excitement. For I knew somehow that this was no declaration of chaste love: the spark that flashed when Sharon's fingers touched my arm was more than electrical static; it conducted an emotional charge as well.

Still shaking with joyous anticipation (and perhaps a little fear), I closed my eyes and moved my head toward Sharon's in expectation of her gentle kiss. When I leaned forward to meet her lips, however, I encountered only empty space. I looked up to find that instead of offering me her mouth, Sharon had retreated slightly, and now stood watching me with narrowed eyes. Her expression confused me: not because it was malevolent, but because it seemed sly and detached, when every scrap of hearsay relating to love had led me to expect that her face would mirror all the unguarded affection and warmth that I knew was radiating from my own.

Wordlessly, Sharon brought her hands to my waist, then unfastened my belt and tore open the fly of my jeans, popping the buttons from their holes with one sure downward tug. Without a pause she slid my pants and underwear to the floor, inclined her body against me for the first time, then brought a leg up between mine. Pressing her face to my neck, she kissed and then bit sharply into the skin below my ear, a tiny nip crimped off between the edges of incisors, like a cat's hit-and-run love bite, but painful all the same. She sucked avidly at the wounded spot, which assuaged its tenderness but did nothing to reduce my bewilderment.

Suddenly she released her lips from my bruised flesh, and I tensed in reflexive expectation of another attack. But when her mouth bent again to my neck, it was only to whisper in my ear—though what she said was perhaps more scathing and provocative than any physical torment I might reasonably have feared.

"I want to fuck you like a boy."

I was stunned and abashed; my head reeled and I felt as though a fist instead of a heart were pounding within my chest. For several terrible seconds a storm of fear and doubt raged within me—until at last I recalled a certain douceur in Sharon's intonation, a muted playful note that seemed to mitigate the crude brutality of her harsh and unexpected words.

I calmed myself and managed to regain some perspective on my situation. What made Sharon's behavior so disturbing, I knew, was that it bore no resemblance to what I'd supposed "sex" would be like; it lay beyond the range of even my imaginative understanding. Yet just as I was reconciling myself to the limits of my comprehension, I was suddenly forced to acknowledge that part of me knew *exactly* what to make of my condition, for I now realized that without consciously intending it, I had responded to the insistent pressure of Sharon's leg by parting my thighs.

With her knee wedged firmly against my groin, Sharon raised a hand to my face, then gently swept my eyelids closed with the tips of her outstretched thumb and index finger: the same formal gesture, I recognized with a shiver, that one would use on a corpse.

There was a sudden rush of movement, and in a fraction of a second my hands were seized, slammed together, and immobilized. I opened my eyes to find Sharon spinning loops of leather rein around my wrists with the practiced motions of a rodeo cowboy hobbling an upended calf. Satisfied that my bindings were secure, she took up the free end of the rein, turned this round a nail that projected from the wall above me, and then pulled it until my hands and arms were drawn forcibly up and over my head. All at once I felt her tongue dart across my teeth and lips; desperate for physical contact, I tried to suck it into my mouth, only to be balked at each attempt by its slippery, teasing surface.

Breaking our kiss, Sharon fixed me with the same sly, objectifying squint as before, and I watched as her mouth formed itself into a slight pout, heavy with lower lip, but louche and self-consumed rather than beckoning. She extended her tongue for a moment in order to moisten a middle finger with saliva, and then lowered her hand to my sex. Before I knew what was happening—for there was neither verbal warning nor the least prefatory caress—she thrust a finger deep within me. Strangely, I felt no pain other than a negligible sting; I only knew that my hymen had been torn when a tiny trickle of blood began to cool against the inside of my thigh. With a gloating smile, Sharon raised her stained hand to my face, then put her fingers in her mouth to suck them clean. Her pride at having robbed me of my virginity was obvious, but so far out on my own erotic current had I ridden that I registered her "crime" almost dispassionately, as though it were a bit of third-party gossip, or an event in the life of a fictional character, instead of my own.

After once more kissing my lips—chastely this time— Sharon dropped to her knees before me. Her hands, palms held together like those of a supplicant, slipped between my thighs and then canted from the wrists, coaxing my legs apart. She paused for a moment, staring at my half-exposed genitals as if in contemplative devotion, a votary before the oread's shrine. Then I felt the wet heat of her breath suffuse my vulva, an advance signature of the soothing conflagration that immediately followed when her mouth, feverish to the touch, was pressed to my pussy. After a flurry of dispersed kisses, she took my clitoris between her lips, at first merely holding it with her teeth abutting its tip, like a sunflower seed about to be hulled, then mildly sucking at it, then lolling it about with soft passes of her fluttering tongue. Soon, however, I began to crave bolder attention: for no matter how they were actually intended, Sharon's delicate pressures and gentle insinuations were becoming a tease. I wanted satisfaction, and notwithstanding my youth and in-experience, I somehow knew that under the present cir-cumstances tenderness—even prolonged tenderness—would never suffice.

I wanted to be devoured, but I'd been ratcheted to such a debilitating pitch of arousal that even had I dared to ask—and such daring was decidedly beyond my power—I would have been unable to articulate my wishes. As if intentionally to compound my frustration, Sharon again pulled away without warning, leaving me to buck my pelvis in a vain at-tempt to press myself against her mouth, now held just be-yond my reach. Then, while looking in my eyes to gauge my reaction, she extended her tongue tip until it barely touched my clitoris, then quickly retracted it away, her face beaming with delight at my travail. I was in an excruciating bind: un-able on the one hand to satisfy a white-hot need; precluded, on the other, from releasing any of the crackling tension which gripped my body.

Sharon continued to flick at my clitoris with her tongue. Once or twice when she applied increased pressure, I felt the muscles of my abdomen tense pre-orgasmically, but she always relented at the very moment when the next touch would have vaulted me into the redeeming abyss. I tried to force the issue by rubbing my thighs together, but this proved ineffectual. A profound despairing shame overtook me: a feeling of humiliation, aggravated by a sense of im-pending failure at my inability either to satisfy myself or to make Sharon satisfy me.

Apparently sensing the advent of my emotional crisis, she abruptly changed her tack.

"Claire," she asked, "are you okay?"—her voice now filled with loving concern. "What's the matter? I thought you liked what we were doing. I'm so sorry if I made you feel bad...we can stop. Do you want me to stop?"

I couldn't answer her. Although I was dying for release, I worried she might use any reply I gave to further her cruel game of denial, which—notwithstanding her gentle words and soothing tone—I was not convinced had ended.

But then Sharon broke the impasse by posing another question, one that for all purposes was rhetorical since I could respond to it in only one way.

"Do you want me to make you come?" she asked. "Is that it?"

"Oh, yes!" I cried, desperation overcoming prudence and fear.

"Are you sure?"

"Yes, Sharon, please—I'm sure. Please make me come, please..."

I knew by her smile, which was both approving and victorious, that I'd at last hit on an adequate reply.

Sharon circled my waist with her hands, then slipped them under my t-shirt. Her fingers strummed across the corrugations of my ribcage before coming to rest on my bare breasts. Finding my nipples, she forsook preliminary caresses, and instead began directly to roll the points between her thumbs and forefingers, applying vice-like pressure until the sensitive flesh was tender-raw and reddened. (Both the roughness of the treatment and my tolerance for it surprised me, for I'd no idea as yet that sexual arousal could elevate the threshold of pain.) Sharon increased the torsion on my nipples, triggering a precritical disgorgement: suddenly my pussy was so wet that for a moment I feared I might have peed myself in my excitement. Smiling with satisfaction, she lowered herself to her knees and began to lap at my vulva, painting it slowly with stripes of saliva, barely touching the tip of her tongue to my clitoris at the end of every upstroke.

This was more than I could stand: I pushed myself down upon her mouth, but this time, thankfully, instead of evading my motions she actively met my thrusts. With her hands on my buttocks, mauling their flesh as she pulled me violently onto her tongue, she at last treated me to that severity which in sexual extremis is the only true kindness. Half a minute more of blissful friction and I came—thrashing, moaning, biting my lips—my pussy shuddering against Sharon's ravenously sucking mouth, all my senses—of time and place, of sound and motion—jumbled and confused, running together like colors, until the border between self and the world dissolved, and for one numinous instant my "I" was absorbed into the purest of imaginable pleasures, and I knew, even before it was over, that I'd tasted something I would no longer be able to live without.

"Open your eyes, Claire."

Like a lotus-eater drifting on the upwellings and currents of an exquisite self-absorption, I had been oblivious both to my surroundings and the passage of time. It might have been seconds or minutes since I'd last registered Nick's presence. Now, as I turned toward the source of his voice, I saw that he'd taken the chair directly in front of mine, and that his hand was tracing the outline of his erection through the faded denim of his jeans. Struggling to emerge from my trance, I smiled at him. Then I parted my thighs and began to play with myself.

"I want to come for you again."

"No, Claire. Not yet: I want to taste you first." Nick pulled his cock—long, slender and rigid—from his pants, and stroking its length in his fist, dropped to his knees in front of me. He bent his head to my sex, but before I felt his touch he paused and raised his eyes to mine.

"Claire, your pussy is so beautiful: a rose in a rose."

His face descended to my crotch, tongue caressing my clitoris, teeth nibbling my labia—then all at once he was applying his lips to the maw of my vagina, kissing it with the tender passion usually reserved for the more public mouth. And these ministrations were no mere courtesy: Nick was reveling in my pussy, indulging the demands of his own orality. Had I still doubted his pleasure in eating me, one glance past his bobbing head to the sight of his hand furiously pumping his cock would have been sufficient to convince me otherwise.

Seized by a sudden inspiration, Nick took firm hold of the cheeks of my ass and shook me sideways so that on each pass my clitoris caught and then slid over his tongue, held rigid and fully extended like the rubber number stop of a roulette wheel. A few moments later I felt a hand migrate from my buttocks to my mons, and then a thumb arched downward to snag the hood of my clitoris. Nick's mouth sucked at the tumid bud beneath—now rendered maximally accessible to his lips—but relinquished it just as I was about to climax, directing his lips and tongue instead to my vagina, where they resumed their palpatory soundings. Convinced I would pass out from the pain of want, I begged Nick to let me come. To my surprise he obliged me, absorbing my clit once again into his mouth, his sucking now combined with rapid flicks of his tongue tip. Only when I was beyond all point of return, my hips flailing and my heart racing in delicious agony, did Nick at last wrest himself free of my locked thighs in order to push his tongue a final time into my vagina. Long after I had come, Nick's face remained between my legs, his tongue passing from the grotto to the channel and back, avidly licking out the fluids released by my orgasm like a honeybee coaxing the last drops of nectar from a blossom.

I awakened to the smell of peppermint and hot milk in my nostrils. At some point I'd been transported to my bed. Nick, who lay shirtless beside me on the coverlet, was offering me a mug of Indian tea.

"How do you feel?"

"Umm . . . Fine. Am I okay?"

"Yes," he laughed, "you're okay. Actually, better than okay —you're terrific," and with a look of protective solicitude he sat watching while I sipped the sweet infusion.

"This was so nice of you, Nick."

"Making the tea? T'weren't nothing, ma'am."

"Mmmm. Yes, it were. Making the tea, yes . . . but also before. Very sweet."

"Well, I only made the tea hoping it might make it easier to take advantage of you."

"Umm, don't you think that's an odd approach to seduction, Nick? I can't imagine it's worked for you before."

"Like a charm. But I used to date a lot of houris and temple prostitutes."

"Oh, well . . . of course you did."

We lay about on the bed for half an hour or so, talking and eating the cookies Nick had ferreted out of my pantry. I was liking him a lot. He was kind and very sexy. And although he was neither as extroverted nor as verbally adept as Andres, I was pleased to find that stiller waters didn't necessarily run shallow.

We had the AIDS discussion, which Nick initiated by telling me he'd recently been tested, and that he used condoms religiously. "I keep votive candles in them," he said.

"I haven't been tested in a while."

"That's not good, Claire. You afraid?"

"No," I said, lowering my eyes to the bed, suddenly uncomfortable with the explanation I was about to offer. "It's not that; it's not fear."

"Then what is it?"

"Oh, well . . . it's just that I haven't had much reason to, really. It's been over two years since I last had sex."

"*Two years?* What's going on, Claire? You ugly or something?"

"Yes, that's it," I laughed. "Now you know why I showed you my naked body so quickly: I wanted to distract you before you noticed how horrid my face was."

"Haha! But two years? Really?"

"Yes. Well ... not exactly. Let's just say I haven't had sex involving contact in two years."

"I have a better idea: let's not."

"We can't just leave it at that?"

"Not on your life."

"Look, I'll tell you—I will. I promise. But later, okay?"

Before he could argue, I leaned over and unbuttoned his jeans. Then I reached into the fly of his boxers and fished out his cock, which twitched rapidly to life again at my touch. After stealing a quick look at the expression on his face, I lowered my mouth to the head of his penis, and with the edge of my tongue slowly circled its corona. Nick moaned with expectancy at the contact, which I took care not to break, even as I extended an arm to the night table, where, obedient to the dating advice consensus of the women's magazines, I had placed a condom in preparation for the contingency.

I stabilized Nick's cock with one hand, brought the wrapper to my mouth with the other, tore it open with my teeth, removed the condom and positioned it for deployment. Then I placed my mouth over the glans, now glycerin smooth and nacreous in its latex sheath, and with my lips chasing the leading edge of the descending condom as I un-rolled it, took the column into my throat to the plinth. I came up for air, then licked my saliva from the shaft and head—Nick's eyes following my every move, his erection raised in staunch approval of my performance.

"Play with yourself while you suck me."

I dug out of the covers and arranged myself so that I could

suck Nick's cock while keeping a hand free to masturbate. Despite the polymer taste of the condom, his penis felt marvelous in my mouth, and because its girth wasn't excessive, I was able to swallow most of it—to his obvious pleasure. Nick seemed pent up, and I was sure my deep sucking would make short work of him. But just as I was spurring myself into what I thought were final efforts, he seized my head without warning and began to fuck my mouth so forcefully that not only were my attempts to suppress my gag reflex nullified, but I had to fight myself free of his pinioning hands simply in order to breathe. For a split second I was petrified. Had I been terribly—perhaps fatally—wrong about Nick? Yet even as I was mentally locating the nearest exits and reflexively weighing the comparative risks of flight versus fight, I realized that the danger had already passed, gone as precipitously as it had arisen. The hands which had trapped me moments before now lay softly upon my shoulders, and when I looked up, half expecting to see a frightful wooden grimace, my eyes found only Nick's gentle, ironical smile.

"Too rough, Claire?"

Unbelievably, my mouth still full of his cock, I shook my head "no." Only a second before, I'd thought I had met the throttling grip of my murderer—*now I was encouraging him!* Plainly I had mixed feelings about fear.

I gradually disgorged Nick's penis, and when my lips finally cleared its head they remained connected across threads of saliva provoked from my throat's membranes by the violent irritation of his thrusts. With meditatively prolonged movements, his fingers detached the clinging webs of spit from his cock, afterwards spooning them back into my mouth as though they were spanning strands of melted gruyère trailing from an onion soup. Taking my face in his hands, he cleaned the straggling drops from my lips and neck with his tongue, then once again (and as forcefully as before) planted his cock in my throat.

This time however I was psychologically prepared for the strike, and absorbed its length with relative ease. Yet before long I understood that it was my choking that most quickened Nick's ardor, and so to indulge him, I forced myself down on his cock until my throat gurgled and quivered in protest. Clearly fascinated by my distress, Nick stared at my agonized face with the unblinking absorption of a cat watching the struggles of a wounded bird. His gaze and demeanor took on a robotic constancy that I couldn't help but attribute to extreme mental abstraction. Presently the fugue became visible in his eyes as a rapid flickering of the iris, a flutter of contractions bandying the focal point to and fro between the foreground of actuality and what must have been some distant horizon of self-engrossment. I knew he was verging on extramundane territory, a place whose physiography, had it been accessible to my view, I would no doubt have recognized from my own sojourns.

As Nick alternately fucked my face and licked me clean, his enthusiasm remained high but utterly, mechanically constant. I began to worry that the end of the cycle might lie too distant, that I might not be equal to the task. My condition was rapidly deteriorating under his attacks, and I feared that despite the pride I took in pertinacity I would soon be forced to give up short of my goal. Catching my reflection in the side of a mirrored jewel box on my night table, I saw that

I was, in fact, a mess: my mascara a sooty smudge across my cheeks, tracked there by tears that streamed from my eyes each time I gagged on Nick's cock; my hair a tangled nest of clumped strands, braids cemented with drying sweat and saliva; my nose running into the ragged smear of red lipstick that marked my mouth like tincture on a wound.

If it is generally true, as Schopenhauer argued, that knowledge does *not* equal power (or scholars would rule the world), one is nonetheless able here and there to make practical use of a bit of book learning. I'd read somewhere about the tricks of courtesans, and tried now to mine my memory for a solution to our current impasse. Before long a venerable intervention suggested itself: while continuing to suck Nick's cock, I licked my index finger and inserted it into his anus. There was no resistance. I found his prostate directly and massaged it with the prescribed pressure and motion. Within seconds my foray into applied theory had succeeded in its main objective: Nick emerged from his introversive jag, coming alive as if suddenly jarred free from a hypnotic state. Animated now, he pulled his cock from my mouth, then gently but firmly laid me on my back, and at last—using my hip bones as handles—flipped me onto my belly.

"Lift your ass, Claire—and spread your thighs. I want to fuck you. Keep your fingers on your clit."

Nick drew me backward onto my knees and then all at once his cock was in me, the head lodged against my cervix. With a finger I trailed wetness from my vagina to my clitoris, which I proceeded to worry between my fingertips. But such were the kinetics of Nick's exertions that soon I found it unnecessary to stroke myself; I had only to draw the hood of my clit forward in order to expose it to the enlivening pull of surrounding flesh.

As Nick fucked me, he held apart the cheeks of my ass with fingers whose grip embossed my skin with bruising pressure. He began to describe the vista that had opened before him:

"... rose pink flower cunt, Claire ... so fucking beautiful ... little pink mouth all wet and open ... little pink mouth stretched tight round my cock ... fucking you, Claire ... watching you ... so beautiful ... long hard cock in your flower cunt ... perfect round ass ... spreading you ... spreading the petals ... fucking your rose flower cunt ... You like me fucking you, Claire? You like my hard cock in your tight little rose flower cunt?"

"Yes, Nick ... Jesus, yes ..."

I was close to coming, my speech halting and clipped. At the penultimate moment, Nick's hands found my nipples and twisted them savagely—exquisitely apposite torture that served only to precipitate the crisis. But fearing the cruel mercy of a silent, glassy descent, I begged Nick to fuck me full force. He answered my call with an allegro of half-thrusts: like a pestle striking a mortar, his cock pounded my vagina with short, percussive blows until, tumbled across the collapsing face of the swell, I lost muscular control, fell twisting and writhing onto my belly, and finally came to rest, splayed out like storm-cast wrack on the draggled beach of bedsheets.

When, blissfully and extravagantly consumed, I at last lay still, Nick slipped his penis from me and rolled me once again onto my back. As I watched, he ripped the condom from his cock, exposing its shining crimson head, slick with pre-come and spermicide.

"Stroke my balls," he ordered, now kneeling astride my hips as he jerked himself off. Nick was splendid at the end: his face frozen in rapture, his muscles rigid, his cock hard and red as an ingot spewed hot from the blast furnace. His penis recoiled violently as he climaxed through three long strokes, casting turbid aspersions of semen in broad, flossy arcs upon my belly, breasts, and throat. Drenched in his warm emission and my own copious juices, I lay back in bed and stretched my sore limbs before curling with satisfaction into a fetal crescent. I fell asleep with Nick's fingers cupping my shoulder and his warm breath on my neck.

5

Nick told people we were "going steady," and in fact it wasn't too long before we were spending most of our free hours together. The habit came easily: we liked each other; we were good at parallel play; we never seemed to argue about how to spend our time, about what movie to see, or whether to raise the cockatiel as a Jew or a Catholic. I'd worried that I might have developed some insufferably rigid habits during my bachelorette isolation, so this frictionless readaptation to couplehood came not only as a pleasure but something of a relief.

Nick quickly sussed out my submissive aspect, and right away set off to chart its tributaries and backwaters. Each night we spent together seemed to carry me to a more remote and primitive station. For Nick, the journey was essentially pragmatic, a way to uncover my desires and their limits ("so they can be used against you," he told me). Yet one of his first discoveries wasn't a limit, but its opposite: as far as we could experimentally determine, my capacity for erotic pleasure was boundless.

I wanted sex all the time, and when it wasn't available, I masturbated—sometimes only minutes after Nick had taken his leave of me. This caused me vague worries that I was becoming dangerously self-indulgent, slipping toward some final, terrible dissolution. Under cross-examination, however, neither my body nor my mind could produce convincing evidence against my appetites. Denial or even delay of gratification seemed pointless, and thus, on those nights when Nick had to work or was otherwise indisposed, I would go online to find Andres.

At first I'd been apprehensive even to talk to Andres about Nick, fearful that, despite his encouragement of my extra-virtual activities, he would ultimately resent the division of my affections. I decided not to volunteer any information, though I wasn't sure I could lie if he were to ask me a direct question.

> PATROQUEEET: Dearest Claire! Hormiga mía! Como ceviche?

> PARAPRAXISTA: *Muy* bien, gracias.

> PATROQUEEET: I take it from the "muy" that the date with your new fella went well?

> PARAPRAXISTA: Oh, yes. Very.

> PATROQUEEET: Grand. So . . . do I have to ask?

> PARAPRAXISTA: Ask what?

> PATROQUEEET: I will, you know: I have no sense of propriety. Or, rather, I have a sense, but it takes a backseat to my documentarian's responsibility to expose the truth—the whole truth, I say,

in all its harsh beauty, shocking filth, and not excluding any of its long, boring, waiting-around bits.

PARAPRAXISTA: Andres, you're a nut case!

PATROQUEEET: Hardly the first time you've so accused me. But I forget: what did you say that other term for Brazil nut was?

PARAPRAXISTA: Oh no! I'm not falling for that one again. Fool me twice and such. Now, what was your question?

PATROQUEEET: Nothing. It's over your head— never mind.

PARAPRAXISTA: *Oh!* Now you're making me mad!

PATROQUEEET: Good. I'm beautiful when you're angry. :-)

PARAPRAXISTA: Haha! Yes, and that's a lovely lip color. New shade?

PATROQUEEET: Thanks for noticing. It's "Brigade Rouge," by Estée Lauder. Tell me you love it.

PARAPRAXISTA: Absolutely. It's you. Your colorist was right: you *are* a "spring."

PATROQUEEET: Thanks, and yes. So . . . did you fuck him this time?

PARAPRAXISTA: I did.

PATROQUEEET. How was it?

PARAPRAXISTA: You really want to know? It won't bother you?

PATROQUEEET. I want to know. Of course it'll bother me: I'm already seething with jealousy. But tell me every detail anyway: I'm nurturing the masochist within.

PARAPRAXISTA: Okay, Andres. I like him.

PATROQUEEET: Grand. Was it hot?

PARAPRAXISTA: It was hot.

PATROQUEEET: Hot how?

PARAPRAXISTA: He made me play for him.

PATROQUEEET: Holy moly! He did? Christ, I can see why you like him—*I* even like him. He's my kind of guy. Is he a landsman?

PARAPRAXISTA: No. A shegetz. But not a goyishekopf.

PATROQUEEET: He makes a living?

PARAPRAXISTA: Haha! Yes. You want I should ask for his financials?

PATROQUEEET: A recent 1099 would do. Fax it tonight so I can run a TRW. What else?

PARAPRAXISTA: He's sexy: he likes it drawn out . . . likes to see me come. And he "dom'd" me a little. In the good way. "Our" way. He was really sweet afterwards.

PATROQUEEET: Ah, Clairest dear. I am very, very happy for you. He sounds like the imperfect gentleman. Exactly what you've needed: good manners, but sexually deviant. A pimp in the parlor, and a dandy in the bedroom. A walk-in-closet transvestite. A libertarian. A commodities trader. A man whose penis reeks of garlic and gun oil.

PARAPRAXISTA: You sure you're okay with all of this? I feel a little strange talking about it.

PATROQUEEET: You look a little strange, too. Might be post-climactic stress. Better watch for onset of the Stockholm Syndrome: as a workers' council representative, you enter the conference room militant, primed to call a general strike: eight hours later your sympathies have all gone over to management. Remember what Jean-Paul Abalone said: "Hell is otters." And one more thing—

PARAPRAXISTA: What?

PATROQUEEET: Call me. I want to hear all about your adventure.

PARAPRAXISTA: Really?

PATROQUEEET: Yes. Call me.

This was one response I surely hadn't anticipated: Andres was actually turned on by the idea of my tryst with Nick; he wanted me to share! But as I pondered this novel possibility, I was suddenly unsure about the ethics of divulging the story to Andres without Nick's consent. Would that be merely gossiping? Or would I be stepping over a line into indiscretion? I hesitated for a moment—then gave in to the appeal of cheap fun, choosing at least for now to ignore the moral quandary.

I called Andres, and we masturbated together as I told the tale minutely and exhaustively, finding for the first time that I could control the narration well enough to assure his pleasure without neglecting my own. We came simultaneously, the sound of Andres' gasps cueing my own powerful orgasm.

"That was great, Claire," Andres said, breaking the post-ecstatic lapse. "*You* were great. I'd have to say that was the best experience I've ever had doing this—being on the receiving end, I mean."

"That can't be true, Andres. You've reached out and touched a lot of women."

"Tens of thousands, of course. But that's beside the point. You're good. I'd say you were the best."

"But?"

"But nothing. That's an idiom."

"Oh. I know. I mean . . . okay. Forget it, Andres."

"Done."

"Shithead."

"Baby."

That began a routine of sorts. Once or twice a week I would recount to Andres the circumstances of my latest rendezvous with Nick. Andres couldn't wait to hear about it, and I was intoxicated with the telling. I continued to disregard doubts about the propriety of what I was doing, because I didn't want to stop using the stories. They were too good, I rationalized, too exciting *not* to be used; and besides, nothing negative could come from my little misdemeanor: I'd taken pains not to reveal any details to Andres that could be used to identify Nick, and Nick remained unaware even of Andres' existence.

As the focus of their combined attentions, I felt I'd been granted prerogatives that were available to very few besides film stars, the extraordinarily beautiful, and the obscenely rich: satisfaction on demand, and sexual variety.

But if there was variety, there was also convergence, for Nick and Andres sometimes exhibited an eerie simultaneity of obsessions that in my more suspicious moments I couldn't believe was merely coincidental. In certain moods, I even imagined that they'd hatched a conspiracy against me, although to what end I couldn't fathom, except to posit a vague scenario of deception ending in my total debauch.

One circumstance in particular fed this daydream of intrigue: Andres and Nick suggested almost concurrently that another woman be introduced to our sex play. Andres was first: while fucking me on the phone, he began to describe a woman seated before us, masturbating as she watched our final labors. I enjoyed the scenario, and was only disappointed that Andres hadn't elaborated it further.

Two days later, Nick broached the same subject. He'd suggested we take the ferry out to Staten Island to visit the zoo. It was a miserably cold and overcast Saturday morning, but

Nick insisted I wear a short skirt beneath my overcoat. Although he was clearly up to no good, I refrained from arguing. I'd learned that honoring his idiosyncratic requests was an investment of trust that usually paid a nice erotic return.

We wandered around the zoo for an hour or so, pausing a while to watch the chimpanzees ignore the taunts of unhappy children, though the spectacle soon incited less amusement than disgust, with both zoos and humankind. Later, we stood in mute sympathy before a svelte jungle cat, a feline Sisyphus condemned to an endless march across the front of her cage. By the time Nick and I stopped at a dilapidated refreshment stand for a hotdog and a tepid beer, I was demoralized, my mood grown as somber gray as the unbroken mass of clouds that loomed above.

At ten to one, under a sky that threatened to piss down rain at any moment, Nick took me by the hand and led me along a walkway to the reptile house, explaining to me, apropos of absolutely nothing, that it once held the best collection of rattlesnakes in the United States. Unconvinced of the sincerity of his sudden herpetological interests, I nevertheless played along and went without a struggle. What I saw when I was about to enter the building, however, nearly made me turn heel and flee. The keepers were introducing rats and mice to their charges at the ends of long forceps: it was feeding time.

"You bastard, Nick. I don't want to see this." I'd stopped short of the entrance, Nick nearly colliding with me from behind.

"Shikes, Claire. C'mon! It's part of nature. You'll get used to it. Besides, all the food is dead: pre-killed. These snakes are completely urban. They're just like us: they won't do any dirty work. It ain't cows—it's steak. It ain't rats—it's rodent tenders. I hear things have gotten so bad the cobras insist on a good white Bordeaux with their meals."

Although I was laughing and allowing Nick to inch me slowly forward into the arcade that ringed the displays, I was less sure than ever that I wanted to be a party to his crazy plan—whatever it was. I was close enough now, however, to see that Nick had been telling the truth about one thing at least: the little rodent bodies were lifeless, their pristine white fur unmarked by any sign of fatal trauma, almost as though they had died in their sleep. While parents looked on stoically, or turned away, their children screamed in delighted revulsion whenever a snake stirred itself to accept a furry morsel.

Nick guided me to a corner of the polygonal structure, then nudged me through a sort of bottleneck formed where a doorway had been narrowed to accommodate the salient angle of one of the large snake exhibits. The passage opened into a small cul-de-sac, walled in wood on three sides and glassed in on the fourth by thick panes that protected an Indian python from the harassing masses. Anyone entering the arcade through the nearest exhibit door would naturally tend toward the wider main portal opposite us, especially after seeing that our tiny side-chamber was occupied. Nick's design was now plain, and I knew him well enough to be sure that he'd previously scoped out—and had likely made use of—the quasi-private cubicle where we found ourselves.

Nick turned his back toward the glass cage and faced me, so that I now faced him, and the snake: sixteen feet of muscle and sinew in a living mosaic sheath of caramel and cream tesserae. Slowly extending a black tongue into the corners of her enclosure, she seemed to sense the imminent offer of food—and indeed, within a few moments a small door opened above her head, and upon the branch that divided her cage, tongs deposited a dead rabbit, its tail and long ears nearly meeting as it bowed limply across the tree limb like a pocket watch in *The Persistence of Memory*.

What followed was both horrifying and fascinating. Because I've never been troubled by animals eating other animals, the horror should have been abstract. But there was something about one creature consuming another whole that struck me as somehow more rudimental and savage than simple carnivory. It disturbed me—exactly the way I'm disturbed whenever I learn that a cat has eaten her newborn kittens. Had I grown up with brothers, I'm sure I would have been inured to this sort of thing. But being an only child, my entire experience of snakes and their feeding habits was from public television programs, and I'd always insisted the channel be changed during scenes of carnage.

"I think you like it," Nick said with smug certainty.

"I don't like it."

"You've been staring at her for at least five minutes. Without blinking. Like a snake—haha!"

"I'll admit it's *interesting*. But that doesn't mean I *like* it."

The python was attempting to stretch its mouth over the rabbit's head. First, rows of recurved teeth shimmied forward until they caught an uningested gobbet, then the rest of the jaw advanced on this toothhold like a rock climber on a piton. From time to time the snake bunched its neck into a compact "S," then abruptly straightened this to an "I," and by these contortions drew another centimeter or two of bunny down its throat.

Suddenly Nick's hands unbelted and unbuttoned my raincoat at the waist, then slipped quickly inside and molded themselves to the curvature of my buttocks. I looked at him in disbelief.

"You're planning to fuck me here? In front of this snake? Sure, Nick."

"Keep your eyes straight ahead, Claire. Don't look at me."

I refocused my gaze on the reptile, then suddenly shivered: Nick was working a cold bead of lubricant into my vagina from behind. I was incredulous: first, at the impertinence, then at my own reaction—for not only was I allowing Nick to finger-fuck me before a feeding python in a public zoo, I was acquiescing to the indignity with enthusiasm. *I've been truly born again into perversion*, I thought to myself— not at all unhappily.

"Listen, Claire: I want you to play for me. Slip your arms out of your sleeves and into your coat, then bring your hands around in front and rub your clit."

Although I was dizzy with excitement, my senses were unusually keen, as if amplified by awareness of the danger of discovery. Heeding Nick's request, I began to play with myself, and my clitoris soon throbbed in response to the movements of my fingers. Nick's fingers, meanwhile, continued to dither me from behind, and now I felt the trousered hardness of his cock rubbing against my belly and thighs. I caught myself involuntarily protruding my buttocks, as though his touch had triggered something ancestral in my hind brain, perhaps the expression of an ur-primate instinct of genital offering. In cruel counterresponse, Nick abruptly removed his dipping finger tips.

"You like my finger in your pussy, don't you, Claire?"

"Yes."

"Too much, I think."

I was about to ask if we could please leave this place and finish elsewhere, when suddenly a man's figure stood in gray half-silhouette at the entrance to our chamber. Although his attentions seemed exclusive to the python—which by now had reached the halfway mark in its labor of consumption— I nevertheless cringed at the thought we'd been found out. Nick held me fast before I could move to break our embrace, then began to address me in whispers:

"Look at me for a second, Claire. Calm down. That geezer by the door has no idea what we're doing. He won't move any closer. Concentrate on my fingers and your pussy. Don't worry about him. Now look straight ahead at our big, scaly girl-friend, and think about how good my hand feels in you . . ."

"But, Nick—"

"It's okay. Trust me on this, please? Just stare at the snake and concentrate on our fingers. I want you to come for me, just like this, standing up. Fuck that bastard—he'll never know a thing. Just focus: bury your face in my neck, and don't make a noise. You can do this."

"I don't know, Nick . . ."

"That's okay, Claire—I do."

Nick's fingers, the index this time paired to the middle, penetrated me to the knuckle. I nearly cried out in surprise, but anxious not to draw our neighbor's attention, managed to muffle myself into Nick's fur collar at the last second.

From the very moment we had entered the snake house,

I'd been host to an internal tug-of-war between anxiety and excitement. The arrival of the stranger at the door escalated this struggle from a stand-off to a pitched battle, a contest that would be resolved one way or the other, through flight or orgasm—which left only orgasm, because Nick had prohibited escape. And therein lay the rub, or rather the question of whether the rub was to be or not to be of any use: for I knew I couldn't come unless I was sure I could come silently and invisibly, a feat of self-control I was far from certain I could pull off. The burden of unrelieved pressure became excessive: I began to hyperventilate, a seep of perspiration trickled between my breasts. Suddenly queasy, I begged Nick for a moment's respite. I wanted a chance to negotiate a way out.

"Nick, please—let's stop for a second. I can't do this. I mean not with him here."

"But you are doing it," Nick interrupted. "Now be quiet and rub your clit: you're going to come for me. Shut your eyes and play while I finger you. I want you to come with my finger in your cunt."

When I had closed my eyes, Nick said, "Wait a second—I want to get behind you"—and his fingers vacated me. He slipped away, and then a hand at the small of my back urged me forward until my face abutted the glass of the cage. My overcoat was gathered to my hip (the right hip, away from the doorway and its Janus) while at the same time I felt two fingers move lazily down the curve of my buttocks, then suddenly dash into my vagina like startled voles going to ground. Once again I found myself sheltered by Nick's body, this time hemming me in from behind.

"Claire, you're doing great. Just keep your eyes closed:

concentrate on our fingers and my voice. I've been thinking about a gift—for both of us. A woman. A friend of mine. Sandrine. She's very pretty. Very sexy. She likes girls—I know she'd like you. I think you'd like her as well..."

As Nick began to conjecture along these lines, a strange garbling urgency slowly crept into his voice. And something else: his words seemed oddly displaced—slightly misaligned with their source, as if thrown by a ventriloquist.

Then suddenly, indeed almost in mid-sentence, his acoustic identity—the agglutinations of tone and timbre that imparted individuality to his speech—underwent a radical transformation. "You step to the bed," he'd been saying, still recognizably Nick, but when he continued, the old voice had been replaced by the new, a voice slow and ethereal, a voice telling a story which seemed to come now from a place in a dream or hallucination, "... *like a bride to be prepared. I unclothe you... kiss you... stroke you. Your body and mind decompress under my fingertips. Your eyes close, lids begin to flutter, moths settling on the warm bulb after the light is extinguished. Before you can sleep, however, I call for her. She approaches, head bowed, silent and beautiful, her lithe body revealed in the flowing gaps of a long, archaic robe—dark silk, satin soutache, and embroidery—the morning gown of a belle dame tied loosely at the waist. Her body seems to emit its own perfume—a chemistry of recollection, scent provoking memories of scent: the maquis in bloom... sage and white myrtle... the turpentine sweetness of cut pine...*

"*I give her a sign, and for the first time she looks at you—and is instantly enslaved to one thought, to one potentiality: your touch—touching you and being touched. The idea of you in-*

flames her; deprivation becomes her consuming fear. She searches my face for permission. Her eyes—large, brown inlaid with hazel—sparkle with intelligence: there is nothing in them of the doe's aqueous vapidity, the cretin's marrons glacés. She searches my face, and I nod, and she kneels at your bedside and begins to anoint and lay hands upon your back. Gently at first, then ardently, lenitive fingers unlock your vertebrae. Your muscles protest, even as their suppleness is repatriated. Sandrine labors over you until her hands cramp and slacken with fatigue. Her desire, however, suffers no such weakness: her gaze, burning with dissatisfaction, is lost in that desolate landscape which is the mind's glyph of the heart's ache. She wants you, Claire. I can smell the ancient hunger between her legs. I can smell the animal in estrus. Her ache is for you: for the heartbreaking perfection that is the curve of your throat; for the incarnadine ripeness of your nipples; for lips she longs to devour like fruit; for your sex. Her hand strays from the hollow of your sacrum: poised between your thighs, it hesitates like a purse-snatcher waiting for a moment of negligence. Sandrine would steal a single, precious touch—but she is too slow, and too late. Become a mantis, I pounce: seizing her fingers, bending them back against her knuckles, then rising with her from the bed, a formal dance whose steps I guide incrementally, with pain. When Sandrine is beyond arm's length, I bind her hands at her sides and order her to stand before us."

I'd been listening and masturbating, Nick's fingers keeping pace with mine. His voice and words were incongruent with their source, but the vision they described was no less spellbinding and no less incendiary—exactly the kind of vision I urgently needed. For I was a very horny girl in very weird and difficult straits, and this tale might just deliver me from my predicament—if only I could suppress my cries, and if only the man at the door would continue to behave himself. But just then—just as I was becoming hopeful for these possibilities, and ultimately, for completion—a sudden rustling noise from his direction startled me out of my wits, and all hope seemed in that instant to be lost. I opened my eyes to investigate, but a hand immediately covered them, keeping me both literally and figuratively in the dark. I went rigid with fear until the steady continuity of Nick's voice and fingers persuaded me that there had been no untoward change in our spectator's interest.

"I part your legs and spread your pussy for her. We will kill her in stages. She is dying to taste you, even if only from my fingers. If she believed she had the faintest chance of moving me, she would beg, she would promise me anything. But she knows my refusal is absolute, that there will be no negotiation. She can do nothing but watch: even as my fingers retract the petals, and trace the flower's concentric ellipses; even as I force the fruit to dehisce, to reveal the nectary within. But when she sees my hand move with purpose to excite you—when the blush without grows milk-shiny, and the cache within wine-dark—she cannot suppress a soughing cry, the whimper of a starving dog at a gourmand's table . . .

"We are killing her in stages. And I know now how this slow murder moves you, for as Sandrine looks on in wretched disappointment, eyes ablaze with impotent envy, you pull my head to your breast and begin to give me suck. With a newborn's blind and exigent hunger, I draw at your teat: your nipple tender-hurt, lengthening and swelling, responding to my *mouth, to my warmth and my need. At last I recognize the pre-cursor, an infant's memory of a singular organic unlocking: the ducts uncoiling within, and then—as my mouth pulls hard at your breast, as the intimate vacuum extends—the let-down. I receive the unguinous hot spray in my throat; I swal-low and draw deeper, and the trophic cascade begins: now there is only feeding and making me feed—only my hunger, and your hunger to give. On and on I suckle, and you give suck, and then—shuddering, and almost despite yourself—you come . . ."*

As the first waves of orgasm broke upon me, I shook my-self free of the hand that covered my eyes, opening them in time to see the python's livid, gaping throat close over a cot-tonball tail. A witness might have found a gruesome poetry in the juxtaposition of the serpent's disarticulated grin and unblinking gaze with my own strained jaw and blind, cli-mactic stare. But I could achieve no such detachment, and a flood of revulsion tainted what should have been the most pure and perfect ecstasy. *A witness!* With a shock, I remem-bered. I looked toward the doorway as a clammy fear seized upon me—and then turned to horrified disbelief: for there, propped casually against the inner jamb, stood Nick.

We took the ferry back to Manhattan in silence. I was drained, my emotions topsy-turvy. Nick said nothing until we were well on our way into town from the ferry land-ing.

"Are you still pissed off?"

"You're kidding, right?"

"No. This is no time to kid. Are you mad?"

"Goddamn right, I'm mad."

"How mad?

"Christ, Nick—are you insane? Give me one reason I shouldn't hate your guts."

"'Cause you don't. And, you came good."

I had no answer to that, so I said nothing. Just exactly what had taken place in the reptile house was still unclear to me, and Nick, I knew, had explanations. For the moment, however, I was determined not to ask him anything at all. Discussion was sure to open the door first to "understanding," thence to pardon—and that was one French aphorism whose truth I was in no mood to confirm.

Not that I could honestly say that Nick was beyond forgiveness. In truth, I wasn't even very angry with him. I'd been manipulated, which irritated me, but mostly I'd come away from the zoo feeling haunted, as from a strange, symbolic dream that obstinately resisted all interpretation. At first, listening to the stranger's narration, ignorant that he'd taken Nick's place, I'd felt somehow intrusive, as though I were secreted in a bedroom closet, eavesdropping on another's somniloquy. Later on, however, it occurred to me that only the voice was truly alien: the images and preoccupations, and even the language, were familiar. And their main theme—a man using my body to excite another woman —seemed indisputably mine. By now I was certain: the parallels to my own erotic universe were too numerous and too close to be accounted for by a lucky pluck from the toy box of generic fantasy. All of a sudden, having answers was more important than reserving the right to punish.

"Okay, Nick. Who was he?"

"A friend. He says he went to Princeton. Now he writes ad copy. And he does voice-overs. I thought he was qualified."

"Great. You have great friends. I suppose I should be flattered that you interviewed for the position. How the hell did he know those things about me?"

"I told him."

"Of course you told him, *dick!* Jesus, do I suddenly look stupid to you? I meant, how did *you* know?"

"Claire, this may come as a surprise to you, but you talk in your sleep. A lot. I had to hire scribes to get it all. And by the way, I think you're on the summer repeat schedule, because I've heard some of these a bunch of times. I was kinda hoping for a special, maybe a variety show—anything to break the monotony. But I guess that's all out of the question now—"

I laughed and then hit him—and then all at once we both shot upward, so that only our shoulder-belts prevented us from colliding with the sunroof panel. Fending off my attack, Nick had driven us into a giant pothole.

"Just a scratch," he mumbled in disgust. "Two grand, at least, for parts—plus labor. Fucking foreign car repair..."

Nick inched the car carefully forward in a bid to extricate us without further damaging the fender. When at last the tire emerged from the rut, the suspension bottomed-out in slow motion, as though shrugging at our ineptitude.

"How much to replace your balls after I remove them?" I asked.

"Haha! We don't replace 'em. I move to Salt Lake. Career

change. They'll take me—I've had choir practice. I could stand a little drying out, anyway. But Claire, tell me the truth: how did you like the zoo? Really?"

"I missed the cotton candy."

"*What?*"

He looked baffled, and I smiled with satisfaction. Of course, the war was already lost: I'd forfeited the moral advantage of victimhood the moment I'd laughed. But I could still try to make sure his victory wasn't a picnic.

"You deaf? What part of 'I missed the cotton candy' didn't you catch?"

"I heard you. Can you explain?"

"Yeah—like I owe *you* an explanation."

"Please?"

"I don't know why it matters, Nick: we're breaking up."

"Okay. For my diary, then?"

"Oh, it's for your *diary!* Why didn't you say so in the first place? That changes everything. Of *course* I'll explain. Once upon a time, when I was a little girl, my governess would take me to the zoo—mostly the Bronx zoo, but also the Paris zoo—and not once would she let me have cotton candy. 'Ben non, Claire—c'est pas possible. Ça abîme les dents.' So after all these years, all I wanted was some freaking cotton candy, and you didn't come through. I hate you for that more than anything else."

"Was it really that terrible?" he asked, his voice almost plaintive.

"No, not really. I had a wonderful time. And it was very educational, too."

"You crack me up, Claire," he laughed. "Have I told you how much fun I have with you?"

"Recently. But I'd like to hear it again." I moved closer to him and kissed his ear. "Oh, and by the way, Nick, did I tell you about my friend from online?"

"Oh, shit!—no you didn't. But I had a feeling . . ."

"Yes, I think you should know about him. His name is Andres. We're very close."

"Yeah?" he bridled. "How close?"

"Like, umm . . . very close." I was giggling, and squirming with pleasure at Nick's discomfort.

"Okay, Claire: enough torture. What's the story with you and this guy? Have you met him?"

"Oh, no. We just talk."

"Haha! I bet."

"It's true, he's a good talker."

"No doubt. Do you have phone sex with him?"

"That depends on what you mean."

"What do you *mean* it depends on what I mean? What else could I mean?" Nick stiffened in his seat, and his hands began to clasp and unclasp the steering wheel. He was riled up, caught between jealousy and curiosity. He was exactly where I wanted him.

"Anyway," I said, "I just thought you might know him."

"How would I know him? What made you think that?"

"You have very similar tastes."

"You mean we both like you?"

"Yes," I laughed, "that too."

Before I knew what was happening the car swerved violently to the right, narrowly missing the bumper of the cab in front of us. Nick brought us to an abrupt halt at the curb and killed the ignition, just as the first heavy drops of the rainstorm we'd attended all day began to thud against our windshield.

"We need to have a drink and talk."

"Not now, Nick. I'm too tired. Being tricked into having sex with your lover's friend is hard work. *Tomorrow* we'll have a drink and talk. Will you please take me home?"

As he silently wended us through the heavy evening traffic, I knew he was hoping for a word of forgiveness. But I wasn't inclined to give him a blanket pardon, and I was too tired to compose a version I could live with. He was just going to have to wait.

6

NICK CALLED THE NEXT DAY AND APOLOGIZED—
not quite for what he had done, but for having upset me. He
got me to admit that I'd found the episode exciting, but I still
insisted that I should have been forewarned about—and
given the opportunity to veto—any third-party involvement.
He said he understood that I was right—"in principle"—but
argued that advance notice would have ruined the whole effect—"like watching a disaster movie when you already know
the ship is going to sink," he said. I let the matter drop for the
time being, and we arranged to get together for drinks that
evening.

Night was falling when Nick came to get me. We walked
to a little neighborhood pub near my flat, where we settled
into a dark corner—away from the pool table and dart board.

"So what's going on with this Andres guy?" Nick asked,
opening the discussion.

"I beg your fucking pardon?" I snapped back. "I wasn't
under the impression we were done talking about what happened at the zoo."

"Jesus. Again, I'm sorry. That'll never happen again—I
mean, at the zoo. Tell me about this guy."

"I already did. He's a dear friend. I suspected you might know each other. That's all."

Nick brought his hands to his face in a gesture of wearied frustration, then fell silent.

"Look, Nick," I began, moved at last to cut him some slack. "I'll tell you—but you have to promise to stop sulking. It's not becoming."

"Sure. Anything."

"That's much better. The story is this: I met Andres online about a year ago. He's a stock broker. He lives in Denver. We became good friends—then I started to have cyber sex with him. Eventually we began talking on the phone."

"He phone-fucks you?"

"Yes."

"You've phone-fucked him since we met?"

"Yes."

"Oh."

"Are you all right with that, Nick?"

"I'm not sure. I think so." He paused for a moment, as if to ponder the implications of his answer, then said, "What if I'm not? What would you do?"

"I don't know," I said, truthfully. "I'm not sure, either. I guess I haven't wanted to think about it—about having to decide. I guess that sounds kind of weird, doesn't it?"

"No, not so weird. Shit, Claire: I'm a dog—remember? The last thing I'm going to do is pull some moral outrage routine on someone for having sex with someone else. You like this Andres guy?"

"I do. And though you're both really different—"

"Different how? He's got a bigger dick?"

"Virtually, yes," I laughed. "No. I mean, I have no idea. I only meant that despite your differences, you seem to have nearly identical obsessions."

"Like what?"

"Like, within the last three days you both talked about me being with another woman."

"Claire," Nick said, suddenly condescending, "this may surprise you, but that's not exactly a startling coincidence. It's a standard boy fantasy in fact. I'm kind of shocked you didn't know that. I mean, every skin flick made in the last seventy years has had to include a lesbian sex scene. It's in the Federal pornography code."

"Smut-Hawley?" I asked.

"What?"

"*Footnotes* you want now, Mr. Smartass? That's something you *earn*." I smiled, glad to have paid him out for talking down to me.

"Christ. You are one gnarly wahine."

"Look, Nick, I know all about men's fascination with lesbians. I wasn't born on a turnip truck. But it's not the subject so much as how you both set it up—the *way* you described it. And the way you both imagined the other woman acting. The similarities were uncanny."

"Yeah?"

"Yeah. Honestly, I wouldn't have thought twice about it if you guys had envisioned me doing Kama-sutra position soixante dix-neuf with some eighteen-year-old stripper. That's right out of male fantasy central casting. But this was different."

"Isn't it 'soixante-neuf'?"

"Nick, I like you—but please don't question the intentionality of my jokes—okay?"

"Ouch. You want another beer?"

"Sure. But first I have something to confess."

"Oh, shit, here it comes. You're really a man—that's it, isn't it? Damn, I was afraid of this. I should have known from the start. The clues were all over the place: your sex-drive, your tastes..."

I laughed, loudly enough that a couple of the bar patrons looked at us across the pool table to investigate the source of the outburst.

"No," I said, lowering my voice, "I'm not a man. If you need proof, I've got video of myself retaining water."

"Oh, so you're not a man—you're a plant. That's a big relief." Then Nick squinted at me, and in a better-than-decent Irish brogue added: "But about that confession, child: what was it you were wanting to tell me?"

"Well," I began, and immediately ran into difficulty, "it's just that . . . you see, I simply wanted to say that . . ."

"Yes?"

". . . that I told Andres about you and me—about what we do together." Suddenly I was ashamed. Now that I'd verbalized it, my behavior seemed starkly reprehensible, even unforgivable.

"Holy shit, Claire! Like details? Like the sticky stuff?"

"Yes. All that."

"Claire . . . darling . . . love of my fiscal quarter—let me just make sure I have this right: you recounted intimate details of our sex life to this guy, in order to get him off?"

"And me."

"What?"

"And get me off. We both got off. Oh, Christ, Nick . . . that sounds so horrible. I feel so guilty . . ."

"Oh, no, Claire—it's fine: don't feel guilty. I think it's kind of cool, actually."

"You *do?* You don't think I'm a terrible person?"

"Hell no, muñeca," Nick laughed. He scooched his chair closer to mine and put his arm around me.

"Claire, I mean, it's more flattering than anything else. How many guys can say that a woman uses what they do in bed to get another man off? Of course, I'd like to make a little percentage on the rights, but we can talk about that later . . ."

Nick was incredibly sweet and understanding. He refused to hear any contrition, and insisted repeatedly that I needn't end my relationship with Andres on his account.

"But," he said, "I do want something in return."

"Sure, of course—anything. What?"

"I want the same deal."

"The same deal? What do you mean?"

"I want to hear about what you and Andres do together."

"You *do?* Are you sure?"

"Yes, I do. And I'm sure."

My conscience suddenly felt light and pure. And now, having at last come clean to Nick about Andres, I could say I'd fully assumed the role—the female third of a triangle— that Andres had predicted for me. Not a "sub" (that loathsome word, with its connotations of servility and inequality), but an "hypoteneuse": the link between two men, the base of the triangle certainly, but sovereign and independent, never merely a passive victim of its geometry.

We left the pub after midnight. Nick, sozzled, swayed unsteadily all the way home. I insisted he stay rather than drive back drunk to his studio. We took a long bath together, and afterwards, as we snuggled in bed, he told me for the first time that he was in love with me. With the thought that veritas as likely lay in lager as in wine, I chose to take the statement at face value.

At eight the next morning, Nick sat bolt upright, looked at me with unseeing bloodshot eyes, and cried, "Late!" He dressed in the kitchen while I made us coffee. He couldn't stay, and suddenly I wanted to make certain it would torture him to leave, so on an impulse I dropped to my knees, unlimbered him through the gap at the leg of his shorts, and began to suck. He stiffened instantaneously, then put his hands on my shoulders and started pumping his hips, his fervor mounting with each thrust. I sucked energetically for a few more seconds, then stopped and pulled him—now ferociously rampant and drooling—from my mouth, licked my lips, and reinstated him into his boxers. Then I stood up and pried the coffee mug from his hand.

"Put your pants on, Nick. And drive carefully. Call me later if you think of it."

"That's *it*?"

"Yes, that's it. You're already late."

"Bitch."

"True," I said, affecting a coquettish smile, "but guess what?"

"More disappointment?"

I tried to look hurt. "No—not that at all. You judge me harshly, good sir. I was going to say that I've been thinking about your offer."

"What offer?" he asked.

"To meet that friend of yours. Sandrine was it?"

"Oh, shit—*yeah*? Really? You'll meet her?"

"I didn't say that. I said I was thinking about it. You're late. Now go work hard and good."

I'd been shooing Nick toward the front door, forcing him backwards at bust-edge, so that he now stood with his heels balanced over the riser into the hallway. Before he could speak again, I gave him a little push and then closed the door in his face, which at last look was confused, a bit puffy from hangover, but brightening with hope.

7

THE IDYLLIC DAYS WITH NICK ACCUMULATED
into months. Indeed, it looked as if my happiness might extend indefinitely, until one day Andres suddenly became unavailable. There could only be one explanation: jealousy, I was sure, had broken out at last.

I wrote Andres several notes containing gently obvious openings for a discussion, all of which he ignored. Nor did he respond to my e-mail asking him to call, which upset me, though I couldn't deny a certain humorous incongruity to the situation. Who would believe, after all, that the cause of such a tumult was my cyber lover's jealousy toward my real-life lover, and not the other way around?

I decided to give Andres some time alone. It was up to him to figure out what he wanted, and what he could live with. Certainly I refused to feel guilty: I'd broken no rules or covenants, explicit or implied, and I'd hidden nothing from him. Intentionally or not, he was being ridiculous. He should have known that his friendship meant the world to me, just as he should have known that Nick could never replace him in my affections. If nothing else, he ought to have recognized that I was too greedy even to consider a choice: I wanted both my men.

He telephoned me late one evening. A month had passed since we'd last spoken.

"Clairest dear . . . I needed to talk to you."

"It's good to hear from you."

"Look—I'm sorry. I know I've been weird. I've been jealous, and I'm annoyed with myself over it, which is why I've been avoiding you."

"I figured as much."

"I want to explain, Claire. But be forewarned: it's not so dreadful."

"A pfennig for your thoughts?"

"It's this way, querida: I've concluded that I'm not jealous of Nick. I mean, I'm not jealous of what you have with him. Does that make any sense?"

"Perfect sense. Please explain."

"I mean I'm honestly happy for you: you've found a good thing. Nick's a great guy, and you deserve that in your life. So, it's not that I don't want him around, or that I see him as some sort of rival for your affections. That would be ludicrous, anyway, what with all those air-miles separating us, me being so cis, and you so trans, and all."

"So what is it, Andres? Please tell me."

"Oh, Christ, Claire . . . I'm such a stunted, fucked-up little man."

"You're six foot four."

"Okay, I'm such a stunted, fucked-up little man trapped in a giant, fucked-up little man's body."

"Andres—please help me here. I don't see the problem. What's wrong?"

"Nothing's wrong . . . it's just different now."

"Different how now?"

"Different because I went and fell in love with Nick."

"Jesus Christ, Andres!"

"I'm serious, Claire. I know we haven't met—and I know the danger in that. You'll recall that I wrote the friggin' manual. But I've done the calculations, checked and rechecked the figures, corrected for the delusional factors. I come to the same conclusion every time: Nick is the one."

"You are insane!"

"Now don't freak out on me, Claire. There's no reason at all for that. I don't want to ruin things for you. To begin with, I don't expect him to reciprocate. Just please explain to him why I've been so distant. And that I'm not going to badger him, or try to win him over. It's enough that we're friends . . . that he knows how deeply I feel . . . how much I groove on him, and stuff. And, as for you, please understand that you're perfectly safe. I have no intention of challenging you to a duel. I never ask for seconds—which, by the way, is how I keep my girlish figure. Still, I can't promise I won't try to take advantage of things if, say, you were to contract a virulent lymphoma . . ."

I laughed, and then I smiled, happy that Andres was finally back.

8

NICK AND I REFINED OUR PAS DE DEUX OF THE
regular and the predictable. Saturday mornings we browsed
thrift stores and antique shops. Sunday's ritual never devi-
ated: we lingered in bed over lox, bagels, schmear, and the
Times until well past midday. Tuesday night was fixed: pizza
and TV at my place. Wednesday lunchtime we skipped
school, splitting the workday with a matinee. Thursdays we
always spent apart.

We were paragons of routine, except when it came to our
lovemaking, which was subject, in particular, to capricious
changes of venue. Nick, for example, planned or found opportunities to sexually assault me in all the city's major department stores. He ate me to orgasm in the men's changing
room at Neiman's, and the women's bathroom at Bergdorf's,
each time cramming a handkerchief in my mouth at the critical instant to stanch my cries. After threading me through a
herd of crazed Thanksgiving Day Sale shoppers at Macy's,
he diverted me into a semi-secluded corner of the home-
wares department, an "L" where defective and display merchandise attended reboxing, and there, while rubbing my
pussy through my pants, had me jerk him off into a large,

non-stick wok. The outcome was fascinating: striking the wok's pewter-hued sides, Nick's semen separated into silvery beads like some animal mercury, slid to the bottom of the pan, then coalesced drop by drop into a shimmery pool.

As we walked away, I caught Nick gazing wistfully back to where he had made his deposit, and shot him an inquiring look.

"That coating's really impressive," he explained. "Great technology—and it's nice to see some civilian benefits from the space program."

I laughed, but vowed never again to purchase any floor model—for any reason.

We broadened our scope to include all variety of retail establishment, although before long Nick developed a clear preference for bookstores. Used, new, highbrow, middlebrow: no bookstore could come within our view but Nick would skip ahead to open its door and usher me in, always with the same hooligan grin lifting the corners of his mouth. Blessed with an almost supernatural gift for finding the optimal place for public sex in any environment, he would unerringly make a beeline for the darkest and most private corner. When there wasn't a suitable alcove or recess—as was sometimes the case with the larger chains and their more homogenous floor plans—he improvised.

One night, for example, we were out taking a stroll, when suddenly I noticed Nick hesitate in his stride just as we came up parallel to one of the large, well-lighted bookstore chain outlets, the kind that has carrels and desks scattered throughout and a coffee house grafted to one flank. Head tilted back, nose skyward like a retriever sniffing the air for the aroma of freshly downed duck, he led me inside, and then together we ran the maze of shelving before entering a sparsely populated area. Along the way Nick must have quietly lifted a name plate from somewhere, for he now replaced the "Reference" sign that hung at the end of our section with a placard that read "Staff Only."

"That ought to discourage the casual browser," he said, "—but we still have to do this quick."

"Oh, no, Nick! Not here! We're completely exposed!"

"It's okay, Claire. Just hurry." Then, pointing to an atlas at my feet, he said, "Bend over and leaf through that book."

I bent as instructed, which made my skirt ride up my hips far enough to expose the tops of my stockings, the thigh-high hosiery that Nick always insisted I wear on our outings, "just in case." Despite my nervousness, I was feverish with excitement. The logistical preliminaries—coming upon the bookstore, choosing our spot, Nick's calmly injunctive way of speaking—had all served as extended foreplay. His hand first touched the back of my right knee, but after a moment slid upward to the top of my stockings, tarrying there to finger the elastic. Nick loved this meeting of flesh and fabric: the bold visual contrast of black silk or nylon against the whiteness of my thigh, the way hose subtly, erotically transformed the resistance and texture of skin. At home he would spend hours simply watching me in stockings, caressing my legs and having me assume various poses. He had a particular obsession with the slight constriction of my thighs where the elastic pressed in at the top. "God resides here," he once said to me—with unquestionable sincerity.

Just now, however, there was no time for such fetishistic dawdling.

"Are you wet enough, Claire?"

"Yes. Hurry before we get caught."

"I want you to come for me: two fingers."

All at once Nick's hand flew to my crotch, then two fingers penetrated my vagina and spread themselves within, as though signing victory to my uterus.

In my current excited state, the most delicate touch would have sufficed to bring me to climax, but instead Nick drubbed my cunt with unflagging, almost punitive severity, so that by the time he responded to my pleas to relent, my orgasm was long concluded, and his thrusts had nearly hammered me to the floor. Dazed, I only made it across the store with the support of his arm. We were a dozen paces short of the exit when an assistant manager interrupted us:

"Is she all right?"

"Yes, thanks," Nick said. "She's just a little drunk—with knowledge."

I held my laughter until we'd escaped outside.

9

I'D BEEN ALONE IN MY STUDY FOR A WHILE, typing to Andres, when Nick suddenly materialized at my back. "Mind if I read your screen?" he asked, rubbing my shoulders.

"*I* don't mind. *You* might, though. It's Andres."

"Aha! El famoso! Give him my regards."

PARAPRAXISTA: Andres, Nick is here . . . he sends his best.

PATROQUEEET: Ah! Convey my felicitations—and condolences."

PARAPRAXISTA: *Condolences?*

PATROQUEEET: Absolutely. Remember, I only have to play with you—Nick has to deal with your shit.

Nick read the screen and laughed, and I pinched his arm until he yelped. "Tell Andres I admire his style," he said. I related the sentiment, feeling a little like a shipboard Morse code operator translating messages between captains.

PARAPRAXISTA: Nick says he admires your style.

PATROQUEEET: You told him about my tie collection?

PARAPRAXISTA: Haha! Of course not. That's strictly between us.

Nick laughed. "I mean, tell him I like the way he makes you hot—the way he gets you ready for me."

"I think it's the other way around," I said. "Andres gets the late night shift, after you're asleep."

"You're kidding me—right?" He looked surprised, and a little hurt.

"No," I said, "I'm not kidding."

"You cyber him after I go to bed? Damn, Claire. Give Andres 'high fives' from Nick."

PARAPRAXISTA: Andres: 'High fives' from Nick.

PATROQUEEET: Back at him. But what was that for?

PARAPRAXISTA: I just told him how you make me come late at night, after he's made me come. I think he was being congratulatory.

PATROQUEEET: You told him *that*? What did he say?

PARAPRAXISTA: Not too much. I think he's okay with it. He's very open-minded . . . and he knows a girl has needs.

PATROQUEEET: I'm jealous.

PARAPRAXISTA: Of what?

PATROQUEEET: Of your capacity for orgasms. Women's capacity for orgasms, generally. It's a source of male envy—particularly for those males, like me, who happen to be older than thirteen.

PARAPRAXISTA: I see. But still, it's not such a great trade-off: we have periods, and the agony of childbirth. Then osteoporosis, and also we outlive you, so the burden of being a burden to our children falls exclusively on our shoulders.

PATROQUEEET: Well, I guess nothing's free in this world, except with purchase.

PARAPRAXISTA: What?

PATROQUEEET: 'Free with purchase'—like those cosmetic spiffs. I've always thought that was a great idea: an advertising claim that contains its own contradiction. But you're right about the childbirth thing. Still, I'd love to be able to come with you—and then to come again, say, half an hour later—with Nick.

PARAPRAXISTA: Haha!

PATROQUEEET: So, tell me: things are still good between you kids?

PARAPRAXISTA: Very good. Couldn't be better, actually.

PATROQUEEET: That's great, Claire. I mean it: you're the happiest you've been since I've known you. Think you'll marry? Have a family? Divorce? Become a dental hygienist?

PARAPRAXISTA: We haven't discussed it. And ixnay on the hygienist ingthay: I look terrible in mauve scrubs. And anyway, I'm going to dedicate my twilight years to writing the definitive biography of Kate Moss. But the truth is we're having such a good time together that I haven't even thought about that stuff. I'm really satisfied, Andres. More than satisfied. After all, I have you, too. :-)

Just then I felt Nick's hand on my breasts, his finger tips rubbing my nipples through my blouse, and I realized with a start that he'd been silently following the conversation the whole time, while I'd been going on as though he weren't present at all. My fingers froze on the keyboard.

"Keep typing," Nick said.

I kept typing, though his caresses made it more and more difficult for me to concentrate. I decided to throw him a curve.

PARAPRAXISTA: Andres, do you think it's weird that I phone-fuck you after I come with Nick? That doesn't make me a nymphomaniac, does it?

"Phone, *too?*" shouted Nick, shaking his head in astonishment. (I'd scored, and apparently with a direct hit.)

PATROQUEEET: No, Claire, that wouldn't make you a nymphomaniac. You were *born* a nymphomaniac. And anyways, I rebel at the suggestion that wanting to have sex more than once a week somehow means you've got a problem. There's no such thing as "sex addiction." It sounds like something Allan Bloom might have cooked up.

PARAPRAXISTA: That would be Allan, *Closing*, not Harold, *Canon*—right?

PATROQUEEET: Allan, *Closing*, right. I always imagine him hunched in a corner of his office, wanking to the *Symposium*, his balls aching with unrequited lust, cursing his students—cursing their youth and their ignorance, their unearned confidence, their frivolousness, their relativism, their rock and roll, their vanity—cursing above all else that runic knockout in the front row of his *Iliad* lecture. Heather, was it? or Tiffany?

PARAPRAXISTA: Tiffany, probably.

PATROQUEEET: Yes, Tiffany. But *he* could never keep it straight—that's the point.

PARAPRAXISTA: Why was he cursing poor Tif?

PATROQUEEET: I was just getting to that. Stop interrupting. He was cursing her because she drove him nuts: her short tennis skirts and her smooth athletic thighs, muscles defined even in repose; her tight little tops and no bra and those big nipples, hard despite the heat of summer session—nipples like accusatory fingers jabbing at his discontent. He hated her—hated her tan, her insolent azure eyes, her high Norwegian cheekbones; hated her blond hair with its swimmer's tinge of chlorine green, and her perfect nose with the faceted gemstone tip.

PARAPRAXISTA: You're saying he hated her?

PATROQUEEET: Yes. He hated her. But—and this is the bloody heart of the matter, so pay attention—as much as he hated her, he despised *himself* even more.

PARAPRAXISTA: He *did*?

PATROQUEEET: He did. Let me finish, will you? There's a rhythm to this thing.

PARAPRAXISTA: Carry on, my little drummer boy.

PATROQUEEET: I'm trying. Where was I?

PARAPRAXISTA: He was despising himself.

PATROQUEEET: Yes. He despised himself because he knew in his heart, with knowledge affirmed by the pyrotic churn and popple in his stomach, with conviction driven home by each agonizing, exfoliating splash of gastric acid (the corrosive wash eventuating, you may recall, in a fatal perforation), that he'd gladly see every extant copy of his beloved *Nicomachean Ethics* burned before him (Nay! he'd put the torch to the pyre with his very own hand) in exchange for a single hour's unlimited dominion over and within Tiffany's—or Heather's—holy of holies.

PARAPRAXISTA: Her what?

PATROQUEEET: Her holy of holies. Her sainted sulcus.

PARAPRAXISTA: Her *sainted sulcus?*

PATROQUEEET: Yes. Id est: her flax-fringed, pearl-pink, honey-dipped, lilac-scented, inviolate little teenaged alligator-snapper squack.

PARAPRAXISTA: Christ almighty, Andres! Where did you get that?

PATROQUEEET: It's from a eulogy I composed on the occasion of Bloom's death. Would you believe *The American Spectator* refused to publish it?

Laughing, Nick tapped my shoulder. "Is he like this all the time?"

"Yes, unfortunately."

"He sounds a lot like you."

"He's me with a penis. That's why we get along so well."

"Oh. Where do I fit in?"

"You don't, really. I'm just using you."

"Great, Claire."

Nick had lucked out. Although I'd described Andres' tirades to him, their full comic effect could only be gotten first-hand. And since I'd very much hoped he'd like Andres, I was cheered by his laughter—even as his hands, pinching my nipples now, and his lips, nuzzling my earlobes, continued to make me hot.

> PARAPRAXISTA: I'm sorry about the *Spectator*. What were we talking about?
>
> PATROQUEEET: Nymphomania. Like I said, you're no nymphomaniac. You're more the "Charming Betty Careless" type. And you've got the kind of legs that I like: feet at one end, pussy at the other. What I'm trying to say is, don't ever change.
>
> PARAPRAXISTA: Haha! Okay, Andres, you've convinced me: I'm not a sex maniac. Still, whenever I read the results of one of those sex surveys, I feel like I'm off the scale.
>
> PATROQUEEET: But you're not! That's just the fascism of statistics. Trust me, if anyone knows from misleading, it's me: I can counterfeit two-factor analysis of variance and Games-Howell post-hoc tests in my sleep. Sex surveys are phony, anyway. You think anyone gives honest answers to the Kinsey field interviewers? I don't. I concoct baroque phantasmagoria starring truffle pigs and triplets, and make 'em believe every last word of

it—the interviewers, I mean. I have a very sincere face and a charming way about me. The fact is that nobody knows what people do in bed. Someone who calls himself a sex expert is like Kropotkin's metaphysician: "A blind man in a dark room looking for a black hat that isn't there." It's self-delusion.

PARAPRAXISTA: Yes. Circularity. I understand. I see it in my work. People tell me what they want me to hear, based on what they've already heard themselves. It's not self-referential, it's a catalogue of the preferences of some Otto Normalverbraucher living in a pollster's database—and nowhere else. I think people are scared of being too different.

PATROQUEEET. Yes, Boswell. Exactly. And if you learn anything at all, it's by omission.

PARAPRAXISTA: By omission, my illustrious friend?

PATROQUEEET: Yes, by omission. Stop repeating everything I say, okay? Look, I'll give you a fer instance: let's suppose that people are having sex with goats. Let's suppose, furthermore, that they aren't admitting it on surveys, but you have proof from other sources. The discrepancy can tell you something about people's attitudes toward goatfucking. And who the hell is Otto Normalverbraucher?

"Ask him what other sources," Nick interrupted.

"What?"

"About the goats."

"Oh, okay," I laughed. "Silly bastid."

> PARAPRAXISTA: Andres, umm . . . aside from surveys, what other sources might there be for goat-fucking information?

> PATROQUEEET: I have no idea, Claire—what the hell difference does it make? *Vet News*, I suppose. I'm sure the veterinarian trade journals would report a rash of goat-fucking. Forlorn she-goats, off their feed, waiting for the day-after phone calls that never come . . .

Nick and I both laughed, then his hands slid down across my abdomen. Andres meanwhile had somehow gotten onto the subject of relationships, and although I wanted to comment, the luscious pressure of Nick's finger against my pussy was seriously restricting the length of my responses.

> PATROQUEEET: I'm telling you, Claire, the most obvious truths are inadmissible in a conversation about relationships. If you don't believe me, just question the notion of affective monogamy— people go apeshit.

> PARAPRAXISTA: "Affective monogamy"?

> PATROQUEEET: Yeah. Ever heard of it?

> PARAPRAXISTA: Honestly, no.

PATROQUEEET: Good. I just made it up. Wanted to see if you were still paying attention.

PARAPRAXISTA: Clever boy. Now, what's it mean?

PATROQUEEET: Gimme a second—I'm still working on that part. This is worse than my poemless poetry titles.

PARAPRAXISTA: Yawn. Fidget. Clacking sound of nails drummed impatiently across desktop. Glance at watch. Humming *Strangers in the Night*.

PATROQUEEET: Christ! Okay, okay. Here it is: Affective monogamy (noun): the idea that you can love only one person at a time. I mean erotic love, of course. Serial monogamy is the social norm, affective monogamy its primary underlying assumption. And since any deviation is heretical, you should never admit to loving two people. You'll be rode out of town on a rail, like Hester Pryne in *The Red Badge of Courage*.

PARAPRAXISTA: You know damned well that Hester Pryne was the heroine of *The Purloined Letter*, and she never left Paris.

PATROQUEEET: You're a pedant, Claire. And all your fine distinctions are beside the point.

PARAPRAXISTA: Which, you'll forgive me, was?

PATROQUEEET: That all is permitted: enemas and vinyl and home dungeon kits—so long as it's within the context of an "exclusive, loving relationship." Now why, I ask, should erotic love be any more exclusive than parental love?

PARAPRAXISTA: No reason.

PATROQUEEET: Thanks. The statement was rhetorical.

PARAPRAXISTA: Is that true—I mean about the dungeon kits? There's really such a thing?

PATROQUEEET: I have no idea. I made it up: polemic license. It could be true—I mean, it's not unlikely. Everything okay, Claire? I'm afraid I've been monologuing. I'm homozygous dominant for the bombast gene. Oh, and I hope I haven't been keeping you from your main squeeze.

PARAPRAXISTA: Not at all. He got bored and left a long time ago. And you're not bombastic, Andres. I'd describe you more as . . . umm . . . a gasbag.

Nick had removed my blouse and skirt, making available new opportunities for purchase and exploration that his hands lost no time taking advantage of. I decided it was time to clue Andres in on what was happening.

PARAPRAXISTA: I'm sorry, Andres: I lied just now. Nick's been watching. He likes your sense of humor, but he's an incorrigible horn-puppy. At this very moment he's crouched beside me with his finger buried in my pussy. Sometimes he pulls it out and licks it.

"Oh, fuck!" Nick exclaimed, with a double take at the screen that rivaled a silent film star's best performance. His incredulity was echoed at nearly the same instant by Andres' IM.

PATROQUEEET: You *aren't* serious, Claire! *Are* you?

PARAPRAXISTA: Serious as they come, darling. And they do—I make sure of it. But you already know that . . .

PATROQUEEET: Haha! Christ—I've created a monster vixen!

And Andres was right—though he hadn't exactly been cultivating sterile soil either . . .

The afternoon's festivities soon gave way to baser amusements. Nick bent me over my desk to fuck me, and while he fucked me, I kept at the keyboard, describing everything to Andres: how Nick had me stand so he could smarm my pussy and ass with lubricant; how, slipping behind me into my chair, he pushed his fingers into my anus with steady, dilative pressure, making me long for his whole hard prick in that dark, secret place, then perversely withholding all but the tip; how he made me beg for him, threatened to deny me should my entreaties lack conviction, forced me to plead again and again in a clear, high voice for his cock in my ass. (Andres thereby discovering what Nick already knew: that in contradistinction to those women who abhorred the practice, or those who suffered it uncomplainingly but without pleasure, there were times when I wanted nothing more (or less) than to be retrogressed into the bleating, bestial, ecstatically martyred "ass-whore" (in Nick's idiom) of a man's most depraved dreams.)

Relenting at last, Nick allowed gravity to exert its force unimpeded, and I slid to the base of his cock, thereby initiating a cycle of penetration and withdrawal that I assisted with my own undulations and contractions. Very soon I felt thigh muscles twitching sharply under the backs of my knees, and I knew (as I reported with due diligence to Andres) that Nick was about to come. Moments later I felt a short series of desperate embowelling thrusts culminate in a spray of hot liquid, a special pleasure to me—more primal than any strictly genital thrill—that was no less sublime for having been expected.

Andres got off next, his hand pulling furiously at his cock while I limned in detail the scene of venery that preceded my own climax: Nick, limp and satisfied, down on his knees, his nose buried in the flowing seep of my ass as he ate me from behind, greedily smacking and slurping at my pussy like a thirsty boy sucking watermelon on a hot day. I left off typing only when the shock of orgasm had rendered me atonic and invertebrate, a jellyfish out of water. Bereft of motor coordination, I collapsed, falling backwards onto Nick who, though forced to bear my crashing weight with the muscles of his neck and arms, never broke the seal between his mouth and my pussy.

10

"WHAT DO YOU THINK," I ASKED, "MUSSELS OR monkfish?" Unsure what to order, I was soliciting Nick's opinion on yet another pair of menu alternatives. "Mussels," he answered. "By the way, did you know that 'moules-frites' is the national dish of Belgium?" Something was up. That "by the way" had been too awkward to be spontaneous. And indeed, I now learned that the bit of gastronomical trivia it introduced had been passed on by "Sandrine—who was born in Liège." I drew a momentary blank before remembering that Sandrine was Nick's lesbian or bisexual acquaintance, the woman he wanted me to meet.

"Have you seen her recently?" I asked, playing along for the moment.

"Last week—we had lunch."

"I see." I wasn't yet prepared to express overt interest, despite the fact that Sandrine "as a concept" had recently featured in several of my erotic dreams. My curiosity was piqued, but I wasn't exactly sure what I wanted, or how far I'd be willing to go, or be taken.

"I talked to her about you, Claire. I hope that's all right."

"Oh, sure . . . yes, of course. What did you say?"

"Only nice things," Nick smiled. "How's your cold?" he asked, changing the subject.

"It sucks."

"Taking anything?"

"Don't start with me, Nick."

"Christ! That was a simple, concerned question—why so defensive?"

"Sorry. I'm raw from too much advice. If you must know, I'm taking a decongestant, an expectorant/cough-suppressant cocktail, and Tylenol. And next week, when the sinus infection starts, I'll be taking antibiotics. And after that, antacid for the sour stomach I get from the antibiotics. Maybe I'm just like my mother."

"She's never satisfied?"

"*What?* No. She's a hypochondriac. A naturalized citizen of the PDR."

"An elderly Jewish woman hypochondriac? In New York? That's news."

"You're a comedian, Nick. But I'm serious—she really is a hypochondriac. They even had to name a new disease because of her."

"What's that?"

"The 'judaeosarcoma.'"

"What the hell is a *judaeosarcoma?*"

"A kind of cancer. Very unusual presentation: it wanders from organ to organ, causing minor aches and pains, lasts a lifetime, can't be verified by any known test, and temporarily vanishes in the presence of a doctor."

"Haha! Interesting. If I didn't know you, I'd think you'd made that up. By the way, mi amor, have you noticed any change in that mole on your left shoulder?"

"Cute."

"Well . . . anyway—she's very interested."

"Who is? Interested in what?"

"Sandrine."

"Oh. You mean interested in *me?*" (Despite my neutral phrasing, the clear implication ("interested in having sex with me?") now floated palpably between us.)

"Yes," Nick answered. "And I told her what I had in mind. She's intrigued by the possibility."

"But she hasn't even met me."

"That's true. But she trusts my judgment . . . and taste."

I paused to study Nick's face for some indication of what he'd thought to accomplish by that statement. I was irked, though not entirely sure why. And I saw that Nick himself understood he'd crossed a line, for he was fidgeting uncomfortably in his chair as though impatient for a chance to explain himself. But before he could speak I silenced him with a dark, disapproving stare. I wanted a moment to work through my own feelings.

I knew I wasn't jealous of Sandrine. According to Nick, she was "almost exclusively gay," a self-described "situational bisexual" who enjoyed occasional scenes that included male participants. She liked what men did to women—or rather the way women responded to men, which she claimed was different from how they responded to her. She also liked what the spectacle of two women making love did to men. But while Nick insisted that he and Sandrine were strictly old friends, I'd always suspected they'd been involved romantically, and so I could hardly say I was blind-sided by Nick's comment that Sandrine trusted his "taste"—an obvious allusion to some sort of shared sexual history.

Neither jealousy nor betrayal, then, could reasonably explain my irritation with Nick. And when I deducted these from the sum of all possible causes for my displeasure, I was left with a difference that amounted to me not liking how happy he'd been waving his past escapades in my face. I was on the verge of ruining dinner over a trifle. At this point I might have apologized to Nick for my overreaction, and probably could have extracted an apology from him for his boorishness in exchange. Instead, giving in to childish pettiness, I sat dejected and vague for the rest of the meal, and the evening ended on a sour note.

Early the next morning, after a fitful night's sleep, I called Nick at his studio. I have a horror of letting bad feeling linger unresolved. It's a core thing for me, nearly obsessive: I can't regain emotional equilibrium after a row until there's some sort of closure.

"Nick? Hi."

"Hi."

"I'm sorry about last night. I was a shit."

"That's okay," he laughed, "You're entitled every once in a while. Just don't go over quota."

I promised, relieved that he wasn't nursing a hangover from my bad behavior.

"I know you're busy; I just called to apologize—and to tell you that I want you to arrange a meeting with Sandrine."

"Whoa, Claire! Wait a minute . . . You're agreeing to meet her because you feel guilty about what happened last night? That's not what I wanted at all."

"No, no!" I said. "This is about libido—not guilt. I *want* to do this thing with Sandrine. Really."

"Sure, Claire. Last night you were cold on the idea, now you're hot. What gives?"

"Nothing gives. I just didn't want any responsibility for the decision. I wanted you to talk me into it. It's hard to explain."

"Hard is good. But this having-to-be-seduced business . . . it's not really you. It's not the way you are."

"Sure it is: you talk me into stuff all the time. But this one is especially hard for me. Which is odd, I'll admit, because the whole idea turns me on. You could even say I've been primed for it. Being with another woman is something I've thought about for years and years . . ."

"So, what's the problem?"

"I'm split, Nick."

"Split how?"

"Split in a weird way."

I explained to Nick about the dichotomous me: the puritanical day Claire (competent, prudent, rational, respectful) and the libertine night Claire (spontaneous, devil-may-care, hedonistic, irreverent)—two halves that recognized each other, but only imperfectly communicated.

"Big deal, Claire. Every *Tom and Jerry* cartoon has a scene with an angel whispering in one ear and a devil in the other. What's new?"

While I had to concede that what I'd described so far wasn't awfully original, I nevertheless insisted that my particular case was more complicated. When I tried to prove the point, however, I quickly entangled myself in a sticky net of disconnected theory and conjectural self-analysis, lamely arrogating in support of my uniqueness everything from my life-long lack of flying dreams to the conflict of the Dionysian with the Apollonian—until the explanation sounded so tortuously labyrinthine and implausible even to my own ears that I was relieved when Nick's laughter finally interrupted me.

"Querida! You're so damned funny when you're serious. But this is way too complicated for my pea-brain. I'd need to make a wall chart just to keep the parts straight. In fact—can you hang on the line a second? I want to go grab a marker."

"Hysterical, Nick. Really. But go ahead, have fun at my expense. Here I bare my soul to you—haul out the contents of my psyche for you to examine, limpet-encrusted treasure from the bowels of a wrecked galleon—and you mock me. I'll remember this, *Mr. Empath.* You think it's easy being me? You think that's so funny?"

"No," he said, not even bothering to suppress his laughter, "you're right. It's not funny. *Limpet-encrusted treasure?* Where do you get this stuff? But okay, go on—I'm listening. And then what happened?"

"Fuck you, Nick"

"Your mama."

"My mama would rip your head off, Nick. Look—I don't want to talk about this any more, okay?"

"Yeah?"

"Yeah. I'm done. Besides, I lost my train of thought."

"Fair enough, but would you mind telling me what any of this has to do with you having sex with Sandrine?"

"I honestly don't know, Nick. Let's all just get together for a drink. Okay?"

"You betchum! Besos, Clara. I'll call you later."

Nick arranged a date: dinner for three, Thai food. Butterflies immediately began to eclode in my stomach. Though I knew this was to be merely an introduction—a preliminary meeting to see if there was any mutual attraction—the anticipation right away set me on edge.

My anxiety expressed itself in an unusual way: the evening of our soiree found me agonizing over what to wear. Unlike most women I knew, I'd never had difficulty selecting an outfit for any occasion, casual or formal. This was one life-skill I could always perform with absolute decisiveness, and I never regretted my choices. Now, however, I couldn't stop vacillating. On the one hand, I wanted my clothing to project self-confidence and sophistication; on the other, sexual allure—contradictory requisites that would have been difficult enough to reconcile without the additional burden of figuring out what it meant to be attractive to another woman. I felt like a high school girl preparing for a blind date with a "handsome exchange student"—from Alpha Centauri. At last, unable to make up my mind, I called Nick.

"Nick. Claire. How should I dress for this thing?"

"You're asking *me*?"

"Yes. I'm frazzled. Help me here."

"Claire—please relax. This is going to be very easy. Sandrine won't be judging you."

"Sure. Haha. But we all judge—don't you remember? Just answer me: what should I wear?"

"Okay. It's very simple. Put on what I like: dark stockings, heels, shortish skirt—doesn't have to be a micro—and wear your hair up. You'll look great. Oh, and also, no panties—but that's just for me."

"Jacket or sweater?" I asked.

"Sweater."

"Angora or mohair."

"Mohair. Mo' bettah."

"Haha! Thanks, bye! You're a lifesaver."

Sandrine was to meet us at the restaurant, a pricey, newish place called "Phuket: Let's Eat." Nick and I arrived early and were seated in a booth. He ordered me a kir, half of which I downed straight off. The minutes crawled with painful disregard for my schpilkes, and for some reason neither Nick nor I seemed able to interest one another in a conversation.

To combat nervous anticipation, I studied the restaurant's interior. A beautiful space: antique Thai furniture, Khmer pottery and sculpture, fine old Indonesian batiks—all bathed in the diffuse light of colored rice-paper lamps, a soft, persimmony glow that seemed to submerge everything it touched under mellowing layers of antique lacquer. I was reminded of Glenn's sensibility: each decorative choice was a visual mot juste—nothing garish or inappropriate intruded, nothing clunky or faddish. (Suddenly I was very happy: I had recalled Glenn to mind without any bad feeling, with neither pain nor anger. For the first time I realized that I'd been completely cured of him.)

A large oval bar in the center of the restaurant was ringed

two deep with customers. The crowd was medium young, within that demographic I had taken to calling "people, you know, our age." They were well-off, mostly straight, mostly white. Studiously casual, they seemed to resent even the minor disruption of cool required to order an Absolut something-or-other from the bartenders. I knew their type: the fin-de-siècle nastier, crueler, gender-inclusive version of the 50's "organization man." Ruthlessness, venality, narcissism —these were the traits that distinguished the taxon. I despised them—but I liked to watch.

Despite these ambient distractions, however, I couldn't calm down. After waiting twenty minutes, I was about to tell Nick that I wanted to back out of the whole thing, make my apologies, and take a cab home, when—as if cued by my cold feet—in walked Sandrine: a striking ash blond in black leather pants and a chocolate suede jacket, all smiles as she caught Nick waving to her from our corner. She paused to hug the mâitre d' before making her way to our table.

Nick stood up to greet her. They embraced, and then Sandrine bounded over to my side of the table, leaned across ("Ah, you must be Claire!"), and gave me kisses on both cheeks that left my face warm and wet with her lipstick.

As I said, she was striking: her eyes were a ravishing pure deep blue, and she had good cheekbones, a high, smooth patrician brow, and a sensuous mouth that arched in the middle to form a winsome chorine pout. I found myself looking closely at her lips to verify that their fetchingly old-fashioned shape wasn't painted on. On the other hand, I noted (with relief, for women who are glaringly more attractive than I am make me jealous and insecure) that her features attained neither the structural delicacy nor curvilinear regularity of the classic beauty: her nose, for example, was too broad at the base, and her chin had a slightly masculine cleft. She was forty-two, though she looked younger by a decade; physically compact, almost tiny; trim but solid, with the toned shoulders and arms of a swimmer. When the waiter helped her out of her jacket, the blouse she wore underneath opened to where it had been buttoned half-way down, revealing a plunge of cleavage and natural, full breasts that bobbed with alluring buoyancy each time she moved. My first assessment struck me as disconcertingly masculine: Sandrine was sexy as hell.

We settled into our seats and Nick looked at me, eyes wide with hopeful expectancy, eager for a sign that I approved of his friend, and hence that he had a chance to realize his fantasy scene. I met his gaze with that blank look one assumes to inform passing strangers that one will absolutely, positively, not be waylaid—for spare change or Jesus or anything else. I wasn't about to offer an opinion about Sandrine before I'd had a long, unhurried opportunity to form one.

Though I'd feared uncomfortable pauses and forced pleasantries, the dinner conversation was spontaneous and easy. Sandrine was charming and vivacious. Something about her—a suggestion of drama, a subtle grandeur in her gestures and expressions—made her extraordinarily attractive, made you want to ingratiate yourself with her.

Sandrine, I learned, was a "garmento"—a designer for a

division of a subsidiary of a monstrously large and ramified women's sportswear manufacturer. She regaled us with sordid tales of greed, betrayal, and pathological egotism from the world of prêt à porter. Although she apparently held a position of substantial responsibility and authority within her company, she took pains to downplay the importance of her own job, and the glamour of the industry.

"I'm a péon, Claire," she insisted. "Well paid, but a péon nonetheless." (Though her English was nearly without accent, she reverted to French pronunciations with certain words.)

"It's really a terrible business—terrible. It attracts the worst people. I swear to you, most of them should be in jail. The garment industry is like the Foreign Legion: it invites all the scum of every nationality to come to make a new life. It rewards criminals. I'm not exaggerating. Even the mafia must be less dishonest. It's disgusting. I'd get out, but they would ban me from the warehouse sales—and I can't live without beautiful clothes . . ."

Nick had assured me beforehand that Sandrine would be discreet and well mannered. She understood, he'd said, that this first meeting was provisional—I needn't worry she would try to make a play for me. True to this characterization, her friendliness never once crossed the line into overt suggestion. Several times she touched my hand in order to emphasize a point or express agreement, but she always withdrew her fingers before they might be suspected of inappropriate lingering. If anything, however, this self-restraint only made her more attractive to me, and by the time the evening ended, my thoughts had turned speculative, with her as their sole subject—how she kissed, how her thigh might bend to the curve of my hip, how her breasts would feel crushed against mine . . .

Nick left first thing in the morning for a business trip to Miami, and returned a week later on a red-eye. He called from the airport, waking me well after midnight to ask if I'd meet him for an early breakfast. From this I deduced three things: that he'd had a chance to speak with Sandrine, that the news was in his favor, and that he was anxious to tackle the final obstacle, me. I wanted to see what sort of elaborate suasive performance he could come up with for the occasion, so I remained deliberately opaque regarding my own impressions. Besides, I was anxious to know what Sandrine thought of me, and I reasoned that the less forthcoming I was, the more I was likely to hear.

We met at a coffee shop, and the instant he saw me Nick began to dance around like a kid with a full bladder. He kissed me playfully about the head and neck as he helped me into my chair.

"Thanks for coming," he began, breathless and excited. "I know you have early appointments. Sorry about waking you last night. I was wired from the flight. I'll get the waitress. You're having the number four, right? Scrambled well, bacon crispy, rye dry? I missed you a lot, you know."

I chose not to be miffed at that afterthought of a "missed you." Nick could be oafish at times; it wasn't part of his charm.

I leaned over the table and kissed him on the mouth. "I'm glad to see you, too."

"Claire—I talked to Sandrine. She told me she wants you."

I was surprised that he'd cut so directly to the chase instead of trying to shmooze me. The report itself, however, seemed contrived, and I decided to challenge its accuracy. "You lie, Nick. Sandrine never said that."

"I swear," he insisted. But after a moment's hesitation he said, "Okay, you're right. What happened was this: I said, 'So, Sandrine...what do you think?'—and she said 'Oui.' That's how it went down. She thinks you're hot. She wanted to tell you how beautiful you were the night we met, but she didn't want to scare you off. The bottom lion is that she wants it to happen."

"Okay."

"*Okay?*"

Nick's face lit up as it dawned on him that I wasn't just acknowledging his statement but actually agreeing to his plan.

"You really mean it?"

"Oui."

"Fuck."

II

NICK RESERVED A SMALL SUITE FOR US AT THE
Saint Regis. "Better on neutral ground," he explained. "And
besides, we'll need room service."

Sandrine was to meet us at ten that night, but Nick drove
me to the hotel a few hours earlier—in order to have time to
prepare me, he said. We checked in, made a quick inspec-
tion of the room, then descended to the bar for a cocktail.
Nick was pensive. I could tell he was busy playing out possible scenarios in his mind. He asked me several times if I was
okay, if I was still up for the plan, if I had any particular worries or requests. I assured him that I was happy to relax into
his capable hands.

"I'm glad," he laughed, "—but just the same, I'd like to
make a couple of things clear right up front. First, I'm not
going to fuck Sandrine—I probably won't even touch her.
Second, she is only going to do what I let her, and that
means she won't do anything you aren't comfortable with.
We'll take it step by step, very gently and very slowly. We only
go as far as you want to . . ."

We finished our drinks and went back to the room. Nick
drew a bath for me, then helped me out of my clothes and
into the tub. He washed me and loofah'd my back and sham-

pooed my hair, telling me the whole time how great I looked, how sexy I was, how hot I constantly made him. Though I was sure most of this was premeditated—as a rule Nick wasn't the gratuitously complimentary sort—it was pleasant to hear all the same. Besides, I reflected, planning and sincerity weren't necessarily mutually exclusive.

Nick toweled me dry and then asked me to dress again, this time without my underclothes. Then he had me stretch out, belly down on the sheets, while he stood at the foot of the bed, looking me over with what seemed to me calculating self-interest, like a brothel habitué evaluating a prostitute. When he addressed me, however, it was intimately—in the low, loitering, gently dictatorial baritone he used to tender his lewdest sexual requests, an approach now eloquently vindicated by a sudden drenching wetness between my legs.

"Spread your thighs a little for me, Claire . . . I want to see your pussy. Show it to me. Yes, just like that: perfect—open and wet. I want to lick you, suck you from the inside. You want that, don't you?"

"Please . . . yes."

"'Please, yes' what?" he taunted. (Nick loved to make me repeat his most vulgar suggestions. Somehow his libido fed off the stressful inner battle it cost me to talk dirty to him.) "Tell me *exactly* what you want me to do to you, Claire."

"Please suck me, Nick . . . I want your mouth on my pussy."

"On your cunt."

"I want your mouth," I hesitated, "on my . . . cunt."

"First you're going to play for me, Claire. Reach your hand under and frig yourself."

Nick leaned on the bed and pulled my skirt up to my waist, exposing my bottom. I rose slightly on my knees, enough so that I could run a hand beneath my right hip bone, then under and across my belly. At last I brought my middle finger up between my thighs, moistened it in my vagina, then took the via interlabia back down to my clitoris.

"Frig yourself," Nick repeated. "I'm going to watch you while I stroke my cock. I want you to come for me." Then, in an aside to himself, he whispered, "Sandrine is going to love this."

While I rubbed my clitoris, Nick diddled me from behind with a finger, but his strokes were only negligent and irregular essays, more like the casual reconnaissance of an ear cavity by one absorbed in a book than a lover's purposeful caresses. He was teasing me, intentionally denying me a coupling rhythm I could ride to climax. Suddenly he stopped altogether. He brought his right hand up to my face—the hand with which he'd been masturbating—and demanded that I lick the pre-come from where it had collected along the inside of his index finger.

"I taste good, don't I, Claire? You like tasting my cock on your lips while I finger your slutty wet cunt, don't you?"

"Yes, Nick," I said, licking avidly at his fingers, excited by the hint of depravity in the act.

He re-entered me, but now his fingers trundled back and forth to the same steady $4/4$ time with which I rubbed my clit, giving me hope that I could bring myself off before he again interrupted. I desperately needed relief, but I knew my chances of finishing before daybreak would be dashed if I were to display the least sign that my crisis was at hand. To deceive Nick, I set my jaw and forced myself to take slow, even breaths. But these efforts were in vain, for at the point where a moment's further stimulation would have lofted me beyond the outermost battlements, Nick suddenly pulled his fingers from my vagina and, seizing my wrist, wrenched my own hand from my clitoris.

"Please, Nick," I begged, burning with frustration, "please let me come." I wanted to cry out, but quashed the urge instead, beating down skirls of disappointment for fear Nick would use any outburst as an excuse for further intransigence.

"Of course I will," he said with a perversely gleeful snigger, "—but you're going to work for it. You're going to fuck the sheets for me. Show me what a horny slut you are by fucking the bed while I watch from behind."

Compliant, I ground my pubis into the bed, awkwardly straining to find a combination of movements that might translate sufficient pressure to my clitoris.

"That's beautiful," Nick said, "—just like that: hump the bed like a dog..."

I turned to find him, stripped naked, watching me while he stroked his cock, oblivious to the doubtful biomechanical feasibility of his request. For although I oscillated my hips as I pushed them against the mattress, and otherwise attempted to increase the area of contact between my vulva and the bedclothes, I succeeded only in sliding impotently over the finely woven cotton sheeting until, sweat-soaked and dissatisfied, I finally realized that my problem was a dearth of surface relief. For remedy, I reached back between my legs and grabbed up a handful of sheets, scrunching these into a longitudinal ridge at the latitude of my crotch, praying that this percale escarpment, shallow though it was, might do the trick.

Nick, meanwhile, still masturbating, had begun to accompany his strokes with a lurid soliloquy. I heard myself transmuted into raw ore for his libido, vivisected into discrete erogenous parts: mouth, breasts, vagina, ass—a sort of ultimate objectification. To my surprise, this carnal litany made me feel more deified than devalued, a Venus exalted through the naming and praising of her separate attributes.

I answered Nick's vile nothings with my own: "I want your hard cock in my mouth when I come, Nick..."

"I *bet* you do," he jeered. "You're a skanky little slut. Push your pussy into the bed. Let me see it... spread yourself wider."

"I need your cock, Nick."

"You'll *work* for my cock," he answered, nearly shouting now, his voice domineering and flinty. "Spread your pussy for me. If you do it right—show it to me the right way—I'll go in you later: with my mouth. And when you come: my tongue in your ass, the way you like it..."

"I'm going to come... *Please*, Nick... cock... mouth..."

"No, Claire. I told you to fuck the bed. Here—this way..."

In an instant Nick had shimmed open my vagina with both thumbs, inserting them knuckle to knuckle as if he were preparing to section a grapefruit. His other fingers lay butterflied out and over my buttocks on each side, but their lightly mantling touch suddenly tightened into a painful raptorial grasp as nails dug for leverage in the flesh of my cheeks. A moment later he slammed me belly first into the mattress, and then—pulling skin and muscle—lifted me skyward with a jerk of his arms. Directing my clitoris into the bed, he once again shoved me down—a violent hoeing he had to repeat only twice before my body, crash-diving in orgasm's deep delirium, went first board-stiff, then tremulously slack, coming to a dissipated standstill with a final shuddering extinction of tension.

Afterward, in the entre'acte before Sandrine's scheduled arrival, Nick and I lay head to toe beside each other on the bed, languidly sharing cigarettes and exchanging long pauses that now and then digressed into short conversation.

"I love the way you come," Nick said. "It's beautiful. 'Le petit mort.' Ever think about that? Sort of a strange conception of death, if you ask me. Very optimistic—seems more American than French."

"The Jews call it 'le petit Mort Sahl.'"

"What?"

A little while later I tried again: "The Mexicans call it 'la mordida chiquita.'"

"It's odd," he mused. "I mean, you're in this blissful afterglow, where you forget all your worries—at least for a while. I guess it's like an idea of heaven. It seems strange they didn't name it 'the little paradise' instead. Do the Mexicans really call it that?

"No, Nick. It was a joke. 'Mordida' means 'the little bite.' It's the vernacular for 'bribe.'"

"I *know* what 'mordida' means!" he snapped. "I'm Latin American—remember?" (He pronounced "Latin American" with touchy pride, as if I had insulted the memory of Simón Bolívar.) A moment later he calmed down. "I thought you were serious . . . that maybe there was some connection between bite and orgasm—like a vampire. They're completely loco over those chupacabras down there."

Silence reigned again for a few minutes, a tranquil spell made possible only because I'd intentionally neglected to arrange forwarding voicemail from my office, and had insisted—not without resistance—that Nick leave his pager at home. Staring at the ceiling, happy to let my thoughts drift of their own accord, I found myself mentally connecting the hairline cracks in the plaster to form fanciful shapes: wild beasts and monsters.

After a while I said, "I don't understand this vampire thing, Nick. I mean vampire romance. Stoker's original *Dracula*? Sure, a good story. But all these heirs to his misfortune? The modern bloodsuckers? The attraction completely escapes me."

"Even *The Lost Boys?*"

I pondered that for a second.

"Okay. Except for *The Lost Boys*."

"It's sex and death," he said, with a serious, sad expression that opened abruptly into a laugh.

"What's so funny?" I asked.

"Oh, nothing. I mean—you just made me think of 'The Goth Incident.'"

Remembering, I began to laugh too, though not so much at The Goth Incident itself—which, in retrospect, wasn't really that amusing—as at Nick's habit of assigning the binomials of geopolitical suspense novels to memorable events—hence, also, "The Macy's Covenant," and "The Staten Island Illusion."

The phone rang, waking us both. Not having meant to sleep, we'd quickly fallen into the deepest slumber, and rousing ourselves was taking an effort. As minds and memories cleared, we suddenly looked at each other and chorused, "Sandrine!"

The ensuing scene was comic: Nick grabbed the receiver while I made a dash for the bathroom, snatching peignoir, makeup bag, and toothbrush en route. I'd hoped to present a sleekly done up and perfectly composed Claire for the occasion, but now there was no time, so I settled for fresh lipstick, brushed hair, and a semblance of calm. I'd just managed to arrange myself into what I hoped was a convincingly languorous pose on the bed—like Manet's *Olympia*, but clothed—when there came the expected knock at the door.

Clad only in blue silk pajama bottoms, Nick got up to let Sandrine in. She entered smiling, her beautiful mouth an alizarin crescent, but then assumed a look of stern disapproval as she took in the room with its disheveled bed and tousled occupants.

"Bonsoir, mes enfants," she said at last, smiling again, winking at me conspiratorially. "I see the show is already in progress." She kissed us both, then from a shopping bag pulled two bottles of champagne, one of which she uncorked and began to pour out before Nick could fill an ice bucket for the second.

Glass in hand, looking hopefully at Nick, she said, "Alors, *la veuve* est là, mais ... Nicky, by *any* chance were you able to—"

"Yes, chou-chou," he said, anticipating her question. He slipped a small fold of paper from the pocket of his pajamas, opened it carefully, and laid it before us on the glass coffee table in the center of the room. With an upturned fingernail, Sandrine scooped out a small mound of white powder, divided this mound into still smaller hillocks, and then with the edge of a credit card drew out the hillocks one by one into parallel lines.

After we'd each had a turn, Nick raised his glass and toasted: "To bubbly wine, el polvo blanco de la sagrada sierra Boliviana, y—sobre todo—present company. Dum vivimus, vivamus."

"'*Dum vivimus, vivamus*'?" I said, "'Let's live life to the fullest'?—The *nuns* taught you that?"

"The brothers," Nick said.

"Jesuits?"

"Homies."

Nick always had recreational drugs. Availability led to experimentation, and I'd found that a certain combination of alcohol and cocaine could induce in me a kind of pousse-café euphoria, layering alertness over sociability over tranquillity. The effect was genial: no narcotic dulling of wits or cannabic personality shift, just a slight softening of inhibitions, a relaxation of my usual off-handed dismissiveness.

We talked for a while, and although I felt sexual anticipation all around, the atmosphere remained amiable, and quite free of the sinister tension I'd expected. It's hard to say when the little kisses and caresses began, or even when we moved to the bed—there was no general announcement or forced segue. The erotic ontogeny was seamless: friendliness to physicality to licentiousness in an organic unfolding that seemed destined rather than contrived.

I think Nick touched me first—my throat and arms. Then Sandrine reached out to intertwine her fingers with mine, and lifting my hands to her mouth, began to kiss my palms. She stroked my face with her fingertips and kissed my eyelids, then leaned past me to press her mouth against Nick's. I heard her whisper to him, "Thank you . . . she's superb," before turning back to me with a smile. An icy thrill shot down my spine at the realization that I'd just been offered as a sexual gift, a present from one lover to another. Commodified, I suddenly felt extraordinarily valuable and beautiful, though these emotions quickly gave way to a sweeping mood of wistfulness they themselves seemed to beget.

I had been under this spell before: awash in a kind of nostalgia, but for places and times I'd never known personally—memories that nonetheless persisted in my mind like traces of the most emotionally concentrated of "real" events. I would suddenly recall an intensity of equatorial sun, rays bursting in reflection upon a sea of saffron silk; or remember a crowded Levantine street market, an ancient, constricted thoroughfare clouded with spices: cardamom, asafoetida, fenugreek; or find myself transported to an English garden, the flow of placid water over round stones, the hushed brisance of sunlit poppies rekindling my love for the natural empirical. These visions were strangely familiar, a kind of déjà vu, but sprung from sources I recognized: passages from books I'd read as a child, lines of poetry incompletely remembered, photographs in magazines long ago turned to pulp. In their aftermath, I would crave for hours what they represented: a world of more richly joyful moments than the one I inhabited. And now it occurred to me that what had brought me to this hotel room—perhaps what had brought all of us here—was more than merely a desire to escape the manic pace and pressure of the modern quotidian. We shared the same craving, the same need for romantic venture, the same compulsion to experience scenes of emotional intensity, to be consumed by immoderate delight.

I believed it was happening now: an almost magical convergence of shared desire, spontaneous and unforced. Not a blending of wills, but a fluid arabesque of three individual egos, separate but contiguous, joined in pursuit of an extreme of pleasure that each knew could only come through the pleasure of the others. Sandrine had begun to kiss me, and despite lingering uncertainty about my true desires, I surrendered to the voluptuousness of the moment and kissed her in return. Her breath was sweet as her tongue flirted with mine, timid probings that grew little by little more audacious. Nick uncovered my breasts in order to give the nipples a quick suck, then rose from the bed to help Sandrine out of her sweater and jeans before returning to my side. After removing my dressing gown, he reclined backward on the bed with only his head and shoulders elevated by pillows, then half-lifted, half-pulled me onto him, so that I lay supine with my head against his chest. Sandrine, apparently reconciled to her observer status, looked on from where she now sat in a low chair beside the bedstead, her distance from us reflecting the limitations of her assigned role.

With the tips of his fingers as his brushes, Nick painted slow feathery circles across my nipples. Then, pattering at Sandrine with the oily optimism of a car salesman, he began to describe my breasts:

"Look at these beauties—absolutely extraordinary. The perfect size and shape, firm as a teenager's... exquisite lines, and—my God, are the nipples sensitive! The second you put them in your mouth, they double in size. Incredibly responsive! She can come just by having them touched. No, no—I swear it's true. I've seen it dozens of times. We'll run her through her paces in a bit. Here's a taste, anyway— watch her face when I pull a nipple..."

My reaction to Nick's pincer grip was bipartite: an unbearable instant of blinding pain, then an extended aftermath of ramping euphoria. As my vision began to clear, I grew aware that Sandrine was looking at me with ardent, lockjawed, almost neuropathically shameless fascination, as if the pleasure of watching my ordeal had flash-frozen her expression at the height of wonderment. I now understood that Nick intended to use her not just to fuck me, but also, catering to my exhibitionistic inclinations, as a second pair of eyes to watch me open up.

"That's impossible," Sandrine was saying, taking care as she shook her head not to break the line of sight connecting her eyes with mine. "She can't really come just from having her nipples sucked. Crois moi. She must be squeezing her thighs."

"No, no!" Nick insisted, rising eagerly to the challenge. "Here, I'll prove it to you: just hold her legs open while I suck her nipples—you'll see."

Before I knew what was happening, Sandrine had leapt from her seat, splayed my thighs apart and pinned them to the bed. Then Nick seized the same sore nipple he had been abusing moments before, hyperextended it between his thumb and forefinger, and stuffed it into his mouth. I recoiled sharply, but his lips held fast with gripping suction, and I only succeeded in adding further insult to the earlier injury. When I tried to decrease the tension on my breast by "giving" a little, Nick, smiling maliciously, thwarted my efforts by tilting his head to take up the slack.

In the meantime, Sandrine had stripped off the last of her clothing and regained her chair. She sat on its edge with her knees parted, staring at me with a concentrated sort of attention now more feverishly interactive than passively absorbed. And when I turned my eyes upon the dusky embrasure between her legs, I understood why: she was tapping rapidly against her clitoris with a finger as she watched me. Her clit was large—twice the size of mine—and prominent; thus erect it projected half an inch at least past its harboring folds. Presently I saw that the clitoral drumming was only one movement of a cycle. After several seconds of rapping at herself like a typist pecking at a spacebar, Sandrine switched to circular manipulation in one plane, her fingers spinning in tight orbits that recalled a hand polishing silver. All rotatory motion then ended when she thrust a finger into her vagina, where it deliberated for several seconds until the entire rondo was begun again with the little taps.

Although I found the sight of Sandrine's distended clitoris faintly repulsive, this slight admixture of disgust somehow intensified rather than detracted from my predominantly erotic reaction to watching her masturbate over me. There must be something fundamentally compelling in the grotesque, for I was soon imagining my own clitoris swelling to the proportions of her prodigious organ. My pussy began to ache, and I thrust my hips forward in an attempt to secure some measure of palliative contact for my clit, which, in the mental schematic I carried around of my bodily proportions and outline, had now grown penis-sized and boldly protrusive. My attempts were in vain, however, for I discovered that I'd been immobilized by Sandrine, who had surreptitiously bound my ankles to the corners of the bed after she had relinquished her handhold on my thighs.

I begged Nick to touch my sex. He laughed, and answered instead by attacking my unattended left breast with his hands while continuing to suck on the nipple in his mouth—now abusing it roughly with his teeth and lips, now lapping at it gently with his tongue. Certainly I was excited in the extreme, though absent a tongue or finger on my clit, permanently shy, I believed, of the precritical plateau. At that moment, however, Sandrine emitted a shrill cry, and I watched transfixed while she attempted to bury her entire hand within her vagina. And as she succumbed to a climactic divulsion of mind and body—the tendons of her neck rigid as strung piano wire, her eyelids twitching like baitfish, her mouth venting a series of throaty grunts—I was overtaken and roundly sacked by my own startlingly unexpected orgasm.

Sandrine recovered swiftly from her paroxysm. Back to playing hostess, she dashed over to the mini-bar for the second bottle of champagne. I sat up, happy at the prospect of a recess, but Nick kept an arm hooked around my waist as if to caution me that the respite would be brief. He handed me one of the champagne flutes, and I was relieved at least for the cool liquid in my parched throat. After we'd all had a glass, Nick casually reached a hand to my pussy and parted my labia, whereupon Sandrine, suddenly attentive, dropped to one knee beside the bed and leaned in close like an eager medical student inspecting a surgical retraction.

Nick was extolling my secondary sexual characteristics ("Isn't she beautiful, Sandrine? The perfect flower: the petals sensuous, but not too fleshy. So tight inside, too: blood-squeeze death-grip on finger or cock. And you'll have to taste her—it's fucking ambrosia, I swear. Always tastes clean—I like to lick her cunt even after she's taken a run..."), while Sandrine pulled at her own nipples: tiny shell-pink caps on very round, very pale breasts. A bronzy spangle reflected from one, and I saw that both nipples were pierced and set with small gold rings. Through these she now threaded her fingertips as she continued to scrutinize me.

"I'd like to fuck her a little," she said suddenly, then looked around with an embarrassed smile, as though startled by her own words. But her eyes remained wild with the hunger behind her outburst, so that I was already squirming with nervous expectation by the time Nick turned to me and whispered, "Are you okay with that, Claire?"

I nodded my assent, but like a first-time home buyer signing a loan document, I remained timorously unsure—beyond the fact that it was momentous—exactly what it was I'd agreed to. Not a minute later I was already regretting my choice: Sandrine had taken hold of the empty champagne bottle and begun to wield it in a fashion that made her intent all too terrifyingly plain. I turned to Nick for succor—although whether I wished for intervention or reassurance I cannot honestly say—but to my surprise he showed absolutely no reaction to Sandrine's bellicose display. When I looked at him imploringly, he remained passively unconcerned; when I beseeched him with my eyes, he stared back at me with pointed disinterest. With a shock, I realized that Nick's indifference was premeditated, that he'd expected both Sandrine's action and my discomfiture. And then I understood that the main steps of this saraband had all been choreographed in advance. The spontaneity I had attributed to its movements and transitions was an illusion, a product of artifice alone.

I was cursing my own gullibility and the gross inadequacy of my theory of the romantic, when all at once a disturbingly gynecological sensation of cold, tubular glass sliding into my pussy shattered my reverie of self-deprecation. Sandrine was on her knees, gripping the champagne bottle with two hands—one on the butt and the other at the middle—applying it to me as if she were loading an artillery round into the breech of a howitzer.

"Fuck her slowly," Nick said, slipping out from under me to take up a new position behind Sandrine. "Do it to her the way she likes it: steady and deep."

Sandrine carried out Nick's orders, but added her own flourish: on each outstroke she gave the bottle a half twist, and the torsion thus produced was so keenly pleasureful it struck me dumb. Misinterpreting my silence as carte blanche, Sandrine forsook the relative restraint of the first incursion and began veritably lunging into me with her makeshift dildo. I braced myself against her attack, but I was surprised to find that instead of suffering under this violent outrage, I started anticipating a strange illicit satisfaction that arose with the shock that terminated each thrust, as if the energy thus conducted had broken through to a heretofore forbidden region of pleasure. Certainly I had entered dark and dangerous territory, for if this were not strictly rape, its reckless aggression nevertheless evoked fantasies of violation.

Closing my eyes, I gave myself over to these fantasies, enjoying them for the first time untainted by any sense of ethical or political transgression. (Perhaps because my ravisher was a woman, both her actions and my responses seemed exempt from criminality.) Suddenly, however, I felt as though all sensation and perception were collapsing in upon me, as if emotion were concentrating itself beyond the limit of safe compression. I was verging on a psychic critical mass. The next stimulus, the next slight movement, was sure to trigger an explosion, an accumulation of erotic energy extravasated in a single cataclysmic instant.

But the awaited plunge of the detonator never came. Instead, as I should have guessed, zero hour was abruptly canceled. Seizing the bottle from Sandrine, Nick yanked it from my vagina with a sharp flexure of his arm. I groaned my displeasure, feeling more violated by this agonizingly untimely abandonment than by the bottle-rape itself. But before I had a chance to articulate my indignation, I saw with relief that I had not, in fact, been left high and wet. Having grabbed up a skein of Sandrine's hair as a handle, Nick was now using it to pull her head onto my crotch. At once a hot mouth superposed itself to my vagina, and then the most wonderful wet exercises were begun inside me.

"Tongue-fuck the little bitch, Sandrine . . . lick her cunt good."

Nick stood over me, facing me and stroking his cock as he encouraged Sandrine. Although I couldn't pinpoint exactly how, the feeling of Sandrine's lips and tongue on my sex was different from anything I had known before—from anything I had known with men, in other words. Alternately boisterous and delicate, she knew exactly how much pressure to apply to my clitoris—and for how long—in order to maintain the trajectory and velocity of my excitement at a titillating constant. Each time I strayed too near the orgasmic vortex, Sandrine's deft oral loxodromy—an expedient adjustment of rudder or trim—would set me again on course. Once or twice, when despite her expert piloting I seemed dead-bound for the cataract, she relinquished my clitoris entirely, and shifting her kisses to my labia and the near reaches of my vagina, drew me back from the beckoning edge of oblivion.

Meanwhile, Nick's oration was shading closer to the manic: "Make her come, Sandrine . . . eat her cunt till she wails. I'm going to spurt all over her . . . mess her pretty face with my come. You want that, don't you, Claire? You want to lick up every sticky drop, don't you?"

Nick wasn't being interrogatory: he'd entered a zone too solipsistic to allow of questions that had any interest in answers. He was playing erotic solitaire, talking to himself while he continued to jerk off with one hand and, as I'd lately become aware, to diddle Sandrine with the other. Suddenly he gave a violent shake, then seemed to go rigid from the ground up: his calves quivered and bunched, his thighs knotted and twitched, the muscles of his arms and torso— sweat-glossy as if dipped in potter's glaze—tensed and bulged. Beautiful in his agony, Nick cried out as a shower of come spouted from his cock, while in the same instant Sandrine, sucking sharply at my clit with lips curled hard against her teeth, at last vouchsafed me my own long awaited discharge. The plangent rush of orgasm slammed through me just as I felt the warm clots of Nick's emission alight, first on my cheeks and eyelids, then on my lips and tongue. When the baptism was over, Sandrine crawled forth to lick the semen from my face, then kissed me deeply and passionately before breaking off with a contented sigh.

12

IN THE WEEKS WHICH FOLLOWED THAT NIGHT
of debauchery, my life—and particularly my erotic life—
sagged. The Thanksgiving to Christmas interregnum, a no-
toriously bad time for patients and their psychologists, had
begun in earnest. For a month at least, every one of my patients believed that she was uniquely alone in her solitude,
and that all of her personal relationships—both romantic
and familial—were false and "dysfunctional." Emergency
client conferences consumed my evenings and weekends,
while my dreams were subject to almost nightly interruption
by calls from my service (coinciding with improbable frequency to the diode-green glow of 2:22 on my alarm clock),
alerting me that one patient or another was reporting suici-
dal thoughts.

Nick, too, was bogged down with work. Squeezed between two overloaded schedules, our reserves of mental and
physical energy nearly tapped out, we barely managed to see
each other once a week. Nick would usually make it over to
my flat Saturday nights, though by then we were often so exhausted that sleep prevailed over sex in the hierarchy of
need. Settling for Chinese takeout and bed by nine, we
began to feel older than our years.

"You want a potsticker, Nick?"

"No, thanks. They bother my digestion. Did you hear about Mrs. Marcus on the second floor?"

"Yes. Terrible. Mort was up to see me. He's passing a kidney stone. He told me Mildred O'Connor's daughter dropped out of Wharton. It's going to kill her father."

"I'm sorry, I didn't hear you."

"I said, MILDRED O'CONNOR'S DAUGHTER DROPPED OUT OF WHARTON!"

"Oy, what a shame! It's going to kill her father. Pass me one of those potstickers, would you?"

Although I was hopeful that the current ebb wouldn't carry over into the new year, it did occasion some hard thinking on the nature of erotism and marriage.

I loved Nick; he told me he loved me too. I wasn't above giving our relationship a little nudge toward some sort of formalization. But when I extrapolated from the current lull in our sex life to what I imagined cohabitation or marriage might become, what loomed there, lamentably, was stagnation.

According to the "enlightened" version of the monogamous ideal, one is supposed to sacrifice the heat of passion for the warmth of intimacy and security, to resign herself to the truth in La Rochefoucauld's quip that "good marriages do exist, but not delectable ones"—and get on with life. But I was leery of the consequences of this horse trade—fearful in particular of becoming like so many of my married patients: dissatisfied, riddled with guilt over betrayals (real or imagined), regretful of my compromises. I wanted a different kind of relationship. And although I didn't envision anything like absolute mutual laissez-faire, and certainly not some perverse confessional compact where (à la Tolstoy) we would torture each other by recounting our every whim or thought or action, I *did* want to start at the pole opposite from traditional arrangements. I hoped for an agreement that gave us each as much freedom as we could tolerate with honest good feeling.

I recognized that my hope was wishful, even utopian—another of the little fictions which sustained me both personally and professionally. It seemed contradicted by history and sociology, by anecdotal evidence and "common sense." On the whole, I realized, I was fairly ignorant of life. Most of what I knew I'd learned vicariously, from reading or from my own case studies. Certainly I had too little experience of the range of human emotion to make credible claims about its flexibility and limits. In other words, I was acutely aware that actual circumstances could very well vanquish my theories. (How, for example, would I *really* feel if I were living contentedly with Nick and he slept with someone else? Was I so sure I wouldn't become the sort of jealous, possessive woman I claimed to despise? And what if I decided I wanted babies? Could I honestly imagine myself as a mother *and* a libertine?)

Nagged by suspicions that my scheme was foolishly impractical, or at least practically unsustainable, I decided that I needed to talk to Nick about our future together—soon, before self-doubt eroded my determination entirely. I would have preferred that he initiate the discussion, but he seemed bound by that stereotypically male attitude toward amorous relations that saw no need to formalize what seemed to be working—ever.

My opportunity came one night at Nick's loft, where we'd somehow ended up, even though my apartment would have offered decidedly snugger refuge from the Christmas blizzard that was punishing the city. We had turned in early, both blear-eyed from overwork, but now suddenly found ourselves awake at three a.m., wired and hungry, unable to fall back asleep.

The night air was marrow-chilling, a Canadian storm conducted directly into the loft through its large rectangular banks of uninsulated windows. Inside it was cold enough to safely age beef. We huddled under piles of bedclothes with only our faces exposed, inhaling each other's vapory breaths. When my pangs of hunger finally triumphed over my dread of bare feet on frigid linoleum, I made a dash for the kitchen. There I scooped up a bag of day-old croissants, some jam, a knife, and a bottle of orange juice, and then scampered back to our toasty hibernaculum in the bed. I made Nick lie on me and curl his feet around mine until my teeth stopped chattering.

We pulled on sweatshirts and sat up, then attacked the rolls as if we hadn't eaten in days. Afterwards, we were more awake than ever. We had plenty of time and little to do before dawn.

"Let's fuck," Nick said suddenly.

I considered the question. "No, let's talk."

"*Talk?* We haven't had sex in three weeks and you want to make a little conversation? Gevalt."

"'*Gevalt*'?" I laughed. "Is that a Bolivian expression?"

"Very funny, Claire. Tell me something: why is it that Jews are always so surprised when the goyim use their expressions?"

"Ah, well . . . that would be for exactly the same reason my close personal friend Nick is always surprised when I pronounce 'arroz con pollo' in proper Castilian. And besides that, you're . . . umm . . . not really a goy anymore."

"I'm not? But the circumcision isn't scheduled until next week."

"Haha! That's only a formality. The actual conversion took place when you started answering questions with questions."

"Okay," he said, sighing with resignation, "since we're not going to fuck, what do you want to talk about?"

I sketched for him my vision of what our relationship might look like. Or at least I sketched it as well as I could, given that I'd never taken time to flesh out the bare bones of the idea with any kind of meaty detail. What I offered instead were foundational principles: maximum liberty, mutual respect, honest commitment—a kind of constitutional framework upon which I thought we might build a life together. I made it clear that I wasn't presenting any ultimata, and that the terms were negotiable. But I didn't fudge, either. I was careful to make sure Nick understood that I needed something from him, some reassurance that we were in it together for the long term—one way or another. He listened with respectful interest while I spoke, interposing agreement here and there, asking me once or twice to clarify a point. But he remained poker-faced throughout, and when I'd finished, I hadn't the slightest inkling what he thought.

I sat for a while in silent expectation, but Nick said nothing. I assumed he was pondering my words, so I sat silently some more, awaiting his verdict. I tried to read his face, but found the effort agonizing, so I closed my eyes. After five minutes of this, I cracked.

"*So?*" I barked, startling myself as much as Nick.

"*Geez!* So *what?*"

"So . . . what do you *think*, Nick?"

"Sounds good, Claire."

"*Sounds good?* What do you mean 'sounds good'?"

"Isn't that pretty self-explanatory? I'm fine with what you said."

"You're serious?" I was incredulous. Nothing was this easy.

"Why does everything have to be so difficult for you?" Nick said, answering my thought. "Would you feel better if I had a problem? What you said makes a lot of sense to me. Why can't you be happy with that?"

Nick was right. I'd been fired up, primed for a row.

"Look, Claire: I love you," Nick continued. "I know I don't say it a lot. Though if I did, you'd probably think I was a girl. I know I should reassure you more—about how much you mean to me. Because you do. That's not a line. I mean...it's a line, but it's also a fact. And, yes, I was serious before. I think what you said—your proposal—is really great. I honestly think it could work for us. I especially like the part where I get to bring home the beautiful Thai waitress without you flying off the handle."

"I figured you might."

"Could be I'm the luckiest bastid in recorded history."

"Could be. But don't forget, Nick: I want some things as well."

"I know," he said, and then, with serious deliberation, as if he were working out just how much he wanted his words to commit him: "And I'm okay with that, too. I never really thought about kids before. But I'd think about it—with you. Not right now. Not right away. I'd want things—life—to be more settled. I'd want to do it right. I mean, *if* we did it."

"That's fine," I said, suddenly very happy. "There's no rush. My biological time bomb isn't set to go off for a few more years yet. Mostly I just needed to know that you'd want me around when it *did*—whatever we decide to do about it."

"Yes," he laughed. "I would. I mean, I do."

Relief came at last with the end of the year. Nick's holiday work rush was over, and I'd made it through another self-killing season without casualties. Tired and a little anti-social from my patients' incessant Yuletide bellyaching, I was in no particular mood for crowds or raucous celebration, and thus I needed little convincing when Nick suggested we spend New Year's Eve at home.

"Why go out?" he explained. "The service always sucks, and the food is third-rate even in the best places. It's rube night—people lined up for abuse. I'd rather eat in. Tell you what: I'll fire up the Hitachi and grill us some burgers. If you think it might turn you on, I'll even wear the frilly pink apron."

I balked at both burger and apron, and as for the hibachi, it was outside growing icicles. Instead, I spent a pleasant afternoon in my kitchen preparing lobster sandwiches and baking lemon tarts.

That night we made love slowly and tenderly. Afterward, Nick admitted that the near celibacy of the previous few weeks had depressed him.

"I know," I said. "It's like a presentiment of the great lukewarm."

Nick nodded in agreement. Then he laughed—his big evil stage laugh—and said he was planning something elaborate for us. He was going to make sure we kicked out the cobwebs in a major way.

A few days later I received a terse, handwritten letter:

Dear Claire,

Hola, favorita. Do me a favor, por favor. Divide a piece of paper down the middle. On the left side, jot down ten fantasy scenes you'd like to do. (That is—lasciva chanchita de mi corazón—if there are any left undone.) On the right side (that's east if you are at the blackboard facing north), write down ten you'd never go through with. Thanks.

I kiss the satiny rat-pink soles of your virgin feet, my love, and hope to remain forever,

Your Humble Servant,
Nicholas

The writing was fun, though I had some trouble with the second column: once committed to paper, certain irregular ideas, extreme notions that were easy enough to indulge in private reverie, seemed more like the tortive products of someone else's dark imagination. I had an urge to disavow them, to deny that I could be subject to such deranged tastes—even hypothetically. They forced me to recognize how alien I could be to my own self-conception.

13

ON A FRIDAY AT THE END OF FEBRUARY, a warm and clear day that hinted of a spring still many weeks away, Nick left a message with my secretary that she was unable to decode beyond the fact that "he said something about 'clearing out the attic.'" I'd taken advantage of the weather and gone out for a morning run. Back in my office, I returned Nick's call. He was polite, but brief.

"No time to talk, chica. I just wanted you to know we're set for tomorrow morning. Tonight I'll sleep at your place, if that's okay."

"Sure. But—"

"Oh! And before I forget—cancel any Monday appointments you've scheduled. You're taking the day off."

"I am?"

"Yes. Trust me: you're going to be needing the rest."

Before I could take issue with his presumption or ask for why's and wherefore's, he hung up. Ten minutes later, I was still trembling with nervous excitement as I stood to shake the hand of my first appointment.

Nick woke me before eight the next morning and instructed me to dress in what had become by this time my standard play attire: silk blouse, short skirt, thigh-high stockings, heels. Although I sometimes found this exclusive reliance on a single ensemble tiresome, I had to concede that what it lacked in variety, it made up for in convenience. In any case, it was nice to be with a man who at least knew what he liked in women's apparel. Today, however, we were making one break with routine: Nick asked that I wear panties. Insisting the choice be his, he began to tear through my dresser drawers, flinging rejects onto the carpet.

"Christ, between your mom and me you own a lot of underwear. Aha! Here's one! The La Perla thong. Beauteous. I'd almost forgotten about this sucker." Nick's refined aesthetic was the product both of enthusiasm and study. Aside from *Car and Driver*, the only magazine he subscribed to was *Intima Collezione*, a slick Italian trade journal devoted to the lingerie business.

As Nick hustled me out my front door at half-past the hour, he paused in the foyer to grab up a large nylon kit-bag I'd never seen before. We came out onto the street, where Nick practically pushed me into the open rear door of a black limousine—and directly onto someone's lap. I turned to find that the lap belonged to Sandrine. She adjusted her legs to accommodate me, smiled broadly, and then kissed me on the mouth. Nick settled in beside us, the door was closed—impelled by an unseen force—and seconds later we were on our way.

They set upon me immediately: hands squeezed my breasts through my clothes, pinching fingers found their way to the exposed flesh on the insides of my thighs and the delicate skin of my armpits. I wasn't amused. The pawing was coarse, vicious even: high jinks gone savagely feral. Then, as if a time-out had been secretly called, the rough handling abruptly ceased.

Sandrine brought a small flask to my lips.

"Tequila," Nick said. "Drink it. Medicinal purposes."

I drank, but the powerful, numbing liquor couldn't arrest the creep of foreboding that had begun in the pit of my stomach as a lurching malaise, and now suddenly localized itself as a choking pressure in my throat, like the thumb of some evil djinn pushing against my trachea. The knowledge that Nick was making me anxious by design (and that his bark likely presaged little in the way of actual bite) weakened but couldn't neutralize my anxiety. I'd never been the sort of person who could simply make up her mind to enjoy fearful anticipation. Even the most unconvincingly realized horror films gave me the willies.

The next round began as suddenly as the last had ended. With neither warning nor apparent effort, Sandrine exercised the muscular arms and shoulders I'd noticed when we first met: she lifted me several inches into the air, then flipped me over onto my belly. I came to rest lying crosswise: my breasts flattened against the tops of her thighs, my knees in Nick's lap, my abdomen bridging the space between them.

I was still trying to determine whether I'd suffered a mild concussion on landing, when Sandrine raised my skirt and attempted to jam a long finger into my vagina from behind. I screamed in pain. I was neither lubricated nor relaxed, and her finger felt as invasively alien and abrasive as a rough dowel. Nick grabbed a fistful of my hair and yanked hard, hissing, "Shut up, Claire"—but in the next instant he turned to Sandrine and no less reproachfully said, "Put some lube in her cunt. She's dry."

Sandrine pulled her finger sharply from my pussy, causing me nearly as much distress as when she'd entered. Lying prone and unable to rotate my head, I found my vision restricted to a narrow vertical swath on my right. I heard Nick squeeze a bottle of lubricant over Sandrine's hands. Then fingers parted the lips of my sex, and Sandrine dove at me like a harrier stooping to flushed game. In seconds she'd worked half a hand at least into my vagina—although this time, thankfully, the ingress was painless.

The unexpected atmosphere of brutality disturbed and bewildered me. This was aggression *realized*, not the implied and stylized version I'd experienced before. By comparison, even the "St. Regis Weekend"—the bottle-rape at Sandrine's hand—seemed more like a performance than a spontaneous attack. And there was another difference: Nick and Sandrine were more wound-up, more high-keyed and uneasy than I'd ever seen them. I couldn't convince myself they were merely acting, and I could no longer explain my way out of being scared.

Yet just as I was concluding that my situation involved real menace, my situation was already beginning to take a calmer, more benign turn. Sandrine had been gently fingering me, and I began to feel a kind of pleasant deep tugging, as if my penetralia seated a sensible spring that was slowly being compressed with each gliding stroke of her fingers. No sooner had these digitally rendered distractions quieted my immediate fear of imminent danger, however, than another sort of worry took its place: that our driver—whose existence I'd so far only been able to infer from secondary effect—might be watching me. Looking up, I was reassured to see that a pane of dark plexiglass separated our compartment from his. Unfortunately, Nick noticed my glance and immediately understood the meaning of my relieved expression. With a raffish, gloating look, he rapped his knuckles twice against the divider, then gave a short, derisive laugh when I cringed in anticipation of being exposed. The split window slid partially open from the other side, and I saw a very handsome, very black face reflected in the rear view mirror.

"Sir, can I help you? Is there something wrong?" The chauffeur's words carried the distinctive lilting accent and sing-song cadence of French Africa.

"No, nothing's wrong at all, Daniel," Nick answered, familiarly. "I just wanted you to see this girl back here. She's beautiful and hot, and my friend is making her pussy all wet. Care to look?"

An ivory smile gradually appropriated Daniel's face. He lowered his sunglasses, peeking over them while he adjusted the angle of his mirror.

"Thank you, sir," he laughed. "A splendid view this morning."

"Feel free to watch . . . Claire loves an appreciative audience."

Nick then shot the divider completely open, and I shrank with embarrassment. Had I been able, I would have disappeared into the seat altogether.

"She's making me very, very hot," said Sandrine to Nick in

a thin, dry whisper. "I need something—*before* we get to the store."

While I waited for Nick to say something that might clarify Sandrine's cryptic reference, I heard behind me a minute, vitreous tapping. Two sharp sniffs confirmed a hunch as Nick extended an arm over my head to Sandrine, who partook.

"All right, Sandrine," he said, "we'll take care of you." Then, addressing our driver, he said, "Tell me, would you like to fuck this little bitch?"—and with a start I realized that he meant me.

"You are serious, sir?" asked Daniel.

"I'm serious. But don't call me 'sir.' The sixteen-year-old girls who serve popcorn at the movie theater call me 'sir.' It makes me feel old."

"As you wish—*monsieur.*" At this everyone laughed, including—despite my uneasiness—me.

Sandrine addressed Daniel in French: "T'es rigolo, tu sais? Appelle lui 'Nick.' Et, par hazard—il est sérieux."

"Sans blague? Mais il est cinglé ou quoi?"

"Non. Pas du tout. C'est pas pour lui . . . Il le fait pour la gonzesse. Elle aime ces choses . . ."

"Ah, c'est *ça*, c'est *ça* . . . ouais. Je comprend maintenant . . ."

"Tell me, Daniel," Nick interrupted, "Do you have a place we can go?"

Daniel appeared to consider this.

"Maybe," he said. "But there is one problem. I share with a couple of guys."

"Ah . . . Well, that's just fine—we'll wake 'em up. Let's go."

"As you wish."

We drove in silence for a while, Sandrine lightly tracing the margin of my ear with a fingertip. The fingers of her other hand, still nestled within me, were for the time being at rest. The hum of the tires suddenly changed timbre and pitch, and then at regular intervals there began a tattoo, a repeated pair of short, dull beats like the chunk of train wheels. We were crossing a bridge.

"Where the hell do you live?" Nick asked.

"Jamaica," replied Daniel.

"A lovely town. Let's not run out of gas."

We parked on the street in front of a row of tenements. Daniel got out and opened the door for us. As we emerged into the blinding sunlight, I was accosted first by the smell of frying meat, and then by a dozen sharp stares aimed at us from stoops and the doorways of bodegas. More puzzled and curious than hostile, the glances were understandable: we must have looked as if we'd come here by accident, taken a wrong turn somewhere, or—closer to the truth, I suspected—like we were slumming.

With a sharp whistle, Daniel called over a tall fellow who had been standing on the opposite corner. Money changed hands, and then the man, thin as a licorice stick under the blousy yardage of his mustard-yellow dashiki, leaned against our car with the custodial insouciance of a born lookout. "Ne vous inquietez pas!" he shouted after us reassuringly as we followed Daniel into the nearest building.

We climbed five flights of stairs—the elevator was broken—and emerged onto a narrow landing. Daniel led us into a small, darkened studio apartment. I saw by the light that entered at the edges of the drawn blinds that four mattresses lay on the floor, two of them occupied by sleeping men. The furnishings were sparse: three chairs, a small table, two footlockers, and a makeshift etagere of cinder blocks and particle board. The room was tidy, its floor and walls spotlessly clean. When I realized that this surprised me, I felt ashamed. Despite my liberal convictions, I wasn't free of the common prejudice that the poor are slovenly.

"We sleep in shifts," Daniel explained. "Everyone drives a cab or limo. Day drivers and night drivers—we're never all three here at the same time. It's a good arrangement—we save money."

"You want to wake your friends?" Nick asked. "I don't want them to be offended. Explain to them what's happening. They can watch, or . . ."

Daniel gently roused his roommates and led them into a corner for a palaver. Heads nodded, then Daniel came back, and I heard him tell Nick that they had agreed but wanted a little money for "the rent of the room."

Laughing as he reached into his pocket, Nick said, "You're a smooth operator, Daniel—very smooth. And hugely underemployed, I might add." He peeled a few bills from a money clip and handed them to Daniel, who in turn distributed them to his friends.

Sandrine took my hand and led me into the center of the room, where she turned me until I stood with my back to our audience. She lifted my skirt from behind, then curved a hand over my ass with a delicately vagrant touch so sensual that it virtually guaranteed my cooperation. Next she began to work my underwear slowly up between my cheeks. I responded by arching my lower back and jutting out my behind—and the room instantly fell silent.

I believe I've always had a fairly accurate physical self-image: confident enough that none of my imperfections was too egregious, comfortably reconciled to being attractive but not beautiful. But for months now Nick had been singing my gluteal praises, and as a result I'd begun to entertain the possibility that my rump had more than average sex appeal. I now envisioned myself as Nick and the others would: the globe of my ass halved by the thong, the pale, smooth skin drawn taut as shrink-wrap over each perfect hemisphere—and my blood quickened at the thought of their admiration and desire.

Sandrine took several steps back, then stood for a while watching me with her arms crossed, like a sculptress checking the rondure of her figure. Suddenly she undid her jeans and dropped them to her ankles. Dancing free of them and her underwear, she stood at parade rest, her legs planted a meter apart. She began to masturbate, her hand a blur of motion over the fine fulvous wisp of her bush.

The impact of this display was immediate and electric. Daniel stripped off his clothing and I watched his penis elevate to the horizontal in bounding stages. Gaping in disbelief, his roommates began to stroke themselves through their underwear. Nick approached me, then took my face in his hands and whispered, "Stand up for a second, baby. Daniel's

going to fuck you. Everything's going to be all right. I promise. Everything's safe. I'm here—I'm watching out."

Then came a sudden peevish shout: "Nick!"

We turned to find Sandrine, hands on hips, glaring at us
in vexation, looking as if she were about to stamp a foot.

"Okay," Nick said, "I hear you." He shook his head and
smiled at her— the sardonic, affectionate smile of a long-suf-
fering but tolerant father. Then he said to me, loud enough
for Sandrine to hear, "Oh . . . and one more thing, Claire: this
time I want you to eat her pussy. I think you're ready—and
you get bonus points for being a good Samaritan, 'cause I'm
pretty sure she's going to explode if you refuse."

Laughing to himself, Nick gestured to Daniel, who came
and stood before me. I hadn't realized how extraordinarily
large he was. Without even touching me, by propinquity
alone, he made me feel as though I were being overpow-
ered—as though I ought to ask for quarter.

"I want you to touch him," Nick directed. "Suck his nipples first . . . then stroke his body."

Daniel removed his cap and sunglasses, and for the first
time I was able to study his face with care. His beauty was
dramatic, and singular—nothing like the generic perfection
of male models. He had elongate, almost Mongolian eyes,
with sea-green irises so large they eclipsed all but the
thinnest halo of conjunctival white. His nose was all angles
and planes, a Euclidean sketch-pad. His lips were full and
well-shaped, his teeth flawless and evenly spaced. His body
too was exquisite, and of a type I had never before known intimately. Whereas all my lovers had been lanky or mesomor-

phic, Daniel was massive and muscular—and yet, because his limbs and hands were gracefully proportioned, there was nothing at all hulking about him.

Taking the initiative, I closed the gap between our bodies, then put my hands on his shoulders and pressed my face to his chest. When I took a nipple in my mouth, his pectoral muscles twitched against my lips and his cock lengthened where it lay against my solar plexus. I rested my cheek against his skin, richly dark and sleek like that of a sea lion, delighting in the way the light modeled its contours, soaking up its delicious smell, warm and slightly sweet, untainted by cologne. His scent and touch evoked increasingly gustatory cravings. I felt as if I were eating a particularly sumptuous dessert, and I wanted to linger over my dish, to wrest all the pleasure I could from each bite. That I could savor a strange man's body so unreservedly was a revelation to me; that I could desire sex before acquaintance, a shock. But Daniel's beauty was absolutely intoxicating. It so captivated me that for the first time I truly comprehended how women's bodies could enrapture and confound men, how physical beauty could be devastating to behold.

"Stroke his cock," Nick said, cutting short my perambulation of Daniel's body and the line of thought that ran with it.

"But—"

"No arguments. Stroke his cock." Nick pushed me to my knees so that the head of Daniel's penis, fully emerged from its collar of unabridged foreskin, bobbed and danced on the tip of my nose. Loading my fingers with the pre-come that already covered his exposed glans, I moistened the rest of Daniel's cock, then gave it a gentle pull.

"Harder, Claire!" Nick exclaimed with annoyance—exasperated, I knew, because he'd once again had to remind me that men like their cocks treated firmly and rigorously. (He insisted that male desire for a slow, light touch was strictly a fanciful creation of women's erotica, a perverted missapplication of the Golden Rule.)

"Stroke it hard, Goddamnit!"

Kneeling corrected, I formed my thumb and forefinger into a tight ring at the neck of Daniel's penis, then briskly pulled the foreskin up and over the head, and then just as briskly pulled it down again around the shaft. As if to confirm Nick's hypothesis, Daniel girdled his hips with his hands and began pumping his pelvis so that his cock met and abetted the active resistance of my hand. Daniel's excited motion soon made me ache for a different kind of touch. Unaware of my needs—or simply indifferent to them—Nick continued issuing orders:

"Stroke his balls, Claire."

I obeyed, enfolding Daniel's scrotum with my hand in order to caress and gently tug at it the way Nick had shown me. Daniel's breathing grew rapid and shallow, then the muscles of his abdomen began to bunch and fibrillate in waves—sure signs that he was nearing orgasm.

Suddenly, however, Nick switched gears.

"Back away, Claire. I want Daniel to fuck you."

I grudgingly relinquished Daniel's cock. He opened his eyes and stared at me with an expression that mixed wild panic and deep disappointment. I almost laughed aloud from the irony: Nick's strategy of excitation and abscission—directed at me—was taking its toll on an unintended victim.

What happened next rattled me. Nick tore a condom from its foil package and placed it without hesitation on the tip of Daniel's cock. I looked at Daniel, but his expression betrayed no hint of surprise or unease as he allowed Nick to unfurl the condom down his shaft. I shifted my gaze to Nick's face, but found only composure there. Certain odd impressions and unanswered questions from the recent past now took possession of my thoughts. Although Nick was the first heterosexual male I had known who had close gay male friends, I'd always attributed this to his constitutional liberality in general. I'd known others who would tolerate gay men—if only out of deference to their status as persecuted minority—but they always maintained a certain physical and conversational barrier. Nick was different. I'd observed him at several "mixed" parties and openings, and not once had I seen him betray the slightest defensive shift of body language, even in the presence of the nelliest flirt or most outrageous queen. One day I'd asked him if he'd had any homosexual experiences as an adolescent.

"Nope, never. Not even experimentally—not even a circle jerk. No funny uncles, either. I'm a flaming heterosexual. I think that's why I'm cool with gay men. It's this way, Claire: I've loved a lot of guys—I've just never wanted to suck their dicks."

I was no longer so sure. There'd been something absolutely, unflinchingly casual in the way Nick had sheathed Daniel. I had a lot of questions, and I would soon be demanding some forthright answers—though not, it would appear, before I answered Sandrine, who I suddenly realized was now telling me something for perhaps the third time:

"Listen to me, cherie! Come on: get up. Come over here to the mattress."

I obeyed her, and then her mimed request that I lower myself onto all fours. First she had me put my head on the mattress and stick my buttocks in the air, then she flopped belly down next to me and brought her mouth to my ear.

"Claire," she whispered, "you're going to lick my pussy. Nick says I can have you. I want you to make me come—you can't stop until then. I'm telling you this because soon it will be hard for you to concentrate—with Daniel fucking you, I mean. You see . . . I want you to try to think about me, to ignore him if you have to. Please do this for me—but don't tell Nick what I said. Pas un mot, je t'en pris . . ."

Like a partisan spy given only seconds to convey a complicated message, Sandrine had delivered her information and her plea in a single rush of breath. This was of course playacting, albeit a very good performance. Certainly its effect on me was real enough. Unable to deny such a passionate request from such a charming petitioner, I pledged myself to Sandrine's cause. I would do my utmost to make her come, even if it meant risking life and limb. *Vive La Résistance!* I thought, laughing to myself.

Sandrine lay in front of me on the mattress with her legs spread and her little underdeveloped pelt inches from my face. Naturally sparse and soft, her bush dwindled gradually at the margins, without the severe outline that marked an aggressive wax job. (I'd once heard Nick say that the current fashionable pubic topiary "looked like a Chaplin mustache on its side—and just as sexy.")

I registered discussion and commotion to my rear. Then

Daniel was on his knees behind me, pulling my underwear aside. An instant later I'd been filled, a tender receptacle accommodating a vital solidity with perfect gliding ease. Daniel's cock fit as though it were the exact casting to my mold, like a missing part of me restored. My breath caught and I trembled as we began slowly to fuck.

But before Daniel had completed half a dozen strokes, Sandrine was already pushing her sex into my face. As she had anticipated when extracting her promise, I would have preferred at this moment to enjoy the passive pleasure of receiving Daniel's cock without being obliged to tend to her needs. But I had already committed myself, and felt I had no choice but to service her.

"Kiss my pussy, Claire. Lips first."

Unsure whether she meant her lips or mine, I began gently to kiss her labia, hoping thereby to cover either interpretation. She moaned, and I felt her wetness irrigate my lower lip. Gathering courage, I slinked my tongue tip into the mouth of her vagina. She responded enthusiastically, whimpering and bucking forward to force herself over my stiffened tongue. Comfortable as I was with my own smells, I'd nevertheless been unsure how I would react to those of another woman, and thus I was relieved to find both her scent and taste perfectly pleasant. On first approach, the cliché of oysters and estuaries seemed surprisingly appropriate, but as I began to lick within her depths, suggestions of sea-life gave way to those of citrus and the acidic bite of green mango. The further I mined her, the more tart and sweet she became. The juices I sucked from her deepest, most succulent flesh only made my mouth water for more.

"Lick her clit," a voice boomed in my ear. I looked up to find Nick masturbating directly over me—though I couldn't keep him consistently in view, for my head rolled each time my buttocks received the force of Daniel's thrusting hips. Daniel remained strangely quiet as he built toward climax—no moan or grunt punctuated the staccato slap of his abdomen and thighs against my ass (a sound like beach sandals being struck together to dislodge sand), nor did even his final desperate ejaculatory lunges (alas, too soon arrived) provoke a single cry or expletive from his mouth. When he withdrew I felt something like regret over life's caprices: the promise of our physical syntony had gone unfulfilled, and a rematch seemed unlikely.

"Have your friends put rubbers on," Nick told Daniel. "They can fuck her too."

"Only Jean-Philippe, monsieur. Alain doesn't want to—he has a fianceé."

"Ah, okay . . . Well then, Jean-Philippe it is. Anyway, he's nicely hung. Claire will like that."

Momentarily redirecting his attention to Sandrine and me, Nick forced his fingers between my mouth and her crotch.

"Lick her clit," he repeated, spreading her labia.

I took Sandrine's clitoris between my lips, trying as faithfully as memory permitted to duplicate the action she had once performed on me.

"*No*, Claire. I said *lick* it, for Christ's sake! That means use your tongue." Nick glared at me impatiently, as if he'd just had to correct a dull-witted pupil for the umpteenth time.

I released Sandrine's clitoris, and began instead to investigate it with the tip of my tongue—finding it strange from this perspective, as though I were approaching human anatomy with the alien sentience of a fly or an octopus. My familiarity with my own body hadn't prepared me at all for the discoveries being wrought by my mouth. Externally delicate and supple, Sandrine's clit seemed as though it ought to have retracted and bent at my touch, like a tiny sea cucumber yielding to a diver's probing finger. Instead it actively resisted pressure: the soft, living coral but thinly covered an extrusive hardness that was decidedly un-feminine. (The clitoral homology with the penis, a scientific commonplace, I now suddenly experienced as fact—as a much more brute and resonant fact, I'm sure, than it was ever understood by the biology professor who first taught it to me.)

"Harder, Claire. Come on, baby—lick it. You're torturing Sandrine. I mean, that's okay with *me*—but she thinks it's *her* job."

When he'd finished laughing at his own commentary, Nick emphasized his point by shoving my face down onto her sex. This time I attacked her clit, lapping at it with the covetousness of a puppy devouring a child's momentarily unattended ice-cream cone. Her hips thrashed so violently I had to pinion them just to keep her genitals in contact with my mouth. A final few caresses with the curling length of my tongue and she came: piercing cries and spastic jerks, then a protracted diminuendo of shallow gasps and intermittent shudderings before peace was at last restored.

Thinking that my cooperation had bought me a moment of liberty, I made to rise from Sandrine, only to have my head forcibly replaced between her legs by Nick, whose conception of the end of act one apparently differed from mine.

"Don't stop, Claire: keep sucking her cunt." I lowered my mouth to Sandrine's pussy—now become a tide-drowned fissure from my recent efforts—and began to suck it dry of her brackish juices and my own spit. My lips slowly and lovingly vacuumed the transuding slit, working northward from the fourchette at its base to its clitoral apex. Sandrine soon gave signs she was progressing toward a second climax.

Unfortunately, our mutual pleasure was spoiled at that moment by Jean-Philippe's bungling attempt to mount me from behind. He had wholly neglected to prepare passage for what—if the terrible pain I suddenly experienced at the port of entry were any indication—must have been a penis of overabundant proportions. Regardless, however, of the actual cause—failure to alert customs, a freighter too broad for the channel, or both—two things were manifestly obvious: his cock had run aground at the harbor's mouth, and no amount of jostling was going to budge it further.

To his credit, Nick reacted quickly to my distress, leaping up the moment he heard my cry, shouting "Off of her, man!" as he pulled the maladroit Jean-Philippe from me before any real damage had been inflicted. He then calmly lectured the now shamed and apologetic Senegalese:

"She's very small. You have to use lube . . . and go very slowly." He looked around as though for words, then said, "Tout doucement . . . that's it, tout doucement—you understand?"

Jean-Philippe nodded.

"You want to try it again?" Nick encouraged.

"Yes."

I first felt the treacly drip of lubricant on my pussy, and then Nick's expert fingers gently working me open. With a gymnastics spotter's air of vigilant concern, he stood by me as Jean-Philippe attempted re-entry, his hands holding me open to ease the way. There was no difficulty this time. I was tight but pliable and could accommodate even a very large member as long as I was sufficiently wet and relaxed. Indeed, as Nick had revealed to me through dildo play, I took a special pleasure in being filled to capacity, in being glutted by cock.

Jean-Philippe began to fuck me, and I breathed relief that the extraordinary girth of his penis was not matched by its length. Incapable of pounding my cervix, he would cause me no further distress.

While Jean-Philippe rocked himself in my vagina, Nick's fingers—which I recognized by touch alone—massaged my clitoris, a keenly agreeable combination. But just as I was mounting the climactic stage, Jean-Philippe suddenly groaned, and I felt his cock shudder conclusively within me. Then—with what I couldn't help but feel was knavishly impolite post-coital male haste—he began to pull out.

"Don't move!" Nick commanded. "Stay in her!"

Nick knew I liked something in me when I climaxed: Jean-Philippe had had his fun and—like it or not—was going to have to submit to service as a stopgap.

On his back now, like a mechanic preparing to inspect a transmission, Nick pushed himself off against his heels, scuffing my belly with the rough stubble of his weekend beard as he leveraged his head under my hips. Suddenly his mouth was on my clitoris, hungrily sucking it like a kid at a dam's teat. Not long afterward I came—a slow, undulant orgasm that whelmed me less with its intensity than with its extraordinary duration.

While thus preoccupied with Nick and Jean-Philippe, I'd temporarily forgotten Sandrine, who, I now saw, had apparently lost herself in a masturbatory trance, her pelvis oscillating in the wobbly circles of a toy top about to topple.

"Come for us, Sandrine!" Nick exhorted her. "Come, you little slut!" With Jean-Philippe out of the way, Nick had returned to his earlier station, on his knees facing us, stroking his cock. All of a sudden he stiffened, his muscles knit from his brow to his toes, and then—just as it seemed he might split his skin from the assurgent stress—he gave out an emphatic "fucking Jesus!" and shot three long strings of lactescent spunk point-blank upon the sopping gash of Sandrine's cunt. The last salvo concluded, he pushed my face into her crotch with a blurt of orders:

"Suck her clit now, Claire . . . eat my come from her hole."

Rubbing my face into the swale, I fished for Sandrine's clitoris with my tongue. She screamed and convulsed, then pulled my head to her pussy with savage determination, grinding herself against my mouth as though the resilience of flesh were no longer sufficient—as though her ardor had grown so extortionate it could only be satisfied by the unyielding density of teeth and bone . . .

We lay about for a while, silent and euphoric, each in his own world. Sandrine spoke first, reminding Nick that there were things to be done, complaining she was hungry. I laughed at her impulsiveness, so childlike and ingenuous, even as I acknowledged that a part of me envied her for it.

Everyone cleaned up as best she could, and then we thanked Jean-Philippe and the abstemious Alain (who, however, I suspected had gotten in a furtive wank when no one was paying attention) for their hospitality.

We emerged once again onto the street, no doubt looking considerably more bedraggled to our sentry than we had upon arrival an hour earlier. Daniel greeted him with a handshake, thanked him, and opened the passenger door for us. With a bow and a "wenches first," Nick began to usher Sandrine and me into the back, when suddenly he stopped and straightened, then tilted his head back as though searching for something low in the sky. It wasn't enemy aircraft that had drawn his attention, however, but lunch. He sniffed the air with his bird-dog look, then his gaze followed his nose straight toward some food vendors who were congregated a few yards from us, their braziers and steam tables crowding onto the sidewalk.

"How's the chow, Daniel?" Nick asked.

"What?"

"The food . . . la—what is it?—la bouffe."

"Oh. I have no idea at all. I don't eat that crap." Daniel's answer rang with haughty disdain, as if the mere question had insulted his dignity. It occurred to me that France's legacy to its former colonies included some of the less estimable aspects of its culture.

"Ever been to Paris?" Nick asked nonchalantly.

"Yes, once. Why?"

Daniel seemed confused by the unexpected turn in the

conversation. But I knew Nick well enough to predict that the digression was setting up a zetz.

"Oh, *good*," Nick beamed. "Then you've had one of those little pizzas they sell everywhere. Soggy slice of old bread covered with a handful of salty cheese and a shriveled anchovy and—I swear!—fucking *ketchup*. You wanna talk about crap? *That's* crap. And the Parisians eat it. Hell, they fucking love it. Nobody in New York would eat that shit. At least not twice. Shows what the frogs really know about food."

Without waiting for a reply, Nick strode purposefully over to the food sellers. After a quick review of their hand-lettered signs, he forged past the Cubans and Puerto Ricans to address himself to a small, gray-haired Mexican man who was standing proudly before his cart in a spotless white apron, a pair of long aluminum tongs cradled in his arms like a prized fowling piece.

"Buenas, jefe," Nick began. "Dé me una docena de tacos de carnitas para llevar, por favor."

"Si, señor. Quiere chile?"

"Seis sin chile—para las gringitas." Nick paused to indicate Sandrine and me with a thumb aimed over his shoulder. "Ya estan bastante piquantes."

They both laughed, and the old man looked at us and smiled.

"Algo de tomar?"

"Tiene horchata?"

"No."

"Que lástima! Okay, no importa . . . tenemos champagne —haha! Quantos debo?"

They completed the transaction with mutual smiles and agradecimientos, and Nick rejoined us, toting a paper bag filled with steaming tacos. We settled into the car and a savory aroma immediately filled the space—with Pavlovian effect. Sandrine and I were famished: two devout carnivores, drooling and begging while Nick, with an air of noble benevolence, doled out the morsels one by one. He then opened a bottle of champagne and signaled Daniel to start the car.

The tacos were delicious. Compositionally basic—just fried pork bits wrapped in corn tortillas with a little cilantro and a squeeze of lime—yet amazingly satisfying. More vindication, I thought, for my theory that one was far more likely to get a bad meal (and infarctoid dyspepsia) from a chichi restaurant than on the street.

While Sandrine and I devoured our lunch, Nick offered Daniel the share of tacos he'd reserved for him. Apparently still smarting from Nick's dig at his hauteur, Daniel refused these with a sullen shake of the head.

"Oh, come on," Nick insisted. "Be a sport; try them. Don't deny yourself a great opportunity just because *I'm* a shithead."

Daniel regarded Nick gravely in his mirror—then broke into a grin.

Nick passed him the tacos, but waited until Daniel's mouth was full before asking, "What do you think? Good, huh?"

Swallowing hurriedly, Daniel replied, "Yes, very good. Of course you were right, *monsieur*. And by the way—fuck you, *monsieur*."

"What?"

"Je t'ai dit 'fuck you,'" repeated Daniel, smiling. "Qu'est-ce que t'as pas compris?"

I waited for Nick to take umbrage at this gross insubordination, but instead he gave a hearty laugh and reached forward to pat Daniel's shoulder approvingly.

Unable to explain their behavior, I chalked it up to some sort of strange inter-guy rapport.

We retraced our path up Queens Boulevard and took the 59th Street Bridge back into the city. I was enjoying myself. The brittle and vaguely insidious atmosphere of the morning had dissipated, and for the present at least, everyone was festive and relaxed. I was in such a dopey haze from the champagne that I paid no attention to our progress. When at length I looked up, I was surprised to find we were cruising some of the cruddier streets around Times Square.

"We're here," Nick announced, for no reason that was apparent from our immediate surroundings. The car came to a halt. Through my window I saw a boarded-up surplus store, an adult theater, a methadone clinic, two pawn shops, and a bar—nothing that I could make as a likely destination. I couldn't imagine what my fearless leaders had up their sleeves.

"Bend her for me," Nick said suddenly, the hard edge back in his voice. Sandrine grabbed the base of my neck and slammed my face into Nick's lap. Victim of their gratuitous roughhandling for the second time that day, I was fuming with anger, though I tried to temper my protest, figuring that a heated outburst was exactly what they wanted.

"Nick," I said, in what I hoped was a tone of self-assured

resolve, "let's back off from the brutality, okay? That hurt just now. I never agreed—"

"Shut the fuck up," he interrupted, breathing fire—and all of a sudden I realized that nothing I could say would mollify him in the least.

I was in the midst, once again, of berating myself for the decision that had put me here, when Nick jerked wide the fly of his jeans and began to stuff his erect penis into my mouth.

"Suck it," he said, and then: "Sandrine, get her ready. It's in there."

I heard the zipper of the tote bag open and then felt Sandrine's wet finger on my anus, gingerly probing at first, then gently and insistently massaging, soliciting me to relax. Fearful that resistance might provoke retaliation (and aware of just how vulnerable I was at the moment), I allowed myself to be dilated. Sandrine pushed her finger firmly into my ass.

"That's enough," Nick said, "She's ready." Sandrine slid her finger out of me, and immediately replaced it with a much larger, more rigid object. Nick choked off the gasp in my throat with the occluding tip of his penis, allowing me to disgorge it only after I'd begun to clutch and scrape in a wild panic of anoxia. I was still gulping draughts of air like a half-drowned swimmer when he and Sandrine pulled me upright between them and prepared to leave the car.

We assembled ourselves on the sidewalk. I was addled, knocked off-center. My head buzzed with what ought to have been a by now familiar dissonance of emotions: resentment and excitement, fear and anticipation. I was inert, planktonic, though not so much devoid of will as unable to act on it. So tentative had I become that when I finally complained, it wasn't to renew my demand for an end to my mistreatment generally, but merely to object to a secondary annoyance: I couldn't walk with whatever it was—dildo or plug—they had fitted into my ass.

"Of course you can," Sandrine countered. "Just don't squeeze your muscles. It will stay in you, and your underwear will keep it from poking out." She giggled then, as if "poking out" were an intrinsically funny thing to say.

"Daniel! Her hands!" It was our field marshal Nick, again barking orders.

Daniel grabbed my wrists from behind. Then I watched Sandrine windmill her arm as though pitching a softball. Instead of a sphere, however, what came arcing toward me in slow rotation was a twist of silvery metal, caught first by a flash of sunlight, and then by Daniel's outstretched arm, plucking it from the air above my head. Someone brought my hands together at the small of my back, and then I heard a bright click as handcuffs snapped shut on my wrists.

An explosive guttural cough diverted my attention to a nearby doorway, where three winos in ragged nylon parkas and woolen caps sat watching us, passing a bottle in a paper bag between themselves. Grimy and destitute, with insolent, bloated faces, they stared hungrily at me and smacked their lips. I felt completely demeaned. Nick laughed at my anguish, then stepped behind me and lifted my blouse, eliciting a trio of rotted smiles from our audience. Sandrine came forward to suck my breasts, each in turn, then produced a pair of clamps—rubber-tipped alligator clips joined by a length of chrome chain—which she swiftly attached to the swollen ends of my nipples. The clamps were tensed enough to grip me securely, though thankfully not so tight as to inflict pain.

As Sandrine stepped back to admire her handiwork, a sedan filled with teenaged boys drove by. Apparently we made an impression, for a moment later they came to a tire-screeching halt, then slowly backed up to goggle at us in disbelief. Ashamed, I turned from them and tried to move away, but Daniel held me fast by the handcuffs. Sandrine then grabbed my shoulders and spun me around so that I once again faced the boys. They hooted and whistled and shouted obscenities, while Nick made a big show of pawing my breasts and pulling the chain that linked my nipples. I felt more humiliated and degraded than ever, but also more excited—such was my state of arousal that the merest touch, the lightest scherzo ever played by a finger on a clitoris, would have been enough to set me off.

I should have been so lucky. Without even a prefiguring glance in my direction, Nick seized the clamps on my nipples and tightened the screws until I cried in pain. Then he drew my blouse back down over my breasts and, leaving me bent in tears at the curb, walked to within an arm's length of the boys in the car, whom he addressed in a fine rendition of one of New York's finest:

"Uh-kay, uh-kay . . . moobit a-lawng. Showz ovah, people. Nuttin leff tuh see heeya. C'mon, c'mon . . . jess moobit a-lawng . . ."

The boys drove slowly away, hollering their disappointment in curses aimed, it seemed to me, more at each other than at us, though clearly we were to blame for setting their hormonal kettle boiling. Halfway down the street the driver gunned the beige sedan—a vehicle so bland and featureless it could only have been a parent's car on loan—and sped out of sight.

When at length I'd recuperated enough to stand again, Nick ranged us all and led the charge: a dozen paces down the block, then a sharp left into a sex shop whose marquee my original survey had somehow missed. On the inside the shop was more starkly functional than truly seedy. Two walls were festooned with skin magazines and dirty books, a third supported sheets of pegboard where sex toys in clear plastic bags hung on hooks, and the fourth opened past a turnstile into a video arcade. On an elevated platform in the middle of the room, a man, presumably the owner, stood behind a cash register, sluggishly decimating a jumbo bag of cheese puffs. He was fiftyish and corpulent, his arms and neck a palimpsest of artless tattoos variously faded with age. He had the air of an ex-biker grown docile and lazy from the numbing routine of very small proprietorship. And although our arrival had nearly doubled the number of customers in his store, he didn't seem happy to see us.

Nick hustled us over to the sex toy display, where he examined various implements while conferring sotto voce with Sandrine. Daniel held me back, just beyond the range of their voices. I think he was also hoping to conceal my cuffed hands from the owner, who was eyeing us suspiciously. Nick selected a few items and brought these to the counter.

"How much for the video booth?"

"A dollar," said the owner. Then he looked us over once again and added, "per person."

Nick paid, and we walked through the turnstile, past a curtain, and into a little private cubicle. The cubicle had been furnished only with a narrow bench, a paper towel dispenser, and a video monitor whose static screen bathed the room an appropriately pornographic blue. The boys fumbled with the tape selector for a minute or two, and then images leapt onto the screen: a slender blond with enormous swagging breasts was taking three heroically endowed men, each in a different orifice.

Sandrine drew the curtain and sat down on the bench between Nick and Daniel. With a silent gesture seconded by a nod from Nick, she instructed me to kneel on the ground facing the troika. Nick now revealed one of his purchases: a large, black, strap-on dildo with harness. I must have looked appropriately nonplused, for he answered my expression with the same foul smirk that had been afflicting his face all day.

"Sandrine is going to fuck you with this, Claire. But not till later."

He pulled my blouse over my head and fondled my breasts, weighing them in cupped hands like a banker hefting pouches of prospectors' gold. Sandrine moved eagerly to help Daniel remove his straining penis from his trousers. After performing the same extraction on Nick, she reclined in her seat, a cock now in each fist, and began to pump her outstretched arms with synchronous strokes like some great, hovering gull.

Nick and Daniel were enthralled by the video and, presumably, by the situation. I'd never seen grown men progress to the point of orgasm so quickly. Within seconds their cocks were leaking pre-come, the liquid atomized about the room by Sandrine's energetic manipulations.

Daniel came first, leaning forward at the crisis to inundate my breasts with a spate of hot semen so viscous it clung to my skin like a thick velouté. Moments later, Sandrine's pumping drew forth its second geyser—this one from Nick —which she again directed at my chest, though this time negligently, so that the moiety at least was drizzled across my chin and throat.

Kneeling there, scumbled and adrip, literally a come target, I went feverish with desire. Wild-eyed and panting, I began to look around in search of relief.

It became quickly obvious to me, however, that my satisfaction wasn't part of anyone else's agenda, for the next thing I knew, Nick and Daniel had replaced their flaccid cocks in their pants and were preparing to leave. I tried to get to my feet, but my legs—cramped with cold from the cement floor—buckled under me. Sandrine came to my aid, and as I leaned against her our eyes met. Not daring to speak my request, I silently beseeched her for some sisterly consideration while pointing hopefully to the roll of paper towels with my chin. She looked at Nick for permission, but he only smiled and shook his head.

"No, no!" I exploded. "*Goddamnit*, Nick! This is way over the top. I'm *not* doing this—do you understand?"

In swift answer to my recusancy, Daniel snatched up the chain that depended from my nipples and jerked so hard I nearly blacked out. It was several minutes before I'd recovered enough to be led from the booth, and even then my steps and bearing were somnambulistic—the body had regained its ability to walk, but the walker herself remained divested of will. In tandem procession, we filed through the store and past a half-dozen leering patrons. Their collective expression turned from salaciousness to disbelief, however, the instant they saw that the dazed brunette who moved so uncertainly before them was handcuffed, her face and neck smeared with semen. I stepped hesitantly through the doorway, but then, suddenly revived by the sunlight, turned back round again into the shop. With an icy, arrogant stare, I caught and wilted six lecherous gazes, and then—licking a dollop of come from my lower lip—I skipped out into the street for good.

14

WRUNG OUT FROM THE MORNING'S EVENTS, I propped my head on Sandrine's shoulder, intending only to close my eyes and rest for a short while. Instead I fell asleep. When I awoke, we were outside of the city.

"Where are we?"

"Lung Island," answered Nick.

"Where are we going?" I was groggy. The landmarks outside my window were only impressionistically familiar. I couldn't seem to place us.

"Garden City."

"*Garden City?*"

I laughed. Nick couldn't have picked a more incongruous destination for us. Garden City was old and sedate, famous only as the birthplace of John Tesh. There was simply no reason to go there.

Hypnotized by the diffracting sibilance of the car slicing the wind, I sat in a half stupor, my brief nap having done nothing to dispel the laziness that sandbagged my movements and thoughts. I felt like a lizard on a cold rock, unable to budge more than eyelids.

Full consciousness came with a jolt when an abrupt right turn nearly sent me flying into the seatback in front of me.

We'd pulled into the porte-cochère of the Garden City Hotel, and now, as we came to rest in front of the valet stand, I made ready to scream rape, murder, and any other heinousness rather than be coerced into entering the lobby looking like I did. As it turned out, I wasn't even asked to leave my seat. Instead, we sat idling while Nick went alone into the hotel. He returned shortly with a large carton that he deposited in the trunk. As we were about to leave, his beeper sounded, and he ran back into the hotel to make a call. Five minutes later we were again on our way.

"Where to now?" I piped up.

"You makin' a friggin' map?" Nick's accent was suddenly pure Avenue "U"—remarkably convincing for a guy who'd been to Brooklyn exactly twice and gotten lost both times.

"Yeah," I answered, "I'm making a map. I'm Henry friggin' Hudson. Are you going to tell me, or not?"

"Okay, okay. I guess there's no harm to it. Lloyd Harbor. But we have to make a quick detour to the Five Towns. I have a package to deliver—some artwork."

I laughed quietly to myself. Somehow I'd gotten signed on for the orgy tour of Nassau and Suffolk counties. Not quite the Loire Valley, I wanted to complain. I resolved to schedule a heart-to-heart with my travel agent at the first opportunity.

We entered the township of Woodmere and began poking our way down a well-shaded and orderly residential street, searching for an address among rows of identical two-story brick houses, all in identical good repair, each fronted with an identical bib of immaculate lawn. Feeling a little like burglars casing a neighborhood, we at last reached our destination. Hands in pockets, Nick performed the cakewalk from *Singing in the Rain* on his way up the front steps. He disappeared behind a half-opened door, only to emerge again less than a minute later.

Once we were back on the parkway, my thoughts resumed their aimless wandering: daydreams, trivial longings, silly digressions lit upon my mind and as quickly disappeared. Feeling very childlike, warmly cocooned in my own small world, I soon settled into drowsy contentment.

"Old Jews."

"What the hell was that for?" Nick asked, startling me out of my dreamy ruminations.

I must have inadvertently given voice to a little joke that had been running through my head, one of a dozen which similarly plagued me. Like those bus-ride epiphanies reported by theoretical physicists, they originated in my mind fully formed, usually when I was in the shower or applying my makeup or drying dishes. And while it comforted me that an identical phenomenology linked my thought processes to those of the greatest human minds, unlike these Wissenschaftlerin, I'd always kept my mental novelties to myself. Until now, that is. Owing to my unfortunate slip of the tongue, I was going to have to divulge this one to Nick, who wasn't about to let my outburst go by without explanation.

"'Old Jews?' What the *hell* are you talking about, Claire?"

"Nothing."

"Bullshit, 'nothing.' One thing I know about you is that nothing is never about nothing. Come on—spill."

"Jesus, Nick—okay. Haven't you ever noticed that whenever you order a pastrami dip sandwich, the waitress asks you if you want it with 'old Jews'?"

Nick looked at me as though I'd gone totally daft. He didn't even smile. Sandrine, on the other hand, was hysterical with laughter. *La Belge gets it*, I thought. Go figure.

We turned off the state route and onto a tree-lined drive. The pavement gave way to flagstone as the road meandered up and around a low wooded hill. Presently we stopped before a wrought-iron gate. Nick handed a plastic card to Daniel, who inserted it into the mechanism. The gate swung open noiselessly. We drove at a gradual incline for another quarter mile, and then emerged from the trees onto a large expanse of lawn. As I scanned the horizon, the word "demesne" occurred to me, although I'd forgotten its exact meaning if I'd ever known it. Ahead of us at the crest of the rise was a magnificent rambling house, sprawled across nearly an acre. Its several wings were stepped at varying heights, though no part of it exceeded two stories. It was modern without the sterility of minimalism. Its construction—stone and narrow slats of painted wood siding—harked back to the best traditional American styles. I loved it immediately, but without covetousness, since I never develop visceral longings for anything that's much beyond my means.

We entered the house and passed through a long entryway into a voluminous living room, which I was surprised to find completely bare of furniture. The property was unoccupied. Nick explained that the house was for sale; it had been made available to him for the weekend by a realtor friend who held its listing. Technically, we were trespassing.

Though I was anxious to explore the house and grounds, I hung back, fully anticipating that the next episode of our saturnalia—what I had begun to think of as my "intemperance movement" (and which Nick, true to form, would soon be calling "The Long Island Progression")—was about to commence. My hesitation was a preemptive tactic, intended for self-protection. Since morning, each time I had tried to pursue my own direction the others had stopped me, ruthlessly. Hoping to prevent an encore, I was determined to wait for my companions' next move. After a while, however, nothing happened. When nothing continued to happen, I grew impatient to begin my tour, and asked Nick for the afternoon itinerary.

"Free schedule. We're going to relax. Have a drink, Claire. The fridge is stocked, and I'm going to order in Domino's. Don't ever say I'm not a classy guy."

For the next few hours I wandered the estate, poking into its rooms and closets, exploring its divers gardens, its koi ponds, its forking paths of decomposed granite, ribbons of gravel in taupe and mignonette. The day had remained clear to partly cloudy, and the windows of the upstairs rooms each framed a slightly different view of the Sound, a suite of variations on blue-gray water dotted with sails and whitecaps, the crests of the short choppy waves pinking into a mackerel sky.

As I gazed out over the ocean, I felt both hopeful and serene. I'm generally incapable of the deliberate and contemplative life (however much I may idealize it), except when I'm anticipating something enjoyable—an upcoming celebration, say, or a night on the town. At such moments I sometimes fall into a meditative calm, a spell of tranquillity cast backwards from the future to the present. So it was this afternoon. The promise of what lay in store allowed me to enjoy the silence and beauty of my surroundings with a plenitude of feeling undiminished by boredom or impatience. Furthermore, during those few perfect hours I remained free of the nagging worry—my spirit's all too common companion—that whatever it was I happened to be doing, I ought to be doing something else.

I watched the sunset from a small deck that gave out from one of the second-floor bedrooms. Lost in thought, I noticed neither the coming of darkness nor a precipitous drop in temperature until I heard my own name being called. Daniel approached, apparently relieved to see me.

"We've been looking for you *everywhere!*" He was a little out of breath; the search must have been strenuous.

"I've been here all day," I said, batting my eyelids angelically. It was nice to be missed.

Back in the "main hall,"as everyone was calling the large, wood-floored living room, Nick and Sandrine were serving up dinner.

"We thought we'd lost you," Nick said. "You must be freezing."

My teeth were chattering as he handed me a man's peacoat and then a plate heaped with delicacies. My nose sorted and classified the redolent medley: garlic, oregano, butter, the sea. Our detour to Garden City finally made sense. Nick had been teasing earlier—we would have nothing to do with cold pizza tonight. Instead we feasted on clams, pasta in lobster sauce, eggplant, garlic bread. I could smell strong hot coffee wafting from somewhere. As I ate, I took notice for the first time of the immense stone fireplace set into one wall of the room. Broad enough to roast a goat on a spit, it had been stoked with oak logs and set ablaze. I offered my back to its flames and at last began to defrost. The electric lights were turned off, and a warm, flickering glow from the fire provided the only illumination for our dinner. The effect was cinematic—very *Barry Lyndon*, I thought, laughing at the poverty of my own store of analogies. Still, I had made a worthwhile discovery: the particular wavelengths of light emitted by burning wood were supremely flattering to the human face. Struck by the shifting incandescence of the flames, our skin glowed with a Rembrandtesque beauty, orange-amber, as though lit from within.

After dinner there was still no rush into activity. Sandrine and Daniel disappeared upstairs for a while, and I sat alone with Nick. Breaking out of character for the first time that day, he put aside his fiendish-satyr affectations and spoke to me with gentle consideration. As we talked, I suddenly became conscious of the degree to which my thoughts had been colored by real misgiving. During the last hours, I had more than once seen my tormentors suffer, if not a full loss, than at least a temporary misplacement of reason. At those times, the line separating role-playing from identification seemed to vanish. Mimesis transformed the actors into their parts, with nothing to indicate the condition was reversible. I had good reason to worry that the coming night would be fraught with serious psychic dangers, or worse. But Nick's words calmed me, and although he never directly addressed my fears, somehow I felt reassured that whatever was to happen, he would respect my limits and keep me from harm.

Sandrine descended the staircase nude. From the last step she beckoned to me with a coiling finger. I followed her back up to a bedroom suite, then past a door of translucent green glass and into a large bathroom. I suddenly stood before an ellipse of fire described by the flames of several dozen long white candles. At the center of this luminous perimeter, a column of steam rose like a ghostly butte erupting from a desert valley. Enchanted by the stagecraft, I allowed myself to be stripped bare by Daniel, who then helped me over the ring of burning tapers—like a bride across a threshold—and into the bath.

I soaked for a long time, confident at last that unlike the day's manic rush, the night was going to unfold with luxurious sloth. After a while, Sandrine joined me in the bath. We touched, but the spirit of it was more friendly than erotic. She soaped my back and kissed me playfully once or twice on the neck. I returned her affection by massaging her shoulders. We hardly spoke, and then only in hushed whispers, as if we feared that this moment of limpid sensuality, constructed as it was of silent movement and vapor, might be too fragile to bear the shock of words.

Daniel, who had been sitting cross-legged on the rim of the basin watching us, now removed his robe and slipped into the water. Caught and slivered by his wet skin, the candle flames flashed against him like comet trails in a time exposure of the night sky. Once again I was deeply affected by his beauty. I ached to touch him, and might have reached forward with my hand had not Sandrine (contrary to everything I'd been made to understand about her) chosen that very moment to back Daniel against the side of the bath and take his penis in her mouth.

I was surprised and confused. Here was Sandrine—Sandrine whose sexual relations with men, I'd been assured, were strictly adventitious, a kind of rompish sideshow to her fundamental lesbianism—sucking the cock of a man—a hired chauffeur, no less—whom she had ostensibly met only that morning. I was confused, but more than that I was fascinated, and jealous. (For I desperately wished it were *my* mouth that held this cock, *my* tongue that cradled its length, *my* lips that parsed its velures and ridges, lovingly testing its growing hardness.)

Emboldened by sharp desire, I sidled through the water until my face was only inches from Sandrine's. The contrast of her pale skin juxtaposed to Daniel's relucent darkness was unbearably beautiful. I could do nothing but look on, awed and yearning. With a glance, Sandrine acknowledged my hunger, and by implication her own good fortune, and then, as if to lord it over me, responded by plunging Daniel's cock to the back of her throat with a vigorous snap of her neck.

If there is such a thing as sexual genius, I was now its witness. With Daniel in her mouth, Sandrine became a virtuoso, his penis her instrument. Her confidence and technical range astounded me: after holding his cock in her throat for what seemed like minutes, she would suddenly disgorge it, spiral her tongue slowly up the shaft, and then fasten her mouth upon the prepuce, sucking at the sensitive fold like a lamprey at a wound, stopping only when Daniel's onset of epileptically convulsive quaking persuaded her that she'd driven him to the brink of desperation. Once or twice his gyrations became inordinately violent, and I was sure then that his orgasm was imminent. But he was never truly beyond Sandrine's control. Her manège was the nearly invisible economy of command used by an expert rider with her favorite mount. Daniel's charge would come when she willed it—and certainly not before.

Yet there was something else to all of this, something beyond the brilliant application of technical skill. Suddenly I saw it: as Sandrine opened her eyes momentarily to return my gaze, they betrayed in that split second a poignancy of feeling that spoke of a deep and soulful connection—a connection that couldn't conceivably have arisen through casual sex with a stranger. On the contrary, I now knew that fellating Daniel was for Sandrine an expression of devotion as much as an act of carnality. And at that moment I became certain about something else that I'd previously only suspected: the web of association that linked Nick to Sandrine, and Sandrine to Daniel, was much more complicated than it had been meant to appear.

Daniel touched a finger gently to Sandrine's cheek. "Sandrine, ça suffit pour le moment. Il faut qu'on attende. La fête n'a pas encore commencer... Je dois conserver ma puissance." He was asking her to stop. With a look of disappointment, she planted a final kiss on his penis, then crossed her arms and sat back in the tub with a pout and a muted *harrumph*.

I seized the moment to confront them with my suspicions.

No doubt Nick had pledged them to a covenant of secrecy, but I hoped that intimacy and bathwater might have dissolved some of their compunction to honor that pledge.

"Sandrine," I began, "I want to know the truth about something."

She smiled and gave a little rueful shrug, as though she could anticipate my next question.

"Look," I continued, pausing to include Daniel with a nod in his direction, "—you don't have to tell me everything, but mama didn't raise no fool, vous comprenez? The two of you did *not* meet for the first time today."

"That is true," Sandrine replied softly, avoiding my eyes.

"And *you*, Daniel, are not a chauffeur."

He said nothing to this, but his face broke into a smile— the same arch, slightly ironic smile I'd first seen in the rear view mirror that morning.

"Daniel owns the limousine company," Sandrine said, answering for him. Then, more solicitous than apologetic, she added, "Please don't be angry with us."

"I'm not angry with you. I just want to know what's going on."

"Daniel and I are lovers," she said, looking up at me now. "Nick introduced us. I have others, but only women."

I started to interrupt, but she raised a hand to stop me.

"I know what you're going to ask," she continued. "But Nick was telling the truth: I was never with him that way. I was married, for many years—back in Europe. But very unhappy. I came here to get away—like everyone else. Nick gave me my first job in New York. That's how we met. I worked as his secretary while I took courses at night—pat-

ternmaking, that type of thing. He ridiculed my accent, but
he hired me anyway—and he didn't fire me when he found
out I couldn't really understand when people spoke English
to me on the telephone. We became good friends. He was
very nice to me. He was involved with someone at the time,
or...qui sait, tu sais? But he knew I was lonely."

"And how did Nick meet Daniel?" I asked. I found it odd
referring to Daniel in the third person in his presence,
though he himself seemed perfectly comfortable with it, as
if he were accustomed to Sandrine acting as his mouth-
piece.

"They did some business deal together," she answered.
"Nick invited Daniel to be an investor . . . to be a partner in
one of his real estate investments."

She pronounced "real estate investments" as if it were an
answer someone had given her to memorize. And then, perhaps because he saw that Sandrine was floundering, Daniel
jumped in:

"I had money before, but with Nick I made a lot *more*
money. And now I owe him forever. If you don't think that's
true, just ask him—he'll tell you. And so, that is why I have
to drive the limousine when he asks, and also why I have to
fuck anyone he wants me to."

He laughed, but a sarcastic note in his voice suggested
that his feelings of obligation were real enough, and perhaps
even a source of resentment.

Though I already had a lot to think about, there was one
question I wanted answered immediately, before we were interrupted.

"Why did Nick lie to me about you—about your relationship?"

Sandrine smiled, and her expression grew tender, almost protective.

"Ah, well, you see, Claire . . . Nick told you that because he knew long ago that what we're doing now—what we are doing today—was going to take place. He wanted to surprise you. He likes things very—comment-on dit?—drama*tique*. He takes care to plan for the future. And he is very good at guarding secrets—so you wouldn't know what to expect."

As Sandrine was drawing a breath to continue, Nick called to us from below. It was time, he was saying. Sandrine's eyes went suddenly wide with alarm, and she whispered something in rapid-fire French to Daniel that I didn't catch. Then she looked at me imploringly and exclaimed, "Shit, alors! Nick asked me to trim you—and I completely forgot . . ."

I didn't argue. She'd been very gracious, and I felt I could return the courtesy by making things easy for her now. We hastened to exchange places. I crawled from the bath and perched myself on its edge with my thighs spread for her, while she stood in the water facing me and undertook to snip away the wet curls of my bush with a pair of small shears Daniel placed in her hand.

"This will only take a minute," she said. "Nick wanted you trimmed a little, not completely shaved. I like it that way too. You can see everything better—it looks very neat, not at all infantile . . ."—but explanation quickly turned to flattery and prattle: "You have a *very* pretty pussy, Claire . . . It's marvelous to be able to see it so closely. Have I told you how lovely it is? I meant to before—it's really very beautiful. You see, what I like the best..."

I was amused by the parallel with my hairdresser—with every hairdresser I'd ever known, in fact. I began to speculate that there might be something intrinsic to the act of cutting hair that precluded silence, that made men and women maunder. A study, it seemed to me, was definitely in order.

The tonsure completed, Sandrine smiled and stood up. "Voilà, comme la mienne!" she announced triumphantly, while simultaneously fluffing her own fur.

I took a final dip to rinse off. We dried ourselves, put on robes—the thick terry kind one is always tempted to steal from hotels—and rejoined Nick downstairs. He was seated in a folding camp chair beside the fire, smoking a joint. This he offered to Sandrine and Daniel, who each took a hit or two.

"Let's start," Nick said, rising from his chair.

First, Daniel removed my robe, then Sandrine held a large black scarf before me—a gesture like a toreador presenting an anarchist flag to a bull, and one that struck me as equally nonsensical until she rolled the silk square into a narrow flat band and twisted it at both ends to form a blindfold. This she lifted to my eyes—but then hesitated, as though she were suddenly unwilling to advance the process. A long minute passed before I realized that she was waiting for me to step forward, to touch my face to the outstretched scarf, and then another minute before I understood why: the gesture would be a sign of voluntary obeisance, a formal acknowledgment to my hosts that my submission was absolutely uncoerced. But now, in the half-light of the hearth's embers, I was intent on searching *their* faces, and for a different kind of assurance. Before I sanctioned their plan I needed to know that they were prepared to take full responsibility for my well-being.

What I saw in their eyes (or believed I did)—sincerity, understanding, basic sanity—satisfied my preconditions, though as I advanced toward Sandrine I nevertheless mouthed a short pagan prayer that my vision hadn't been too falsely sweetened by desire. She bowed the blindfold across the bridge of my nose and then knotted it at the back of my head.

My other senses immediately strained to compensate for the sudden loss of vision. The effort seemed to evoke latent abilities, adaptive mechanisms as ancient as the Olduvai. All at once I was endowed with the australopithecine's early-warning system against night-prowling predators: ultra-sensitivity to smell and sound, to fluctuations in temperature and the slightest variations of touch. When my wrists were elevated and bound, I knew from the faint scent of calfskin and the plush sweep of silken corrugations across the backs of my hands that my manacles were two bands of Spanish leather, velvet lined. Alerted by the fire's irregular crackling, I could anticipate by seconds the fall of a charred branch in the hearth. And I deduced from a single amphoric *whoosh* that the narrow implement which had just divided the air was flexible, a length of willow or bamboo, rather than a rigid cane.

Small, soft hands—evidently Sandrine's—were on my bottom, herding me with little pats toward the center of the room. Chains were attached to my wristbands, and then I heard the zipping clatter of steel links running through the grooved rim of a pulley. As the slack was taken up, the weight of the length of chain depending from my wrists began to lift, and in seconds my arms had been hoisted above my head. An upward adjustment of the rigging left me suspended just far enough above the ground that I experienced an uncomfortable tension at both extremities. In order to stave off the sensation that my arms were being pulled from their sockets, I had not only to stand on tiptoe, but also to hold the muscles of my arms unnaturally flexed. Though short of agonizing, the effect was certainly alarming, since I doubted that I could long maintain such a position without losing mental equilibrium. These fretful speculations were cut short, however, when fingers parted the lips of my pussy and Nick, in tones grown hushed and reverential, began to speak:

"My God, Sandrine, it truly *is* beautiful, don't you think? I'm always surprised. Each time I see it is like the very first . . ."

"Yes," she agreed, spreading my labia further. "It was brilliant of you to have me trim her. C'est tellement génial . . ."

"She's very sexy tied up like that, too," Nick continued. "I like the way it makes her hollow the small of her back. I hadn't expected that. Let's have a look at her ass."

Sandrine took hold of my hips and swiveled me around until I faced away from her. Nick lightly stroked a cheek of my ass, then let his fingertips glide along the crease formed by the juncture of my buttock and thigh. When he reached my groin, he fanned his stiffened fingers across the length of my vulva.

"She's wet already."

Nick spread my cheeks, and Daniel and Sandrine voiced their approval. Then all three began to laud and compare my physical merits, as if I'd won best-of-breed at the county fair. The examination was at close quarters: while they spoke I could feel humid breath condense on my perineum.

"She's all yours, Sandrine," Nick said after a while. "Got any plans?"

"I'm going to fuck her with the strap-on, while Daniel fucks me from behind." Her reply had come without hesitation, as though she'd been counting on the question.

"You don't sound sure," Nick laughed, and I imagined Sandrine rolling her eyes. "Tell you what," he continued, "I'll tongue her cunt while you fuck her. But first she needs to be warmed up. Go get the switch for Daniel. He's going to whip Claire while you suck his cock. Keep him excited—I don't want him going easy on her."

I didn't know how frightened I should be. I enjoyed the heightened sensations produced by certain kinds of pain during erotic play, so the idea of being whipped *per se* didn't seem particularly harrowing. Nevertheless, the present situation diverged from my previous experience in two significant respects. For one, I had never before been so completely helpless. For another, in the past I'd been subjected to pain only after I was already well aroused—it had been an element introduced into the midst of ecstasy, not a precursor to it.

Despite plenty of adumbration, the first stinging cut of the switch across my ass came as a hurtful shock. I cried out in protest, but Nick silenced me with a threatening growl. Expecting nevertheless that he'd caution Daniel to temper his attack, I was aghast when he shouted instead, "Harder, Daniel! Let's see you raise some welts."

The next blows—three in rapid succession—felt as if they were ripping my flesh, each one slashing progressively closer to the bone. I nearly fainted. Certain my skin had been shredded, I imagined warm blood spilling from the cuts as freely as the tears of hurt and anger that streamed from my eyes. I wanted to scream my horrified indignation, to excoriate them all—and especially Nick—for their cruelty and presumptuousness, but before I could gather my wits enough to reclaim with appropriately high-flown fury, Nick took me into his arms consolingly, and began to kiss the tears from my face.

"It's okay, Claire . . . you're okay."

"I'm not okay!" I cried. "For Chrissake, Nick—I'm bleeding."

"No you're not, Claire. Look—"

He brushed his hand over my buttocks, then brought his fingers to my lips.

"Taste, baby: no blood. My hand is dry."

Nick was right. Pricked by fear, my imagination had exaggerated the physical severity of the flogging, whose effects had already dwindled to nothing more catastrophic than a tingly warm astringency across the skin of my buttocks.

With relief I snuggled my face into the side of his neck, but my respite was short. His fingers, which for the last few moments had been gently toggling my clitoris back and forth through a small arc, began suddenly to berate it with militant fervor. My cries and moans were a tocsin to Daniel, calling his arm to arms, in a manner of speaking. Once again I heard the thin, whining stoop of the switch, and quivered as it cut a welt across the same transverse crease at the top of my thighs that Nick had been so tenderly fingering only minutes before. But at the exact moment of impact, Nick slid his thumb into my pussy—opposite stimuli that synergized with curare-like effect, paralyzing my diaphragm and attenuating my agonized scream in mid-breath.

The strokes of Daniel's switch now alternated with the thrusts of Nick's fingers—first one, then two—into my vagina. Sandrine fellated Daniel with audible enthusiasm (much slurping and smacking of lips) and fierce effect (for in his frenzied excitement, he threw greater and greater force into his blows). As the flogging continued, Nick began to shunt his fingers within me from side to side, and soon I felt that increase of tension which precedes the orgasmic plummet. But when at last I attained the ecstatic verge—my eyes staring blindly ahead, my mouth contorting in a rictus of agonized anticipation—Nick tore his fingers from me with a single cruel motion, and I dropped instantly back beyond all reach of liberation.

I heard Nick's footsteps recede into the distance, then felt one more stinging cut from Daniel's switch before he himself walked away. Sandrine was last. She kissed me—her mouth had a slightly chlorine taste of semen—and then, without a word, she too disappeared beyond the range of my hearing.

I was alone in the darkness, my muscles knotted by frustration and the imposition of my restraints. After perhaps an hour had gone by, I grew forlorn enough to call out for help.

In an instant Sandrine was at my side, as though she had been near at hand the entire time, waiting for my cry. She pressed the rim of a glass of ice water to my lips, and then something slipped in the pulley above my head. The chains had been caused to give out a little, and suddenly I was able again to stand normally. Sighing with relief, I shook out the pain in my arms and legs as best I could and thanked Sandrine. She cautioned me to keep silent, explaining in a whisper that by coming to my aid she was breaking with the men.

Was this hugger-muggery truly necessary, I wondered, or only another stratagem in the battle plan? Certainly Sandrine's motivation was not without self-interest—as I understood the moment she began, with exasperatingly infinitesimal pressure, to draw her moistened lips across the skin of my neck and breasts. I ached for her to suck my nipples, but she continued on her austral course—traversing my belly in a straight line, scaling the scrubby versant of my freshly depauperate mons, descending its opposite slope, her tongue extending forth to investigate the liquescent vale below. All of a sudden her nails dug into the raw skin of my bottom, then it seemed her entire face was pushing itself into my vagina. Snuffling and licking, guzzling in my pussy like a starved trencherwoman, Sandrine pressed a gluttonous attack that momentarily filled me with the sickening feeling I was being rooted in by swine. After a short time, however, she lifted both her mouth and her attentions to my clitoris.

While her lips tugged metronomically at my clit, her tongue performed a sinuous glissade along its distended length—an alliance of gestures that quickly transported me into a feverish clutch of expectancy. But as I began to come—heaving my pelvis against Sandrine's face, bearding her with the frothy spume churned by my lurching gyrations—she pulled away, short-circuiting my orgasm. Half mad with passion, I cursed Nick for his evangelizing and begged Sandrine for mercy. She laughed, then brought her lips to my ear. "Claire, darling," she whispered, "You're a hot little cunt. Stay that way a while longer."

Then she was gone.

Despite my frustration, I welcomed the solitude of this next intermission. I'm not sure precisely how long it was before I became aware—not without some feeling of resentment at the intrusion—that I was no longer alone. Someone had come into the room and begun heaving logs on the andirons, reviving the fire which had been allowed to burn down to occasionally sputtering coals. Footsteps approached, and I heard the blade of a pocketknife snap open. My blindfold, suddenly seized and severed, fell away from my face. As my eyes grew accustomed to the light, I began to make out the forms and disposition of my three captors. Daniel knelt at my feet, where he was fitting leather bands to my ankles, while Nick stood a few paces beyond, assisting Sandrine with the dildo harness. As I watched, he inserted a black rubber cock through the circular brass terret in front, and then helped her with the straps that secured the contraption to her waist and thighs.

The dull report of metal striking leather recalled my attention to Daniel, who was connecting one end of a yard-length of narrow pipe to the cowhide band that encircled my left ankle. He attached the opposite end to my right ankle, so that I now stood with my arms held apart by the chains above, and my legs forcibly separated by the pipe between my feet. To anyone happening upon us, I would have appeared as a saltire cross—a living ordinary "X"—silhouetted against the blaze of the fire.

No longer able even to clamp my thighs shut, I was left completely susceptible to attack—something Nick and Daniel seemed to notice, concurrently and approvingly. Pausing from their labors, they gave me the once-over, and their cocks simultaneously ascended to identical ultimate angles (and I was suddenly reminded, through some strange eidetic association, of dockside cranes in the quayscapes of Pissarro).

Daniel and Sandrine approached first. Daniel began to jerk off, and Sandrine mirrored his movements, stroking the hard black dildo projecting from her loins as though it were her own flesh. Licking her lips, she watched with fervid eyes as he inserted a finger into my vagina.

"She's ready," Daniel said, reporting to the group. Sandrine positioned herself confidently between my legs, touched the dildo's tip to my vulva, and with a sort of flexuous abdominal thrust, smoothly insinuated its head. The device was wickedly thick, but by means of copious lubrication and patient incremental pressure, she made slow but steady progress. Daniel helped too: lowering himself to the challenge, he took my clitoris in his mouth and sucked while Sandrine pushed the dildo home.

Sandrine now had her chance. I expected an immediate show of force, but instead she resumed with an anemic, slow rocking of her hips— unavailing motion that displaced the dildo no more than a shallow inch or so in either direction, as if she were testing its fit before committing herself to any larger action. Daniel, meanwhile, took up a position behind her, shuffling forward until his pelvis underthrust her buttocks. A moment later I felt him snap his hips, and so his cock, into place. Trembling, Sandrine flexed her own hips, propelling the dildo deep within me. After a few moments she reversed herself, drawing the rubber prick slowly from my vagina. And thus Daniel fucked Sandrine, and Sandrine fucked me—and I would have been elated, but their cycle was too feeble to satisfy my passion.

I was given no opportunity to dwell on my disappointment, however. An enormous blow from the switch, followed by two more of equal severity, brutally redirected my concerns. Nick was wielding the instrument now, and with far more devastating effect than Daniel—for he directed the point of contact with searing precision: on my buttocks, but also on the sensitive skin of my inner thighs, laid utterly open to his aim by the chain-and-tackle contrivance that restrained me.

Screeching with pain, I felt as though I were rocketing upward through deep water, my depleted lungs on fire, hoping my breath would hold out until I surfaced. Nick and I had agreed upon an emergency protocol (Nick's favorite joke: Q: When did you stop beating your wife? A: When she said the safeword), though I had sworn myself to use it only in case of obvious and immediate danger, a set of conditions which had not so far arisen. For while Nick had often danced me to the very margin of the tolerable, we'd never yet lost our footing. I'd had every reason to believe that he knew how I worked; knew that at the most basic level what got me off was mundane: cocks, fingers, and tongues; knew that for me pain could only ever be the accomplice of pleasure, not its substitute. But the force with which he now flogged me was unrelenting, so that with each agonizing clout I found it more and more difficult to deny a terrible apprehension that he'd somehow fallen prey to an insane delusion, that he'd become truly and maniacally bent on enucleating my will.

As it happened, however, Nick proved once again that he knew my limits and capacities better than I did myself. For when at last Sandrine began to fuck me as unrestrainedly and zealously as I'd earlier hoped, there was a rapid displacement of sensation from the abraded flesh of my buttocks and thighs to the tender integument of my clitoris; and suddenly, instead of the strokes of the switch, I felt nothing but a ravening demand for satisfaction, a demand I now laid at the foot—give or take an inch—of Sandrine's stiff machine.

Daniel climaxed first, pulling his cock from Sandrine's pussy in order to effect an exterior and visible discharge. This time his spout was short, slow and laborious; it came forth with a choking sort of gush, then spent itself in torn shreds all across her buttocks. Clear and thin, like tepid egg-white, the last drops had barely trickled from his cock when he encunted Sandrine once again, fucking her until an apoplectic twitching of her facial muscles betokened her own orgasm.

Taking up the switch from Nick, Daniel stepped back as if to measure his reach, and then began to flog Sandrine while Nick exhorted her to finish me off.

"Fuck her hard, Sandrine! Make her beg like a dog, then fuck her till she comes!"

Sandrine became an engine of siege, squealing and panting as she rammed the dildo into me with a wild rolling scend of her hips, her passion so overwrought it recalled the purchased enthusiasm of a porn actress. The room echoed our exertions, and to the whine of the switch rending the air, the slapping of damp bellies, and the muffled crunch of colliding pelvises were soon added my own cries as at last I came—and then came again. Sandrine detached herself from me, leaving me to hang limply on my chains like a sail dragging from the mast of a becalmed ship.

Daniel removed my bindings and wrapped me in a blanket, then walked me over to a futon which had been laid out before the fireplace, within its radiant arc but beyond reach of errant sparks. He eased me down gently, and I stretched out with relief upon the softly yielding cushion. I wanted sleep, but my mind was alive, busily assembling images and editing impressions of what had just taken place, events that were already growing nebulous and jumbled in my memory. *Here* (I thought excitedly) *was the mythopoeic process in action!*—a rare view of the middle ground of consciousness forging a cogent accounting of "what really happened," a serendipitous glimpse of the ego transforming memory to suit itself. It was all very fascinating, I said to myself, yawning. I'd have to make some notes—but in the morning, when I was fresh. It was always best to do science in the morning. . .

15

SANDRINE WOKE ME BEFORE DAWN, AND AS I sat up she gently balanced on my lap a small wooden tray upon whose japanned surface were set a cup of coffee, two prune rugelach, and half a nectarine. I could have been back at my aunt's house in Bayside—or at a bris.

"What time is it?" I asked, groggy with fatigue. "Are we leaving already?"

"No, we're not leaving yet. You have to get up, though. It's almost sunrise. Nick wants you."

This confused me. I'd been under the impression that our debauch had ended the night before—and to everyone's satisfaction. I had assumed we'd be leaving for the city at daybreak. Now, even under the very best of conditions, I'm only semi-functional in the morning, so the pending prospect of an involved epilogue at such an ungodly hour left me somewhat less than enthusiastic. Also, I wanted to brush my teeth, and I needed very much to pee.

I grumbled all this to Sandrine, who agreed to let me wash up in a downstairs bathroom, on condition I was quick about it. "One thing you should know, Claire," she said when I returned, "No whips this morning"—as though the information were certain to console my bad mood.

At the mention of whips I reflexively brought my hand to my bottom, finding the skin still sore but the welts nearly gone. Then Sandrine conjoined my wristbands (and thus my wrists) and secured them with a small padlock. After once again blinkering me (I was now well beyond mere annoyance with this perpetual chiaroscuro of the blindfold), she led me to the center of the room, where she chained me to the ceiling as before. She kissed me hard on the lips just once, and then vanished without another word, leaving me to wait, nude and shivering, in the pre-dawn cold.

Before very long, however, Nick entered the room, bade me an obnoxiously chipper "Morning, Claire!" and kissed me. His hands wandered over my body as he made one-sided conversation. I was cranky and taciturn, but he seemed too cheerful to notice. So different was he from the day before, so flirtatious and complimentary, that I had the impression he was wheedling me for something—until, after a moment's reconsideration, I saw how preposterous the idea was. I was naked and chained, after all; Nick hardly needed to charm me to obtain my cooperation.

"I know it's early, Claire. I'm sorry about that. But I wanted to fuck you this morning. I miss it. I miss you." He leaned into me then, and I felt his erection pressing between my thighs.

"I'll wait till you're wet, Claire; then we'll fuck. I need you. I've been hard since yesterday, watching Sandrine fuck you. That was so beautiful—thank you for that."

Nick's hands grabbled lightly over my flanks, skin barely grazing skin. He kissed my face and neck, then for a moment I felt nothing, and then his breath against my belly, and then on my sex.

"I'm going to spread you a little, Claire. I'll just look for a while. I want to see you get wet for me."

He knelt at my feet, silent except for his breathing. He held me open, and I knew he was watching, his eyes lavish of appreciation.

"I'm hard for you, Claire. I couldn't sleep last night thinking about putting my cock in you. Ah, *there* it is. . ."

Nick had made me wet by voice alone. He stood, and then my arms were wrenched upward with a jangling of chains, and then he was hauling me up by the buttocks until my legs girded his ribcage on either side and my crotch was even with the bottom of his breastbone. I was just about to remark on the odd tickling feeling of his chest hairs against my denuded pubis, when the chain above suddenly disengaged and I experienced an abrupt sensation of falling, like the dead-air sinking feeling you get in a pocket of turbulence. Certain that the slack would run out before my feet reached the ground, I anticipated a jolt at the bottom of the descent. Instead, Nick's cock spitted my vagina, and the padded ring of bone at its base broke my fall. Then, like some depraved circus performer, he proceeded to fuck me by pitching me upward and catching me on his cock, all the while regaling me in the dulcet mode—"darling Claire," "sweet Claire," "my love," "querida"—tender blandishments wholly inconsonant with his rambunctious athleticism.

Suddenly the unmistakable crunch of tires on gravel filled the room, freezing us both in mid-thrust. I began to stutter and squirm, but Nick drew the blindfold from my face and met my frantic look with a tranquil smile.

"You know who's here, don't you?"

My first thought was that a caravan of realtors had come to inspect the property. Although Nick's friend had assured him that our privacy would remain undisturbed, the house was, after all, for sale. It was not impossible that a renegade group of "sales associates," intent on confirming first-hand the magnificence of its dramatic cathedral ceilings, the Old World charm of its manorial stone fireplace, and the solid craftsmanship of its four-panel maple doors, was about to barge in on us.

It was perhaps the look of juvenile mischief on Nick's face that made me reconsider this theory.

"You invited Andres?"

Nick nodded in the affirmative, his hair now softly gilded by the donserly light. I shook my head in amazement. (For although such a meeting had indeed been an item on my fantasy requisition list, I'd discounted the possibility as impractical and unlikely.)

A car door slammed shut, and the sound of approaching footsteps echoed in the emptiness of the main hall. At last a figure stepped from the corridor, but before I could catch more than a vague glimpse, I was enveloped in darkness. With a single swift and unforeseen movement, a magician's legerdemain, Nick had replaced the blindfold over my eyes.

He disengaged himself from me and greeted Andres with an effervescent "Good morning! I'm Nick!"—like a cruise director welcoming a new passenger.

"Pleased to meet you. I'm Andres. May I say first that you have a very lovely country. Oh, and that must be your daughter, the youngest Wallenda—hanging over there . . ."

The voice and manner were distinctive, and certain memories suddenly buffeted my mind, and then, with even greater intensity, my body. I was too excited to follow the conversation, which faded in and out of my hearing like radio signals on a tuner set to scan.

"... with many her age, so of course it's not at all surprising. However, she's lovely, and she'll make a fine aerialist—if she ever learns to apply herself ..."

"... yes, and marvelous genes, Andres, so the potential is undeniable. Still, I question her desire. Honestly, though, what do you think of her? Is she anything like you expected?"

"... quite beautiful, indeed—and physically, at least, she's made for the trapeze. But, as you say, she has to want to make it her life. I see it more as a question of commitment and self-discipline than of raw talent, and only time will tell. By the way, it looks like you've had a good show here. Working without a net, too. Don't you hate the fucking clowns, though? Not bad enough that they're touchy and bibulous, but what a guild of Slobovians, too. Look at this mess!"

In my mind's eye I saw Andres sweep his hand to indicate the condition of the room. The floor had been strewn with the detritus of the day before: empty bottles and food containers, discarded clothing, wet towels, the dildo and harness, the bamboo switch.

Nick laughed. "What can I say? We've been ... busy."

"How was she?" asked Andres, serious now.

"Incredible. I'm sorry you couldn't be here yesterday. Wait!—stay there for a second—let me show you something."

Crooking a hand under the knee of my right leg, Nick

lifted and drew it away from my body as though opening one side of a swinging gate.

"I was just fucking her when you drove up. She's ready for us. But first I want you to see how fast she can come—I can't believe it myself sometimes. Watch this."

Nick sklathed two fingers into my vagina. "See how hot she gets?" he said, muddling them within. "She really likes this, Andres—it's even better for her with you here. I can tell—she's dripping."

"Watch her nipples," he continued, his docent's tour of my sexual idiosyncrasies as blasé as if he were narrating a filmstrip on colonial-era franking privileges. "They get hard by themselves when she's about to get off."

Storming me suddenly from behind, Nick began to fuck me with such savage zeal that each thrust of his cock drove the breath from my lungs. Within seconds I was rushing toward a blissful spasm, heedless of anything but my own desire. But as I was about to come I tensed—the bird gathering herself for the launch into space—and Nick pulled away.

"Fucking bastard!" I shouted, "You fucking bastard!"—my voice a strangled wail.

I was seething with what felt like resentment over an injustice. The emotion, I knew, was inappropriate to the situation: I had chosen my circumstances, and my discomfiture was an expected part of the program. None of this, however, consoled me in the least, and, crying and cursing, I began to shake with anger. Then through my sobs I heard Andres making anxious inquiries:

"Is she okay, Nick? Maybe this is too much for her..."

"She's fine," Nick said. "She's just frustrated—wound up a little too tight. All she needs is some hard fucking." Then, to me, "Claire, you're okay—right?"

"No," I said, though even to my own ears I sounded more petulant than aggrieved. Nick laughed at me.

"*No?* Fine, then—we'll leave. Andres, I was wrong, amigo. Claire doesn't want to be fucked."

"No!" I screamed.

"Which is it, Claire?" he asked, laughing uproariously. "You want us to fuck you—or not?"

I knew I had to be unequivocal—anything less would spell deprivation.

"I want you to fuck me," I got out at last—only to find that I'd again confounded myself, for my answer came across as little more than reluctant.

"That's not good enough, Claire. I want to know *how* you want us to fuck you—exactly how."

"I want," I began haltingly, trying to steel myself for the job, "I want *you* to fuck me in my ass, and Andres in my pussy—both at the same time."

At last it seemed I'd gotten it right. Nick once again bore his cock against me from behind (but obliquely this time, without penetration), and then it was Andres' turn to approach: I felt him bend low for a kiss, then his lips on mine tenderly, the tip of his tongue shyly inviting itself into my mouth. He pressed against me, squeezing me between himself and Nick, then began to rub the head of his penis across the top of my vulva, as if he were a restorer with an eraser, and my clitoris an anachronistic blot on a rare manuscript— too delicately, in other words, to have much effect.

"*Please!*" I urged, impatient with all the preliminaries (never had a woman been so disinclined to foreplay as I at that instant), "Both of you! Fuck me now!"

After preparing the way with a finger, Nick slicked his cock with saliva, then quickly and painlessly rode it into my ass. The aft encroachment complete, I turned my attention to the fore, where Andres was using his hand to introduce the head of his cock into my vagina. On their marks now and set, they fell to transfixing me by turns: first Nick, his breath hot on the back of my neck, his hands moving from my belly to my clitoris, fingers chafing it between them; then Andres, driving forward on Nick's outstroke, pulling my head to his chest, *his* hands on my ass, one on each buttock, spreading my cheeks.

"I love the way you fuck," Nick whispered, his lips brushing the down of my earlobe.

"I love the way you feel," Andres said, his pubic bone grinding Nick's fingers into my clit.

The cycle of their alternating thrusts suddenly and simultaneously quickened, and I recognized with distress that they were both about to come—with distress, because my own orgasm, despite the steady action of cocks and fingers, was lagging behind.

"Nicky...Andres...not yet...another minute—*please*..."

Heeding my request, they contained themselves, slowing to await my cue. I caught up, and then outdistanced them, coming before their cocks recoiled. By the time I felt the twinned surge of their ejaculate, my cries had already died away, and the room returned again to bird song and the faint clang of a distant buoy.

Nick cut me down by sawing through the leather that bound my wrists. The gesture was theatrical—the straps could just as easily have been unbuckled instead—but it served to signal unambiguously that the games were officially concluded. I removed my blindfold and looked up into Andres' eyes for the first time.

I wasn't disappointed by his face, and as we talked—and we talked more like old friends getting reacquainted after a separation than two people meeting for the first time—I soon recognized in Andres all that I'd most valued in Patro: the same honesty and empathetic intelligence, the same caustic humor and gentle irony. And while the carnal Andres and the virtual Patroqueeet were certainly not identical (the person before me was more a romantic than a roué, and much less audacious than his remote counterpart), somehow—strange fact, given the central place of sex in our relationship—that didn't seem to matter to me.

The morning spent itself all too quickly, and at last the time came when we could no longer put off our goodbyes. With the lingering warmth of Andres' last embrace still upon my shoulders, I watched as his car looped its way down the hill toward the trees. I felt the first pangs of separation before he'd even passed from view, and then I began to cry, tears of regret and farewell for this oh-so-sweetly depraved man who had made possible my rebirth to joy.

16

DANIEL AND NICK PACKED UP THE CAR WHILE Sandrine and I took a last slow promenade through the back garden. I'd grown tired, saddened by Andres' departure, downcast and a little world-weary. Then a droll notion made me laugh. I must have been half-consciously performing a mental tally of the last twenty-four hours, for it dawned on me suddenly that we'd failed to enact a single fantasy from the second column of the list I'd given Nick, the subset I'd presumably wished to remain unrealized. Had he suffered a loss of nerve? How could he have failed to construe the things I'd written in that note—*everything* I'd written in that note—as fair game? This was unacceptable. Erotically, Nick was my perfect match: I was as dependent on his sexual audacity as on the air. It was incumbent upon me to destroy incipient weakness. I could permit no slacking off, no retreat, no surrender to fear. Something would have to be done, and soon.

The horn blared twice. Reluctantly breaking off our lazy perambulations, Sandrine and I gathered ourselves and our things and bade farewell to the garden, sunwashed and shimmering now without its cloak of morning mist. We rounded a corner of the house, coming out onto the loop of the driveway. At its opposite end stood our car, and beside it—in full livery—stood Nick. As we approached he opened the passenger door for us, tipped his chauffeur's cap, and smiled. Daniel was waiting in the back seat, cutting the foil on a bottle that rested between his knees. He smiled contentedly as we stepped in, and then the door was closed and Nick started the engine.

We drove in silence until we reached the end of the private drive. Before we turned onto the highway, Daniel tapped the glass divider, which then slid open a handbreadth. I saw Nick's face in the mirror.

"To the city," Daniel said to him. Then he closed the divider, reclined into his seat and added, to no one in particular, "Le plus ça change, tu sais, le plus ça change . . .